Say Yes to the Dress!

Jolene Marselis

Auntie Katie

♡

BRAY

xo

ISBN-10: 1496073878
ISBN-13: 978-1496073877

CONTENTS

ACKNOWLEDGMENTS

I owe everything about this book to my editor, Alice. Honestly! You wouldn't be reading this book if it wasn't for her, because the idea would not have even been born. We were just talking and saw this picture of this fabulous dress that we were both drooling over. Totally over the top of course – you could never wear such a thing in public, doing your groceries or going to work. The only thing you could possibly wear it for was a wedding – but for that you would need a groom.

That got me thinking about what a shame it was that we need to wait for a man to fulfill a dream . . . that actually has nothing to do with him, because most men could care less which dress you are wearing. Not that I have anything against men. Don't get me wrong, I like them very much – as Alice will tell you.

So I invented Izzy, a lady that – just like us – fell in love with a dress. And as she finds her courage, she will let nothing stand in her way of wearing that ultimate dream dress.

So thank you, Alice, for giving me the idea for this story, and for doing this fabulous job on editing it once it was all written.

CHAPTER ONE

It was love at first sight. All Izzy had needed in the first place was a picture to fall head over heels. But that was nothing compared to the real thing. There it was, right in front of her. She could see it through the window in all its glory.

She could not just go in there, could she? She had no business there. Yet the magnetism was undeniable. This had to be destiny – she had even had a dream about it. So how could she not go in? Her heart was beating in her throat – she could hardly contain herself as she opened the door. Her fingers tingled as she pushed against the cold hard marble of the door handle – she could hardly believe she was really doing this.

Just across the room was the object of her affection. She had never imagined that she would see it for real. Slowly, almost out of breath, she moved closer. In awe, she stretched out her hand – she was almost close enough to touch it. It was really there. Up close, it was even more beautiful than she had imagined. Such opulence and wealth. Such detail and eye for perfection. Beyond her wildest dreams, really.

"Would you like to try it on, miss?"

The shop assistant's voice startled Izzy, and she needed a second to compose herself. The question had been asked though. Would she like that? It wasn't her right to do so, but she was right there. The chance to wear such a magnificent gown. This might not ever happen again. Nobody had to know that she did not really belong here. She could just try it on and leave again. Nobody would have to know about her little indulgence. "Yes please." She could feel a blush rise to her cheeks. Calm down now, she was this close to fulfilling this dream.

A second assistant was called for. "Marie, we have a client who would like to try on the dress in the window. Can you help me get it off the mannequin?" Together the two shop assistants started to take the dress off the clothes doll. The process clearly took quite a bit of effort. Should she put a stop to it? Izzy wondered, feeling more guilty by the minute. They were going to an awful lot of trouble, and the outcome was already clear. There was no way she could buy it. But the dress was already off now, and it was too late to object.

"Would you like to follow me, miss?" asked the first shop assistant. She was led through to a fitting room. "By the way, my name is Antoinette, but you can call me Ann."

Ann – that was Izzy's mother's name. Was it a sign? But a sign of what? Izzy knew her mother she would not approve of this sort of frivolity. It was just a dress, though. What harm could there be in just trying it on?

"When will the wedding be, if you don't mind me asking?" Ann wanted to know.

There was the question Izzy had been dreading. Her mind raced, and she felt her blush deepening. Now she had to lie on top of everything else. "In . . . uh . . . about six months. March 27th." That would be her 35th birthday, so it was a fitting date.

Ann smiled and seemed delighted, which only added to Izzy's guilt. "Wonderful. A spring wedding. It's the perfect dress for it. Here we are, and here is your dress. I will leave you to get changed. Once you are ready, please call me, so we can help you to lace up the back."

Left alone with just the dress, Izzy took a minute just to admire it. It truly was a vision made of ivory and gold. A beauty for beauty's sake. Every detail was exquisite. The bodice was beautifully embroidered with golden thread, beadwork, pearls, and the tiniest little flowers. The skirt was a cascading waterfall of ruffles, one overlapping the other in different fabrics and textures that perfectly complimented each other. All together, the dress was a work of art that looked as if it could have belonged to Marie Antoinette. Yet it was distinctly modern somehow – the neckline, the exposed arms, even the way the dress fell was modern, not antique. It was a dress that belonged in a dream, and she felt a bit of envy toward whoever had dreamed it up.

Still, doubt niggled in her stomach. Should she really be doing this? Not only was she here on false pretenses. By trying it on she could only disappoint herself. She could never wear it for real On the other hand, she was already here with the dress. Running out of the dressing room now would be strange. She had to try it on, there was no other choice. And it was not like it was a hardship . . .

It would be completely and utterly rude of her to leave now, as the shop assistants obviously had gone to the trouble of getting the dress off the mannequin for her to try. She started stripping out of her winter clothes, kicking her boots off and hanging her clothes on the available pegs. Luckily, the dressing room was warm and comfy, and the shivers up her spine were only due to excitement. Then it was time to try on the dress.

Despite the fact it was by no means small, it looked very fragile. "You break it, you buy it" lingered somewhere in the back of her mind, though she could not decide if that was a bad thing. Really touching it for the first time, the fabric was so much softer than she had expected. It felt soft and silken. Her hand followed the sways of the fabric. Gently she lifted the gown off the hanger, wondering how she was going to put it on. It was so massive that simply stepping into it was not an option.

"Does mademoiselle require assistance?" a voice behind the velvet curtain asked.

Had they been watching her? No, the curtain was closed. It felt a bit awkward, and the lingerie she was wearing was by no means her best, but if she were to get in the dress she did not have an option. "Yes please," she had to admit.

Both the assistants came into the rather large dressing room. "We should have told you straight away. This is not a dress one can put on by oneself. Sorry about that, miss," Marie assured her.

Inadequately trying to cover up her modesty, Izzy gave a wry smile. "It's alright. I wasn't exactly prepared myself for buying a wedding dress today."

"Ah, you saw it and fell in love. How lucky! I tell you, miss, that is often the best way," said Ann. What would Izzy's own mother have said about this, though?

"Does it happen a lot?"

"Not really, but it should. Usually people bring their families, and then it turns into a quarrel. To calm things down, the bride ends up buying something she did not want to buy at all, just so she won't have to argue with her soon-to-be mother-in-law or even her own mother before the wedding. It's very sad. We're in this business to make dreams come true, not to have them ripped apart. Your wedding should be magical in every way, and that starts with the perfect dress."

Izzy nodded. "Yes, I imagine so. Well, I saw this from the window, and I just had to come in for a closer look." It was the first thing she had said that was the truth. If she had really been shopping for "the" dress though, she would not have been here without her mom.

Ann expertly unfastened the bodice from the skirt. "Well, we shall see what it looks like in a minute – it is truly a gorgeous gown. It's a new brand, and we just got it in." The skirt was lifted over Izzy's head. So that was how you got in it. Then the corset was wrapped around her and laced up. It hugged her like a warm embrace, and it was so much lighter than she had expected. She felt like she could dance in it. In fact, she was tempted to give a twirl.

The red curtains opened, and she was led to a mirror. It was truly breathtaking. She had never felt this beautiful, and that was without her makeup or hair being done. Well, of course she wore a little bit of makeup, but just the day-to-day, nothing that did the dress justice. It did not matter though – the dress was so perfect, it just seemed to bring out the best in her. The more she looked, the more she fell in love with it. Sweet details, like silk roses peeping out of the folds, made it even more special. It wasn't just a dress, it was a piece of art. She never wanted to take it off again.

Looking at Izzy, both the ladies smiled. "You glow, miss. Quite the blushing bride. Your fiancé is a lucky man, and I bet that he will be breathless if he sees you coming down the aisle in that dress," said Ann.

"And it fits so perfectly – just look at it! Tailored to your body," Marie said, backing her up. It's like it was made for you – no alterations are needed. That almost never happens. You look stunning, miss."

Of course, they were telling her exactly what she wanted to hear, but she had to agree with them. It wasn't just that the dress itself was beautiful – it made her look beautiful as well. She just couldn't stop staring at herself – her gaze was locked on her image in the mirror. Never had she felt quite like this. This was the first time she had thought of herself as being beautiful without hesitation. That was strange, wasn't it? That it took a dress to see that. She wanted to capture the moment and just bottle it.

Reality sunk in though. And in that reality, there was no fiancé. She had to put a stop to this, before it went too far. "I don't think I can buy such an expensive dress."

This only seemed to encourage the sales lady. "Well, then this might be your lucky day. Because we are trying to promote the brand, this one is specially priced at $8000. They normally cost $11,000. So a $3000 discount, isn't that wonderful? "

"And I am sure it's worth every cent. Unfortunately, I don't have that kind of money," Izzy said, trying to come up with an excuse that could get her out of this, knowing she could not possibly buy the dress, even if she could afford it.

"That would be such a shame. You are a vision in that dress." Ann paused for a moment to think. "You know, since you don't need any alterations at all, we could make it $7500."

Ugh. That was the exact amount of Izzy's new car fund – she had gotten a bank statement this morning. Knowing that so much beauty was within her reach it made that much harder to say no. The money she had saved was for a car though . . . which she could, in theory, put off buying for another couple of years. In that case, she could buy the dress.

What the heck was she thinking? A dress over a car? Something completely impractical over something she used daily? Surely she was too sensible for that. On the other hand, cars had never made her feel like this. There was nothing wrong with the car she had now – she could easily get a few more of years out of it. Enough time to save for a new one. She had a good job, and not much else to spend her money on. This dress was "once in a lifetime." It gave a feeling she had never had before. Some people invested in art. This masterpiece of a gown could definitely be considered a work of art, if only judged by the amount of work that had gone into it. It was an investment in her happiness, and she deserved that. If her car broke down, there were other options – she had money saved for a rainy day.

Then reason won out. "I'm sorry, I can't," Izzy said.

But if she had thought the shop assistants were going to let her off easy, she was mistaken. "We only have one of these – when you come back, it might not be there anymore. I understand you want to bring your family but it might not be here by then. That would be a shame. The dress is just made for you!"

She tried to resist, but deep in her heart, she just wanted the dress so badly. It confused her. Her heart said "Buy it!" although there was no rational explanation for it. Izzy found it harder and harder to come up with excuses not buy it, even to herself.

"Think about it, miss. We will give you some privacy." They led Izzy back to the changing room and closed the curtain, leaving her alone with the dress. "If you need help undressing, call us. It's much easier taking it off though," Marie promised.

Izzy scrutinized herself in the smaller mirror in the dressing room. Somehow her complexion looked fairer. Her waist was tiny when strapped in like this, and her bosom had never looked . . . fuller. At the back, she looked graceful – there was no way to tell how big her bottom was through the layers of fabric – she looked tall and statuesque, like a china doll.

It was like she was a princess in a fairy tale. Only there was no prince. She needed to keep that in mind, and then maybe she could step away. The guy she was dating was more like a toad. He wasn't horribly per se, just … she did not feel herself around him. She started to wonder if there had ever been chemistry between them. He looked handsome and had a good job, but they had no common interests, and at times he could be extremely bossy. They had been together-ish for three years now, but most of the time she felt like she was with a complete stranger. She wasn't even sure why she was still with him. Soon she would forced to make a decision, and she felt most likely that they would break up.

So there was absolutely no reason to buy a wedding dress. It was silly. Why was she even wearing it? Because she was turning thirty-five next year? Maybe it was just her biological clock ticking. She had always thought she would have been married with children by now. And she hadn't even jumped the first hurdle.

What if she bought it as a reminder? A promise to herself that she hadn't given up on true love and all that. That she was beautiful and worthy of being loved. That she deserved to be admired. The last couple of years she had been working hard, without real enjoyment. Stuck being a dutiful employee, a dutiful girlfriend. This dress reminded her of her other side, the girl with hopes and dreams. She could not let that girl down any longer. She had the money, so why not?

The more she thought about it, the more it started making sense. Some teenagers bought promise rings – why not buy a promise dress, to promise herself that from now on she would be better to herself and achieve the goals she really wanted to achieve, not just trudge along doing her duty. Suddenly she wished that she could somehow wear this dress and never take it off.

She had to though – she could not keep it on forever. Soon the store would close, and the employees would want to go home. And she needed to get home too – she had obligations with the formerly mentioned boyfriend. He had a work do that required a "plus one." Lately these events were the only times they would spend time together. She was not looking forward to it.

One last look at herself like this, then she would take it off. It pained her. A mirage, a vision of perfection that could not become reality. She knew exactly how silly she was being, and in that respect it was a relief that she was in here by herself. In her mind, she could think of a thousand reasons NOT to buy the dress, but the little girl in her kept screaming "want, want, want" …

But she was a grown woman, she reminded herself. By now she should be able to resist such temptation.

Izzy unlaced the corset, and then carefully crawled out of the skirt. It was heavy – she nearly got stuck in it, and it took a lot of effort for her to find the way out. But she was not going to call for help, as a tear was slowly rolling down her cheek. She chided herself – it was just a dress. Getting back into her own clothes, she fought to regain her composure. Deep breaths. She could not let anybody see her like this. They would think she was mad, or worse, pity her.

Finally she felt calm enough to leave the chamber. She would thank them and tell them that she would consider it but that she could not possibly buy it at that amount. The shop assistants had been so helpful that she could not turn them down just like that. But she could not buy such an extravagant item of clothing either.

"Sometimes you see a dress on a person and know it is meant to be. You have such a glow about you, miss. I have only rarely seen that, but you definitely have it. It's like you waited your whole life for this dress. I would hate for you to lose out … so, I just talked to the manager. How about if we make it $6500? I promise you, you won't regret it," Ann tried to convince her.

Izzy could feel her resolve crumbling . . .

CHAPTER TWO

The back seat of Izzy's car was now completely filled by a huge bag that had the hook from a very fancy padded hanger sticking out at the top. What had she been thinking? She should go back there right now and plead insanity. After all it was insane to buy a wedding dress without a wedding, wasn't it? That was something only crazy people did. Which meant she was losing her mind.

She had no time to think about that now though. She was already running late and that meant John was gonna be pissed off as hell, like he always was when things did not exactly go his way. He'd be like a three year old with a temper tantrum, and she was not looking forward to listening to him mope all night long. Why did men have to be so childish? Life did not always go as planned – you just had to roll with it.

Although rolling along would have been nice right now. Traffic was completely jammed, and so far every light was against her. She would never be ready on time.

Once she got home, she still needed to get changed and get ready. The dress was laid out, but she did need to freshen up and touch up her makeup so it would be party proof. There would be no time to grab a bite to eat, though. She had been to John's office parties before, and the food was "special," to say the least. Whoever booked these events was a fan of molecular gastronomy. It was like Frankenstein in the kitchen, with food resurrected from the dead. Whatever you ate, it never tasted like you'd expect. An adventure maybe, if it had tasted nice. But no. Izzy was always happy if she managed to survive the night without getting poisoned.

Darn it, she was only three blocks away from home, but at this rate, walking would be faster. It was unfortunate that she couldn't just leave her car there in the traffic jam. The line in front of her was moving so slowly that the light had turned green three times already without her passing through. All she could hope for was that John would be stuck in traffic as well and not waiting impatiently for her in front of her door when she got there. Finally, she made it, only to find that there were no parking spaces left in the street. Such was the price these days of coming home just a little bit late. There were far too few spaces for the number of cars that needed them. Luckily John would want to drive his car to the dinner – as usual – so she would not have to worry about finding parking in the middle of the night. At last Izzy managed to find a space a block away in a side alley – it was so far away, she might as well have left the car back at the traffic jam. Alright, just lock up and hurry up. If she was lucky, she still had twenty minutes till John arrived.

But … the dress. It was not like she had forgotten about it. But as she caught a glimpse of it through the car window and she realized that leaving it there was not an option. It was obvious what it was, and, as it was worth more than the car at this point, it was clear that she would have to take it with her. However, getting it into her apartment building unnoticed was an entirely different matter. Hopefully, Sam would not see her. That was one person's opinion she did not want to deal with tonight.

Being stealthy with such a huge package wasn't easy though. It seemed to fight her every step of the way. To top it off, the wind started picking up, and the bag began to act like a huge sail. She had to hold on tight in order not to lose it. It made it almost impossible to reach the front door. She could just imagine the front page article, headlining "Woman flies through air with wedding dress," with a quote somewhere at the bottom from friends that were wondering what she was doing with it in the first place, and told how she was obviously mentally unstable.

Finally Izzy made it to the door in one piece, as did the dress. As she got it up the stairs – not the elevator, of course – only one neighbor saw her. Luckily, Mr. Beeton kept pretty much to himself. He would never even say as much as a hello when he passed her in the hallway, even though Izzy always did. He just was a grumpy old man with a grumpy old dog – but for once she was glad of it. Sam seemed to be stuck in traffic too somewhere, as there was no light coming from under his door. Good.

Getting to her apartment and closing the door behind her, she now had to hide the dress somewhere. The last thing she needed was for John to find it by accident. He would probably freak out and dump her on the spot. Hmmm, that would make breaking up with him very easy – she would not have to do a thing. But she still had an event next week where she needed him to return the favor as her "plus one." He did dress up quite nicely.

Only ten minutes left. She was never going to make it. Izzy opened up her closet and started pulling out clothes, throwing them on her bed to make room for the wedding dress. She then hung the dress, still in its bag, in the back of the closet, pulling other clothes around and in front of the bag to hide it as well she could. She closed the closet door with a momentary feeling of relief – but now there was a huge pile of clothes on the bed. Seven minutes and counting.

She pulled her hair loose from the bun she had worn it in all day and stripped. Now, where was the dress that she laid out this morning? Of course, at the bottom of the pile. She just hoped it wasn't too wrinkled.

Digging through the pile of clothes, she noticed how many black items of clothing she owned. Was she really turning into her mother? Well at least her new dress was anything but black. Aha, there it was – her little black dress, or at least, one of them. She quickly pulled it over her head only to hear the doorbell ring.

Just great, that meant John was here already. How did he do that in this kind of traffic? Pulling the dress further down, she headed for the intercom and pushed the button. Now she just needed to find her stockings in that pile.

"You aren't ready yet," John stated as he entered her apartment.

As if she didn't know that. "I got stuck in traffic." It wasn't a complete lie, but it wasn't exactly the truth either.

"I told you, you should have left early." The tone in his voice said it all – he was going to be in a rotten mood all evening.

"Yeah well, sometimes life happens." And, in this case, wedding dresses. "Can you zip me up?"

He did as asked. "How much longer do you need?"

As long as it took to get dressed. She was going as fast as she could, for god's sake. "About fifteen minutes – it doesn't start until 7:30, right? It's hardly past 6:00 yet." Shoes, shoes. Black or red? Red. Time to live a little and not be this dull little mouse.

He was standing there like a strict schoolmaster, about to give a lecture to a tardy student. "You know I hate being late . . . You are not gonna wear those shoes, are you? You'll look like a cheap tart."

Well, thanks a lot. She should dump him right now and get it over with. Then she would have the night off, and she could enjoy the evening with a nice glass of wine and not risk food poisoning. Instead, however, she did what he asked . . . or rather, commanded.

"Wear the pearls I gave you." He was checking his watch again and again, like that was going to make her go faster.

She quickly brushed her hair, put on some makeup, and grabbed the pearl necklace. All the while, he was standing in her hallway, sighing disapprovingly, arms crossed.

"Almost done?" There was that tone again.

All of it had hardly taken ten minutes so far, and she was almost done. One last check up and she was ready to get out of there. The face in the mirror looked familiar, but lacked all the glow she had seen earlier. It looked tired and dowdy. She did, however, look sophisticated, and that was all John cared about. This would have to do.

"Ready." She stated

"Finally . . . You look lovely." The way he said it sounded more like a reproach than a compliment. But at least they were leaving. John usually was nicer when there was other company. Then he had his mask of civility back on. The one he had when she first met him. Apparently she was so familiar now though that she wasn't worth that.

They got into the car. "How was your day?" she asked, trying to start a conversation and get him in a better mood.

"Fine," was his answer. After that, that it went quiet, and it would stay that way for the rest of the journey. It gave her time to reflect

Of course, despite the fact that they were there later than planned, they were still one of the first to arrive. Nobody came to these do's on time, except for John that was, and they would probably stay till the last man left.

She guessed that now was as good a time as any to ask him to accompany her next week. "Next Thursday, I have a company party . . ."

He didn't even let her finish. "I can't come with you. I need to work late that night."

"Can't you do that the night before? Or after? This one is really important to me."

"I'm not gonna turn around all my obligations just to go to another one of your tea parties." No, he just expected that she took off from work an hour early at the end of the day so that he could be the first to arrive. She felt like kicking him. But finally, more people started to arrive, John's boss among them. John went to him immediately, leaving Izzy to stand there by herself. She decided to get a glass of champagne to dull her senses. The events John attended were always so dull and stuffy. Maybe not surprising, as he was an accountant. But right now, she wished she were anywhere but here. The only surprising element at these do's were the food – but that was not necessarily a good thing

"Has he left you alone again?" a deep voice beside her asked.

"Hello Mike." Even though he was a colleague of John, he was one of the few people that were not dull. "Yeah, you know what he's like. He's off schmoozing with the boss again."

"And leaving a lovely lady like you to fend for herself? What a fool. Any man might think you were available. And who could resist a lovely gem like you." So what if Mike was a bit slick – at least he was always nice to Izzy. And complimentary. It made her feel a lot better

"Are you trying to flirt with me?" she laughed.

"I wouldn't dare. But you look ravishing tonight dear. Just … the pearls are maybe a bit too Audrey Hepburn. You are too young for that," he noted.

She rolled her eyes. "How did you guess? John insisted I wear them."

"You should never leave decisions like that up to him – you know men have no taste when it comes to fashion."

"All men except you?" Izzy laughed.

He winked. "I'm special, dear."

So he was. And a much better conversationalist than the guy she had come with.

John, however, charged in. "Is he bothering you?" he asked, pulling her away from Mike.

"Mike? Never." She could handle Mike, and she knew he would never cross the line.

"You *know* I don't want you hanging out with him," John hissed, taking Izzy's glass from her hand and downing her champagne in one swig. The empty glass was thrust back into her hand like she was a busboy.

"I can decide for myself who I hang out with. At least he paid attention to me. You abandoned me the moment Mr. Thompson came in."

"He is important to me, to my career, you know that. My promotion could happen any day now. That does not give you the right to go gallivanting off with other men." John was turning slightly red with anger. She could care less at this point.

"I was hardly gallivanting. He only said hello, and we started talking."

He was holding her by the shoulder like a father scolding his teenage daughter. "He is a womanizer, a skirt chaser. Do you know how bad it looks for me when they see you consorting with him?"

Really, that was what he was worried about? Just looks, not that she'd run off with the guy? Maybe she should, just to spite him. "I don't want to argue with you here John, but if you don't shut up and let go of me now, I will cause a scene you will regret very much. Understood?" she warned him.

"Fine. Let's find our table," he said storming off and dragging her along.

They had been placed at the same table as John's boss, Mr. Anton Thompson, Jr.

Izzy watched as Anton held the door for his wife and pulled out her chair for her as she took her seat. In contrast, Izzy could barely avoid getting hit by the door as John charged through first and sat down without even looking at her. Focusing on his boss, John went back to ignoring Izzy completely. She would have liked to say that behavior like this was a one-off … but lately, this was pretty much how their dates went. She had tried to talk about it, but he simply blew her off. Luckily, she hadn't seen much of him lately. But what kind of woman hated seeing her own boyfriend? Unspoken resentment had been building up for months now, and the break-up seemed more and more unavoidable.

Her thoughts wandered back to the dress – not the way it looked, but what it represented. A wedding dress. Made for a wedding. She was not getting any younger. She didn't want to become an old spinster with twenty cats. But did she have to stay with this man just so that she wouldn't be alone? It didn't seem right. Soon a decision would need to be made.

Getting back into the dating scene was another thing, though. She had hated it in the first place, and to do it all again, at her age . . . Oh god, now she was really starting to sound like an old lady. Maybe she should just started adopting cats now and get it over with.

Well, for now, she just needed to get through the night. At least she had Claire, Mrs. Thompson, to keep her company. Claire was a lovely lady only slightly older than Izzy, and in a few months, Izzy was doing a gallery opening for her. Hopefully the conversation tonight wouldn't be just about work.

"The food tonight isn't too bad, is it?" Claire whispered, smiling at her.

"Yeah, it it's almost edible compared to last time. But that could be because I did not eat beforehand this time."

"Busy day?"

Izzy sighed. "Not really, but got stuck in traffic getting home. And you know John, he wants to be here before anyone else is."

"He really should learn about being fashionably late. It's all the rage these days, you know?"

"Thanks for the tip Claire, but John and "being fashionable"? You are kidding right?" Both women laughed. The men were so deeply immersed in their conversation that they did not even notice.

"Get some kids – I swear you'll never be on time for anything anymore. They are worth it, though. And Anton is wonderful with them. He loves them to bits and never misses the important occasions. He has even stopped working late so he can play with them after work – I never thought I would see that happen."

She wondered what kind of father John would make. He certainly wouldn't get home early to play with the kids. More likely, he would work late the rest of his life just to avoid them. John had no patience with kids – he found them obnoxious and intolerable. When they got near him, he froze, and if they stayed in his vicinity for longer than five minutes, he started to shout at them. He had frightened the life out of poor Lily that way. Izzy had still not forgiven him for that. No, she could not see herself having kids with John. If they did have them, raising them would be left completely up to her.

That was not how she saw her future. She desperately wanted kids, but not with a guy like that. She wanted someone like Sam. He would do anything for his little girl. Well, so would Izzy, for that matter, even though she was just an honorary aunt. She loved Lily to bits.

The father to her children should be hands on, involved, Izzy thought to herself. To be there for her and the kids. That just wasn't John, and she doubted if he could change.

The conversation with Claire had moved on without Izzy noticing. "At our opening I want edible stuff. Cake! I want there to be so much cake, people think they are at a wedding reception," Claire said.

"Hmm?" The word wedding confused her. The dress swam back into her vision, with an altar in the distance … but no man. Then she realized the remark had nothing to do with weddings, but with cake. As in the thing Marie Antoinette loved. "Oh that might work. Who doesn't like cake? Maybe keep it small but delicate. Petite fours."

"Well anything has to be better than this. It's not Anton's choice, you know. His father, however, insists. He fell in love with this "cuisine chemistry" and now tries to infect everybody with it. I'm just afraid that he'll poison us all one day."

Izzy laughed. "Me too."

"At least Anton is treating me to real food after this. A nice steak."

The mere thought made Izzy salivate. If only John did the same. He loved this stuff though. Or at least he said he did to please the boss. He probably believed it too.

"Enjoying yourselves, ladies?" John interrupted, tearing his attention away from the boss for a second. She knew it was his not-so-subtle hint that they were making too much noise.

Claire, however, was oblivious to that. "Yes John, thanks for bringing my friend. I wouldn't know how to make it through the night without her," she answered. John had no reply for that. Not quite satisfied, he turned his attention back to Claire's husband. Poor Anton – stuck with John all night.

Dinner continued, and more culinary "delights" were served. What was wrong with simple good food – in its natural state? Everything here tasted so chemical and unpleasant. Anything had to be better than this. Maybe a cupcake . . . with chocolate glazing and a strawberry on top, Izzy fantasized. Right now, even a plate of Brussels sprouts would have sounded tempting, even though she usually hated those. It couldn't be a good sign if you were daydreaming about food during dinner.

Now Anton turned his attention to her. "You and John have been together quite a couple of years now. When will you two finally tie the knot?"

Izzy nearly choked. Something got caught in her throat, and she started coughing.

John was beside her and patted her back. "Stop it, everybody is watching!"

Well, thanks a lot. That was really the thing to worry about when your girlfriend was choking. Izzy was fighting too hard to get her breath back to protest though.

Claire handed her a glass of water. "Are you alright darling? Maybe best if we do not ask that question again, right?" she asked looking worried.

"It's okay. I'm fine. Just not used to this sort of haute cuisine." This sent Izzy into another fit of coughing, this time to hide her laugh. She could hear Claire giggling as well.

CHAPTER THREE

It was amazing – but not in a good way. Even something as perfectly simple and delicious as chocolate mousse could be utterly ruined. Fast food restaurants even managed to produce a decent version of what had become a staple for women in need of a pick-me-up. This, however, had tasted curdled, and Izzy was scared to eat it. Maybe it was supposed to taste this way, but she wasn't going to risk it. Besides it might ruin her love of chocolate mousse for good.

She felt utterly disappointed. Well, at least it wasn't the worst disappointment of the night. Looking at John, she wondered how she could have ever thought he was the right man. Something about her was different tonight – it was like she was seeing for the first time how he really was. Of course, he had always been this way. But up till now, she had simply ignored it. Blamed herself – even when he was in a rotten mood.

The mousse had been the dessert, so at least that meant there weren't any other dishes that could be ruined. Now it was just another three hours of cocktails, and then John would bring her home, where she could have some proper dinner … if she did not faint beforehand.

Back in the reception hall, a small jazz band was playing. Izzy got herself another glass of champagne and went back to chatting with Claire.

"Is everything alright between you and John?" Claire asked delicately.

Better prepared for the question this time, and with John at the other end of the room, Izzy managed to hold her drink this time. "I don't know. These days I feel like we are completely disconnected. He doesn't even ask how I'm doing anymore. I'm just an accessory to take to these events."

"Sounds what you two need is a good long talk."

If he'd actually listen. "I tried. He never has time."

Claire put her arms around Izzy. "I'll miss you if you two split up, kiddo. I'll lose my partner in crime for these events."

"At least Anton pays attention to you … But you are not rid of me yet. We still have an opening to plan together, we will see lots of each other. And I would like to stay friends after that. You are one of the few people that make going to these nights bearable. You and Mike, even though John never allows me to talk to him for more than five seconds straight."

"What, why not?"

Izzy sighed, and threw her hands in the air. "He has gotten it into his head that Mike is a womanizer and is after me. So every time he comes and talks to me, John charges toward us and chases him away."

For some reason this made Claire break out in a coughing fit. When she got her breathe back all she could utter was, "Tell him he couldn't be more wrong." What she meant with that was not exactly clear, and she did not explain it further.

The music wasn't quite your regular dance music, but the ladies decided to dance together anyways. Halfway through, Anton, charming as he was, cut in to dance with his wife. John was standing on the other side of the room, pretending his nose bled. He could dance – he had even learned ballroom dancing in his youth for one of those fancy-schmancy high society coming-of-age galas where the hobnobs of the ruling class were introduced to each other. But of course, there was no way he would come dance with Izzy unless he absolutely had to. Fine – then she would dance by herself. No matter how silly that looked.

Luckily, he wasn't the only man who could dance. "May I have this dance?"

She smiled "Yes Mike, of course you can."

"We were so rudely interrupted earlier," he winked, and led her out onto the floor.

"Rudely is what John does best."

"Do I detect trouble in paradise?"

"More like impending doom. Oh wait, here it comes." Over Mike's shoulder she saw John charging toward them.

"May I cut in." It wasn't a question. The distaste in his voice was palpable. She could not handle another sermon without screaming. Something in her had changed. Normally, she would have felt guilty for angering him.

She hoped Mike would say no and kept dancing with her, but of course he did not. He stepped aside like the perfect gentleman he was, letting John step in. John looked at her weirdly. She couldn't quite read his face. He was angry for sure, but he seemed to be holding back for some reason. He did not look at her or speak as they swayed around the floor. It was like dancing with a dummy.

"Would you like to leave and go out for a drink?" he all of sudden asked.

It surprised her. Not to be the last ones there? In fact, to be the first to leave before any else did? That was so very unlike John that she wondered if he were feeling ill. It was, however, too good an opportunity to pass up. "Yes, gladly."

Again it surprised her that they were actually moving toward the door. Getting their coats and saying their goodbyes, they left, they actually left.

The wind now was even colder. She shivered, but John kept walking at a fast pace that was unsuitable for the heels she was wearing. She struggled to keep up.

"There's a nice bar around the corner, shall we go there?" he suggested. Ah, so this was probably a temporary outing – they would pop back to the party later. She should have known. He would never really have left the party early.

The only reason he was taking her aside was probably to scold her for having talked to Mike again. No, now she was being negative. It wasn't fair on John, but she was so used to this kind of behavior.

"I think we should talk."

She wondered where the sudden epiphany had come from, seeing as she had been saying the same thing for months. Had Anton clued him in or something? It had Claire written all over it. But if John wanted to talk, she had plenty to tell him. First though, she wanted to know what he had to say.

They arrived at a small cozy looking bar called O'Keeffe's, with brown leather booths and soft lighting. It was quaint, an Irish-style pub … not something John would normally ever set foot in. He liked high-end designer places, with seats that left you with an aching back at the end of the night.

They sat down in one of the stalls, and John ordered a single-malt whiskey for himself and a white wine spritzer for her. Ugh. Izzy hated white wine spritzers. But, she decided to let that one slip, and hear him out first. Pick your battles, she reminded herself.

He stared into his glass without saying a thing. Some talk this was. Well at least the expected scolding hadn't showed up yet. She waited a few minutes until the silence became unbearable.

"How do you see your future?" She was very aware that she did not say our.

Finally he looked up "Well, I am going to get this promotion sometime in the coming months. I put all the hours in, and they practically promised it to me. After that is through and I am partner, I think we should start thinking about getting married."

Izzy's stomach turned. So that was why he had left the party early and brought her here. Wait a minute. Was he proposing? This sounded more like a business proposal. It was typical of him to ask her just like that, as if it was not a big deal – just another transaction. And now he expected an answer from her.

Marriage. Wasn't that what she had been thinking about all night? Turning 35, marrying Mr. Right? It had been on her mind since she had left the wedding dress shop. Then why did the idea of marrying John make her feel ill?

In her heart, she knew why. She was not in love with John – not any more, at least. But to dump him now? She needed to think, get her mind together. One rash decision a day had to be the limit, and she had already bought the dress – which was like the ultimate rash decision of a lifetime.

"What do you say? We should at least think about living together. Mr. Thompson asked me the other day about it, and I did not have an answer. It was embarrassing. After all, we have been together for two years now." The familiar accusatory tone returned to his voice.

To be with John 24/7. The image that brought up was even worse than the idea of marrying him. Still, she couldn't help correcting him. "It's been three years, actually." All that time wasted on a selfish jerk. "Are you suggesting we move in together?"

"Well, not right now – I am far too busy to let your paraphernalia clutter up my life. We would need to plan it carefully after my promotion."

Like hell they would. "Well, I'm busy as well. I'm not sure if I can plan you in." Ouch, that sounded even more bitter than she had meant it to.

"Well, I am sure you can make time for it. Just work around it. I'll be very busy, Fergusson has asked me to look into his clientele list as he's retiring, it's a major opportunity …" And there he went again, acting like his job was majorly important and hers was just a trifling plaything.

The urge to dump him on the spot was growing stronger by the minute. But Izzy had made up her mind. One week to get her head together. She'd give him one more chance . . . one more shot . . .

"If we get the Morgan account, I'll be made partner. It's quite a high profile. . ."

And several shots of vodka if she was going to have to listen to this drivel much longer. "I'm gonna get us some more drinks," she said, getting up from the table. The other option would have been hitting him over the head.

"What? Oh, Glenlivet again."

She went to the bar. "A shot of Glenlivet, and one cocktail that is sickeningly sweet and very high in alcohol."

The bartender looked at her with pity. "Dump him. He's not worth it, dearie. You are far too pretty to spend even a second on the likes of him," he said with a kindhearted smile.

Izzy sighed. "We have been together for three years."

"Ouch. Sorry. Sometimes it's better to rip off the band-aid than to let the wound fester though."

He was right. But one more week shouldn't matter much. Although the decision was pretty clear. She needed to prepare herself though, before she told John. It wasn't something she could do out of the blue. Knowing John, he probably wouldn't even notice if she told him straight out now . . . or he would treat it like it was a whim and ignore it.

"Drinks are on the house."

"Thank you, that is very kind, but it really isn't necessary."

"Oh, yes it is. I hate seeing a pretty lass like you look so sad. So take my advice, dump him . . . and maybe take a chance on me if you do. No strings." He pushed forward a piece of paper with a phone number on it. "Enjoy your White Russian."

What did he mean by that?

"Your cocktail."

Oh. . ..

Tucking the phone number away in her purse she took a good look at him. He looked a fair bit older than her – roughly late forties, Izzy would have guessed – but his face was full of character, with a manly stubble and shaggy hair that was going sophistically gray at the sides. He had a friendly face and was very good looking . . . but she bet he gave his phone number to all the girls. Still, if she did decide to dump John, why not? This guy looked like fun. And he did have a gorgeous accent …

"Thank you. I will think about it," she said, giving him a smile. At least he had somewhat calmed her fears about going back into the dating world.

Getting back to the table, she saw John looking very uncomfortable. She wondered if he was thinking of going back to the hall to do some more schmoozing with his colleagues and business partners.

"What took you so long?" he said, irritated.

"I was getting our drinks," Izzy said. Like she had said she was going to do. She took a sip of her drink. Sickeningly sweet just about covered it.

"And what were you looking at that guy for?

"I think it was the other way round. Really, are you jealous? At least he complimented me. Can't a girl get a compliment every now and then?"

John got defensive. "No, of course not."

Was that a 'No' to being jealous or to her getting a compliment? Well she could fill in the answer to that one, really.

She had promised herself to give him one more shot, though. So one last chance for John to redeem himself. "Do you see children in your future?"

"Yes, of course," he said, if it was completely logical.

Wait. . . Really? He wanted kids?

"They can be essential. The best way to reach the parents is through the kids – you let the kids play together and talk about business in the meantime. Plus, kids' parties are great for networking."

Izzy felt herself going from a slow simmer to a boil. It was not worth it. One more week. It was becoming like a mantra. One more week, and she'd be rid of him.

"I think I am ready to go home," Izzy said. She would start packing his things as soon as she got home.

To her surprise, John did exactly as she asked without protest. On the way home, he was still chatting away about his prospects for a promotion. This time, however, Izzy wasn't in the mood for talking. It was over between them – she knew that for sure after tonight. She just wished she had realized it sooner.

"That was a good time tonight," John said.

Yeah, right – if you liked dentist's appointments, perhaps. In her mind, she was making a list of John's belongings. Luckily, he hardly ever left anything at her apartment. A long time ago, he had said to her that leaving a toothbrush at someone's place was a sign of commitment. She should have seen the warning signs long ago.

"We must do something like this again soon."

"How about that event I have to be at next Thursday?" she asked sarcastically.

"Isabelle . . .you know I can't."

She hated it when he called her Isabelle. "Well, I'm busy the rest of the week with work." And your exit, she thought.

"Fine. I'll walk you to your door."

"I can manage."

"And I'll come up for a coffee."

That meant Izzy would have to wait even longer to get something to eat. But she couldn't stop him – it seemed he was determined to come up. Well, it would be the last time. Thirty minutes, then she would kick him out if she had to.

Once inside though, he started kissing her in a harsh and unromantic way. Trying to pull down her dress, he began pushing her toward the bedroom. But Izzy wasn't about to have one last fuck with him just for the hell of it.

"Whoa, what do you think you are doing? I'm not in the mood," she said harshly, pushing him off her.

"I thought you wanted babies? You're not getting any younger."

Forget dumping him – how about strangling him? "You thought wrong. Just go home. I've had enough."

John stepped back, shaking his head. "This is just not working," he said. "I think we should break up."

Wait a minute – that was her line. She was supposed to prepare for a week and then call him all the names under the sun that she had been bottling up inside. "What?"

"I met someone else … someone that I feel much happier with."

"A second ago you were trying to . . . to fuck me, and now you are telling me there is someone else?" Izzy should have been glad, but the curveball John had just thrown had caught her off guard.

"Yes. She gives me what you can't."

He was lying. Who would want to date such a pompous ass? But wait . . . this was what she wanted . . . she was dumping him . . . well, vice versa, really. "Is that the reason you can't come with me on Thursday? Because you are going out with her?"

"No, uh … of course not." John said, averting his eyes. He paused, and then looked back up at Izzy. "I was hoping we could work it out. This break-up could really put my career at risk, you know. Mr. Thompson and his wife like you. How about if we don't actually break up? Just see other people. We could still be each other's dates for events. I'll take Thursday evening off and come with you – how's that?"

Sure, now he had time for her on Thursday. So typical – he just cared about what the people at work would think. She was so sick of him. He probably had only said that he wanted to break up in order to scare her and make her more compliant. "Oh no you don't. You are right – we are over. You don't care about me, and I certainly don't care about you anymore. Leave! And don't come back."

"Isabelle . . . I do care." He tried to touch her again, but she yanked her arm away.

"About your career, yes. Unfortunately I don't give a damn. I am sick of you belittling me. You can do that to somebody else from now on. I had a good time tonight . . . every time you weren't near me."

"Now you are just being spiteful."

"I haven't started yet. Honestly, I can't remember the last time I had fun in your company. Now if you don't mind, this is my house and I would like you to leave."

"But my stuff?"

"I'll mail it."

John just stood there, trying to think of a response and clearly failing.

"Get out, John! Get it through your thick skull. I never want to see you again."

He remained there, looking quizzically at her as if he really didn't believe she was doing this.

"Get out!" Izzy pointed at the door.

He still wasn't moving. Izzy tried to think of a way to get him to leave. She picked up a plate, and threw it at him. "Get out!" This last bit finally seemed to get through to him – he got the point and left. As she heard the click of the door lock, Izzy felt she could finally breathe again.

He was gone. For good, hopefully. Izzy wasn't sorry, but she noticed that she had started shaking.

She picked up the phone and dialed the one person that she knew would be there for her. "Sam, can you come over?" she asked trying not to sound panicked.

"Can you come here? Lily just fell asleep. She's been having nightmares lately."

"Um . . . yeah, ok." Right now, Izzy didn't want to go anywhere – she just wanted to curl up into a little ball . . . but it was just ten steps from her door to his. She could manage that, right? She could do it.

Sam knew her like nobody else did – even over the phone he could tell. . . "What's the matter?"

"I'll tell you in a minute."

CHAPTER FOUR

Sam was Izzy's best friend. Well, technically, he was her best friend's brother, but since Sophie lived on the other side of the country these days, and he lived across the hall, he had been promoted. She had known Sam since the day he had been born – both girls had been six at the time. He had gone from being their living doll, to being a pesky little brother that bothered them as they were experimenting with makeup, to being an irritable, moody teenager that even tried to spy on them once or twice. Then she had lost sight of him for a decade when she went to college and got her first job. She would still see him at Christmas, though, and by that point, they got along a lot better than they did as kids. He grew into a handsome young man, getting a girlfriend and then getting married. Unlike her. Boyfriends had come and gone – but "The One" had not been among them.

When Izzy had gotten the job offer of a lifetime, the choice was easily made. Being the event organizer for one of the best companies there was – that wasn't something she could turn down. Knowing it that was in the same city where Sam was already living made it easier too. She'd have a friend and would not completely be on her own. They had met up so he could show her around, but pretty soon it became clear his marriage was on the rocks. He and his wife had just had a daughter, but the mother had no interest in taking care of Lily. She saw the little girl as a burden. Izzy became Sam's confidant, giving sisterly advice where she could. At first they had wondered if his wife was suffering from postnatal depression, but it soon became obvious that she just lacked the mothering gene.

Sam stepped up to the task, trying to be a good husband to his wife and be both mother and father to Lily at the same time. However, his wife seemed to be jealous of any time he spent with Lily. Trying to please everyone nearly killed Sam, and so in the end they broke up – leaving him to take care of Lily completely on his own. Lily's mother did not even visit her on weekends. He did everything for Lily – taking care of her, feeding her, dressing her – even braiding her hair. Of course, Izzy thought, with that last bit, he actually had quite a lot of experience. She could not count the number of times they had dressed him up as a girl and did his hair when he was still a little boy, but it was a slight miracle that he had not become a drag queen. It was also a miracle he still had a full head of hair, for that matter. Especially after the flat ironing incident when they had accidentally burned off his beautiful brown curls. She was happy they had recovered.

Now he lived just across the hall, which was great. It was like having a male version of her best friend, and though Izzy would never admit it, often his advice was often better than Sophie's. The marriage, the divorce, and being a father had matured him a lot. She and Sophie still tended to act like kids whenever they met, probably because they had so much past together. She wouldn't trade Sophie for the world, though. Or Sam.

The door was already open, and Sam was waiting for her, his brown curls looking almost golden in the light that poured from the door. "John and I just broke up," she said as soon as she saw him.

"What? Come here, sweetie. Tell me what happened." His arms enclosed her, and he kissed the top of my head.

They sat down on the couch. Comforting gray eyes told her everything was going to be alright. She didn't want to cry, John wasn't worth it. So instead she snuggled up against Sam.

"I think tonight, for the first time, I saw him as he really is, you know. Not like I didn't know it, but I was choosing to ignore it until now. It was convenient to have somebody to come with me to all these parties that I need to go because of work. Oh my god, that sounds awful doesn't it? Together so you have a 'plus one.'"

Sam stroked her back. "Not at all. I bet you are not the only one who does this. After all, John was doing exactly the same by the sound of it."

"That's true. He was even suggesting we get married and have kids tonight, because it would look good to Mr. Thompson, and kids can get him invited to parties . . . I don't think he loves me. He just thinks we look good together." The clearer the picture became, the more painful it was. Years of her life she could not get back. Which she could have used to find the right guy.

"If one guy ever deserved a vasectomy . . ." Sam didn't finish his sentence. "So that's why you dumped him?"

"No, he dumped me . . ." She still couldn't believe it. "I wanted to dump him, but I decided to give him one more week. Mostly so I could mentally prepare myself for dumping him. You know him – if I had told him straight out, he probably would have ignored it. "

"Yeah, I know him alright." Sam's face turned to thunder. He had been trying to hold back so far, but he couldn't stand John.

"Still not forgiven him for yelling at Lily, eh?"

"Never. He frightened the life out of her only because she was singing. Kids make noise – as a grown-up, you deal with that. She was not trying to be obnoxious, she was just happily singing. I could have throttled him that day."

"Me too. I haven't forgiven him for that. I think that was when I first started seeing him for who he was. We have been rocky ever since." It was true – by yelling at Lily, John had shown his true colors. Of course, he had been mean to Izzy before, but she had reasoned that away. Hurting a person she loved was different, and that had been the beginning of the end.

"So what happened?"

"We had an awful time at that dinner – he was ignoring me completely. It had already started out bad because I was late, according to his schedule."

This made Sam huff. He could not stand how John took Izzy for granted.

"No need to get mad now dear. We are already broken up, and I am never going back to him. Ever."

"Good." Sam was still looking angry, though.

I know you are practically my brother, but you can't beat him up, okay? It would set a bad example to Lily," she said with a mocking grin.

This brought a grin to his face "Might be worth it though. Knock off some of his smugness . . . So what happened after that?"

"Well, about the only thing that was pulling me through the evening was talking to Claire. Then, all of a sudden, he asks me if I want to go with him somewhere for a drink, and we end up at this pub. I ask him how he sees his future, turns out I am just a peon in that, and I am getting more ready to dump him by the minute. We get back here, and he tries to get me into bed. I say no, and he dumps me. Even said there was somebody else he likes better."

"Just like that?"

"Pretty much. One minute he is trying to rip my clothes off, the next he says it is over. Took me completely by surprise."

"Asshole," Sam hissed.

"Well to be honest, I was glad. Saved me the trouble of trying to get rid of him. Though he did try to get back with me straight away. Our breaking up wouldn't look right to Mr. Thompson. At that point I threw him out."

Sam got up. "So why are you so upset. Sounds to me like we should be celebrating. Let's crack open a bottle of wine."

"Oh please, no more booze. I have hardly eaten, you know what dinners at that company are like."

"Ah, yeah. Celebratory omelet then?"

"Yes please." Sam cooked a mean omelet. He was a pretty good chef overall, seeing he needed to feed Lily every day and his wife had never even touched a pan.

He moved toward the kitchen. "Parmesan and cheese?" Looking in the fridge he got out the ingredients. "I got some leftover salad too."

"Lovely. Thank you."

"For what?" he asked cracking the eggs and whisking them. A skillet was put on the stove with a knob of butter, and he added in the other ingredients before pouring out the mixture.

"Taking such good care of me."

"You're family, or at least as good as. Come here." He put one arm around her as he kept his eyes on the pan. "That guy wasn't good enough for you. I'm glad he is finally out of your life."

"I should have done it sooner, shouldn't I? I mean, three years of my life . . . wasted on a jerk who just saw me as a trinket on his arm, something to show off."

"He looked okay in the beginning. Then again, so did my ex, so maybe I am not such a good judge of character."

She sighed. "Neither am I, I suppose."

"Well at least we have each other." He gave her another hug.

The omelet was done. He let it slide onto a plate, and they sat down at the kitchen table as she dug in. It was delicious. Good simple food, no frills, just made to perfection with love. She nearly wolfed it down, it was so good. Especially in comparison to what she had been served earlier that night.

"Glad to see you like it."

"I wish you had been the chef there instead of those laboratory cooks from the restaurant. Who wants to eat frothy snot? It should be a crime to serve that stuff."

"Sorry, I am perfectly happy with the career I have," Sam apologized. He worked as a photographer and cameraman. Right now, he had a steady job doing an afternoon talk show that allowed him to bring Lily to day care in the morning and pick her up again in the afternoon. Every now and again, Izzy would hire him as the photographer at one of her events. He was the best there was, capturing people as they were, finding their inner beauty. "Explain one thing to me though. If you wanted to dump him and you are not sorry about him being gone, then why did you sound so upset when you were on the phone? And you were shaking when you got in. I could feel it"

"All the emotions, I guess. It was quite an evening, I had hardly eaten. I feel like I am still processing . . . Oh, and I threw a plate at him."

"Good for you. I hope you hit him."

"No . . . probably should have, he deserved it. I didn't do it out of anger though. He just wouldn't leave, so I thought I need to do something so he'll go away. It was a rational decision, and I felt completely calm as I did it. And it worked. He was surprised, but he left. Is there something wrong with me? I mean, you are supposed to do such things in anger. Am I a psychopath? I feel like I should be feeling something – hurt, anger, resentment – but I feel nothing. Just relief that he is gone."

"You are not a psycho, Izzy. You are the sweetest woman I know. I think you have been heading for this break-up for a long time now. That is why you feel relief."

"And the plate?"

"Good call, I'd say. Next time, aim better."

"It was one of my best though. Villeroy and Boch. I should have grabbed a different plate." She shook her head. "Ugh, now the set is no longer complete. Think I can replace it?"

"Sure, and if not, people are always selling stuff online. I'm sure you'll find one . . . Probably from some other woman who threw half the set at her lousy boyfriend."

That made them both laugh.

Suddenly there was scuffling behind them. "Daddy?" a little voice asked. "Aunty Iz?" Lily rubbed the sleep from her eyes as she clutched the teddy Izzy had given her as a baby. Out of all her toys, Mr. Peebles was her favorite.

"Hey there, sweetie! Nightmares troubling you?" Izzy asked. "Come over here."

The little girl nodded her head and climbed into Izzy's lap. "You too?"

"Sorta, yes." She was pretty sure that all future dreams with John in them would be nightmares.

"Daddy is good at chasing nightmares away."

"I know he is. What got you so scared?" She softly stroked Lily's curls. Lily had her father's hair.

"You and daddy were gone. I got shouted at by a scary monster, and I fell very deep in a dark cave. Then I woke up."

Izzy could almost feel Sam grit his teeth, and she did not need to look at him to see his jaw was clenched. She just wished she *had* aimed that plate properly and hit John in the head, or better yet somewhere it would have *really* hurt. "We are here for you, sweetie. And we are not going anywhere. So anyone who wants to shout at you will have to go through us. We are not gonna let anybody hurt you."

Lily yawned.

"It was just a dream, princess. But now you need to go back to bed," Sam said.

"I don't wanna. What if it comes back?"

"Shall I come with you? I'll read you a story and stay with you till you go back to sleep," she suggested.

"Yes please, Aunt Izzy," the girl begged.

"Softie," Sam whispered in Izzy's ear as they all got up and went to the little girl's bedroom. "She has you wrapped around her little finger."

"Just look in the mirror, 'daddy,'" Izzy replied, softly so Lily couldn't hear.

Sam picked up his little girl in his arms and carried her off to bed as Izzy chose a book off the shelves filled with fairy tales.

"Love you, daddy."

"Love you, little ladybug."

They were so sweet together, so perfect, Izzy thought, standing in the doorway.

"Fairy tale, please!" Lily chirped, as Izzy came over with the book she had chosen – a big book with golden lettering. "You tell them so well, aunty. You do all the voices." High praise it was, and Sam winked.

It was getting a bit chilly, so instead of sitting on top of the bed, Izzy slid in beside Lily under the warm covers. Turning on the little night light so she could read, she opened the book. Cinderella, the girl who got the perfect dress from her fairy godmother so she could woo the man of her dreams – who was perfect in every way, of course. It seemed a very fitting way to end the night. If only it was as easy in real life.

CHAPTER FIVE

The next day Izzy woke up to the sound of a camera shutter. Everything around her was pink, except the girl in her arms. This wasn't her room. She was still in Lily's.

"What are you doing?" she asked sleepily, seeing Sam move from the corner of her eye. He was clearly taking pictures, and she had a rough idea what state she was in. If she looked as bad as she felt, she dreaded the results.

"Shhh, stay like that for another second. You two look perfect." Sure, Sam. Well, leave it up to him to find the beauty in everything. He was a true artist with a camera, so maybe it would look alright.

She was too tired to move anyways. Trying to hide her face as well as she could, she let him be. Lily started to stir next to her, waking up as well.

"Hi aunty," the little girl said immediately, smiling up at her. That was at least one person that never suffered from a bad temper in the morning.

Izzy snuggled closer. "Hi sweetie, did you sleep okay?"

"Great!" Lily gave her a hug and jumped up to hug her daddy as well.

"You two fell asleep around the same time, and you looked so sweet together that I decided to let you stay there. I hope you don't mind, Izzy."

"Sleep with my favorite girl in my arms? Not at all. So have you been taking pictures of us all night?"

"No, only just now. I just got up, and the light hit you so beautifully that I just had to catch it."”

"I just bet, with me looking all disheveled. Ohhh, my head . . . I wasn't that drunk last night, was I?" Last night's events started to come back to her.

Sam shook his head. "Not at all. And you look lovely as ever."

"Must have been the bad combo of liquor without food then. That White Russian didn't feel good going down."

"White Russian?"

"A cocktail. Very sweet."

"You gonna stay with us all day, Aunt Izzy?" Lily asked. She smiled so sweetly, begging her with those big brown eyes, that Izzy just melted.

She couldn't, though. "Um. . .there are a couple of things I need to do today, Lily. But I'll come back later, alright?"

She didn't want to wait for John to come by and ransack her house looking for his stuff – she would rather find it all herself. Ideally, she'd mail it to him so she didn't have to face him at all. It was not that she was afraid of him or her own feelings. She just didn't want to talk to him ever again. She was sick of his lecturing and his condescending ways. And it would be worse now that they had broken up. Either that, or he would realize his mistake and would try to win her back, and that was a definite NO. She was way too happy to be rid of him.

It felt like a burden had fallen off Izzy's shoulders. No more obligations to handle. That was exactly what John had become: a duty, a chore. The number of times that he had been useful to her had been extremely limited, seeing as he always seemed to have had to work late on the days she needed him. Which reminded her of something.

"Sam. Is there a chance you could accompany me to an event on Thursday? I would go alone, but this is one occasion when you really need to bring a partner or you end up looking odd."

"So you are asking me?" He grinned, with a boyish twinkle in his eye.

She laughed, feeling better already. "Yeah, well, any man is better than none, dear. And with a bit of effort, you do scrub up well." Very well indeed if he wanted to.

He looked pensive for a moment. "I'll need a sitter for Lily."

"Of course. Look, I'll go alone if I need to. I would rather have someone as support though."

"I'll see what I can do. If possible, I'll come with you."

She got up and hugged him. "Thank you."

"I can come too!" chirped Lily, looking up at Izzy with a helpful smile.

"Sorry kid, this is for grown-ups only."

"Not fair!" she pouted.

"I know. Well, we will have a 'just girls' day over the weekend to make up for that, alright?" There were some things a daddy could not do, or at least, not that well, and Izzy was happy to step in as a female role model for Lily now and then. She was very aware of the influence she had on Lily, and tried to set her the best example possible, though she was sure she was failing here and there.

Alright. Time to get started, and ban John from her life. After a pancake breakfast that Sam made and that Lily had insisted she stay for, Izzy went back to her own apartment.

The plate still lay broken on the floor as she came in, shattered in so many pieces that gluing it back together wasn't an option. It was a perfect symbol of her relationship with John, and part of her wanted to leave it there as a reminder. She couldn't though – all those sharp shards were far too dangerous. She got a dustpan, swept up the pieces, and threw them away in the trash.

A quick shower, and then to work with the "de-John-ing." It felt good. The only thing that saddened her was the time she had wasted on him.

There was precious little of him around, anyway. A few DVDs from movies she had not liked, a CD from Celine Dion that he had copied and she had hated, a forgotten necktie. No toothbrush, shirt, or anything like that. She combed through her closets just to be sure. She even got the pieces of jewelry that he had given her. Should she return that as well? She looked at them. A golden tennis bracelet, a pearl necklace, a white-gold heart-shaped charm, diamond stud earrings. She definitely didn't want to keep them – she didn't even like them. They were expensive-looking, but so generic that they meant nothing to her. He might as well have bought them for a random stranger. She had found them ugly and had only worn them when he insisted. If he had known anything about her, he would have known that she liked things that were quirky and vintage. She was sure though, that the things he had given her were the real deal and had cost him a lot of money. Money, after all, equaled status to him. Maybe she could sell them – it would serve him right. Though, on the other hand, she did not want to stoop to that level.

Then there were a few small things he had given her: a stuffed bunny, a heart-shaped pillow, a shapeless t-shirt with the words "Hey Sexy". Again, all meaningless, only bought because he had to, because it was Christmas, Valentine's Day, or some other celebration where gifts had to be produced. She was keeping the wine though – it was the only good gift he had ever given her. In fact she would probably polish it off tonight. She looked around to see if there was anything else . . .

Oh, the molecular cookbook. She had forgotten about that. It landed in the box with a bang. Like she was gonna keep that. Well, maybe if she had needed tips on poisoning him, it could have come in handy . . .

One last check of her wardrobe. There was that awful dress that he insisted she wore to his cousin's communion. Izzy had looked like a granny. Well, he could have that too. Otherwise, she would have to ritually burn it, and that was not easy, living in an apartment. It tended to set off the smoke alarms. She yanked the offending item off the hanger and threw it in the box as well.

And there it was. The dress she had bought yesterday, when nothing had seemed the matter. Well, except that, technically, she had not had a fiancé or a wedding planned when she bought it. And the chance of that ever happening seemed even slimmer now than it had yesterday afternoon. It was ridiculously expensive and impractical, not to mention the fact that it was taking up half of the closet. Reason told her she should return it.

She opened the bag to look at it once more. All the emotions she had felt when she had first seen it returned. Her heart filled. It was so beautiful, so delicate, so perfect – it just filled her with happiness. And that was merely from looking at it.

Could that feeling really be worth $6500? Izzy wondered if she would ever tire of looking at the dress. If she could look at it and not be filled with joy – if that was the case, she would have to return it. But even if she never tired of it, could it possibly be worth spending so much money on it?

She thought of the chest of clothes that she used to have when she was a kid and she and Sophie would play "dress up" with. Half of them had been costumes and the other half had been old clothes her mother had worn in years past. Izzy's favorite had been a short white lace dress that had belonged to her mother. At the time, it had reached the floor when she put it on. It had been perfect to play wedding in. The best time was the one her mother had baked a cake for them especially for "the wedding." Sophie had been the minister, and Izzy had been the one walking down the aisle, getting married to Sam, who was four at the time. As the only male available, he had been promoted to groom, no matter how hard he had protested. Though he had agreed, when he had heard that there was cake to be had. The old jacket of her father's they had put him in had been way too big, and he kept running away to play with his toys. And when he had to say "I do," he started crying. She wondered if Sam could still remember it, as he had been so little at the time. It was one of her fondest memories.

This dress gave her the same feelings she had had when dressing up as a kid, but ten times better. What if she kept it – to look at, to wear at home occasionally just to feel beautiful? Was that worth the extravagant amount of money she paid for it? What else was she to do with it? Well . . . the least she could do was put it on and enjoy it while she could. Dress up for grown-ups.

Getting in the skirt was easy – well reasonably easy. The thing weighed 25 pounds and, because of its size, was not easy to maneuver in. The top, however, needed to be laced shut, which was near impossible for Izzy to do by herself. First she tried to do it behind her back, which wasn't an option. She couldn't see what she was doing, and it ended up a jumble. Then she tried to lace it up by turning it back to front, and then turning it back again once laced up. Now it was too loose, and since the knot was at the top, she couldn't reach it to try to tighten it. A third try, lacing it from top to bottom did work, although she could not lace it as tight as it had been in the shop. It was good enough for now, though.

Her own mirror wasn't as big as the one in the shop, but it didn't matter

– the feeling was the same. And with nobody watching her, she could do what she liked. Her posture looked better, she looked brighter. But most of all, she felt happier than she had in a long time, and it showed. She decided to do her hair and makeup as well to get the full picture.

It was probably very vain to stare in the mirror for this long, but she was positively in love with her own reflection and it had been a long time since she felt that way. She was a like a princess, sitting at her dressing table and combing her hair with a silver brush. Putting in a few pins she managed to put her hair up. All she needed now was a servant to bring her a glass of wine and it would be perfect. Or tea and cake.

Unfortunately, she had no servants, and it was still a bit early for wine. So she made herself a cup of tea and poured it in the prettiest cup she owned. No cupcakes, but she did have macaroons. She felt about seven years old again, having a tea party. She felt she should really invite Lily but then she would have to let Sam in on her secret, and he would never understand it. She wasn't even sure if she understood herself. Sure she liked pretty things, but it was not like she was obsessed by them. Yet she could not let go of this dress. The idea of returning it filled her with dread.

The doorbell rang, and she looked at the security camera screen. It was John. She should just ignore him . . . Or not – some idiot downstairs opened the door for him, allowing him in the building. So much for security.

She panicked. She could not let him see her like this, wearing this dress. But at the same time, it would be a good opportunity to rid herself of his belongings. Luckily, he still needed to come up, which bought her some time. She grabbed the box and scribbled a note. "*Here is your stuff. Don't call me. I never want to see you again.*" Dammit, that sounded like a jilted lover that was pining for him. Still, no time for a do-over – she only had a minute until he would be here. "*Don't get any ideas, we won't be getting back together.*" Now that sounded downright bitchy, but it conveyed her feelings. She didn't like him anymore, and if it were up to her, she would never see him again. And you needed to be blatantly obvious in order for him to understand these matters. "*Mail or text me if you are missing anything. I'll see that it gets delivered.*" Now that was a nice ending to it, right? Instead of trashing his belongings, he could get them back. He was even getting the jewelry back, which he really didn't deserve.

She shoved the box outside the door and put the note on top. As she closed the door, she could hear the elevator beep. She braced herself against the closed door. The spy hole could technically work both ways, and she did not want to risk the chance of him seeing her in this dress. Silently, she listened to what was going on. The footsteps went to her door. Then there was a little shuffling – he was probably reading the note. An annoyed sigh and what sounded like cussing. This door was really more flimsy than she had thought – she could practically hear his every breath.

"Isabelle . . . Isabelle! Open up!" He banged on the door as if he were going to kick it in. The sudden fright nearly gave her a heart attack.

Dammit. She hadn't thought he'd make a scene. Well, she wasn't planning on opening the door no matter what happened, so he could bang the door all he liked. She just wished he'd give up soon. Sitting here in her knees made cramps shoot up her sides, and she was afraid she was going to fall over at any second.

"Isabelle come out! I know you are in there!" Well, no shit, Sherlock. Who else had left the box out there?

She could hear a door open. "What are you doing here, pal? She is not interested in you anymore." Sam's voice. Could this get any worse?

"Oh, there we have it, Sam to the rescue. Don't you have better things to do?" John's voice dripped with sarcasm.

"Than protect those I care about? I don't think so. Get out of here before I make you."

"So you can finally get into her pants? I don't think so."

"You are a disgusting loser, do you know that? I'm so glad she finally sees you for the arrogant prick you really are."

"She still wants me, alright. Unlike you. How long have you known her exactly?"

She had to get out there and put a stop to this before someone got hurt. This couldn't get out of hand. She pulled the cord of the corset – it came loose, and she could get it off. Now the skirt. Carefully, she slid it over her head and tossed it in the corner. Even if the door was opened, no one could see it. Now, the only problem was that she didn't have any clothes on. Though this would probably stop both men dead in their tracks, she decided against confronting them like this. Dashing to her bedroom, she put on the first thing she could find: her pj's. Well, at least it was better than nothing.

Taking a deep breath she opened the door. "Get out of here, John. The note says it all. If I never see you again, it will be too soon."

"But we can make it work."

"No we can't. I feel miserable every time I am with you."

"You can work on that."

What??? Of all the self-righteous, arrogant, egotistical . . . "You're not worth it. Goodbye John." It sounded calm, collected. She stared him down. It was not like she had a choice. Going back inside would mean leaving him alone with Sam, and she could see in Sam's face that he was trying to hold back the urge to suckerpunch John. So was she, for that matter. The other option would be to pull Sam inside with her, and leave John standing in the hall. The problem with that was that then he'd see the dress.

John in the meantime was seething and looking for a comeback, but finding none. Snarling and cursing, he went back to the elevator. Izzy silently prayed it would be the last time she saw him.

When John finally had left, Sam came and stood next to her, putting an arm around her shoulder. He winked. "Really, can't I punch him?"

It pulled her out of her negative thoughts. "No dear, that would send a bad example to Lily – remember, we talked about this. Speaking of her, you should probably get back."

"Yeah, she is probably worried sick. She heard John's voice and cringed, my poor baby. That's why I came out. And because I was worried about you."

"Go to her. I'll be with you in a second, and we'll spend the afternoon together." As soon as she put the dress safely away.

She looked at the empty hallway. Dammit, the box was still there. Well that was it – she was pawning the jewelry. The money could go toward her new car fund, so that she could feel less guilty for keeping the dress. Because she was keeping it.

CHAPTER SIX

For the next week, Izzy could not stop thinking about the dress that was hanging safely in her closet. She was now convinced that she wanted to keep it, even though she had no idea what to do with it. Looking at the dress made her happy though, and she needed that. She hated to admit it to herself, but John had chipped away at her confidence over the course of three years. He had started off complimenting and flattering her, but soon that had turned in to more and more negative comments about things she had to change. And she had. More and more she had given in to his tastes and requests. More and more she had changed herself when they were together to meet his standards and not be scolded for them.

Well no more. The old Izzy was getting back with a vengeance. It was hard to believe she had let it come to this – she had always sworn she would never let a man change who she was, but it had been so gradual. She had really dodged a bullet by cutting him out of her life now rather than later. It was time for a radical change though, so she could get back to her true self. She had removed all clothes that even had the slightest hint of John about them and went shopping. Bohemian, sexy, confident, stylish. That was what she liked, who she was. Not miss prim and proper. Not things her gran could wear. Although . . . she made an exception for some of the things her gran might have worn back in the day. She simply loved that 50's pin-up style. Her clothes became fun again, though none could match the dress. Every day, just before going to bed, she would look at it. It brightened up her day, no matter how dreary it had been.

She needed an occasion to wear it. And the only occasion you could wear it was a wedding. Unfortunately, you could not just pick a husband up at the supermarket. Well, you could, but his wife might disagree. And Izzy was not the homewrecker type.

It was about more than just a day to wear a dress, though. Izzy did not want to grow old alone – she wanted somebody to share her life with. For that she needed to go out again, start dating. Which was scary. Dating, trying to find out if somebody liked you, only to find out they were not the person who you thought they were . . . But then again, not all men could be like John, could they? That would be terrible.

The number written down on a napkin by the nice bartender was lying by her phone, but so far she had not had the courage to actually call it. Of course, it didn't help that she did not know his name. This weekend, she would get her nerves together and call him though, she promised herself. He would be a good first date, to get her toes back in the water. At least he liked her . . . or pitied her. Well, she would find that out this weekend.

Now it was time to make dinner, though. Wednesday night was her night to cook for Sam and Lily. She ate there most other days of the week, so it seemed only fair to return the favor at least once a week, even though Sam was definitely the better cook. But he had a busy life too – as a cameraman, he was always running from here to there. Luckily, these days he had a contract, which meant it was nine-to-five most days. When he could not be home in time, Izzy would pick up Lily from preschool and take care of her. Cooking for them on Wednesdays had become a tradition, and no man could come between that. Not even John had managed that, and she knew that had annoyed the hell out of him. She should probably cook more for them now that she was single. No more dates with John meant more free time, and since the way to a man's heart was through his stomach, it might come in handy to test her cooking skills on Sam, as well as Lily.

Tonight they were having a simple pasta dish with plenty of vegetables. Lily was in the living room, playing with her dolls, while Sam sat with Izzy in the kitchen as she chopped tomatoes.

"I got Mrs. Halford from upstairs to babysit for Lily tomorrow, so I will be able to escort you to your gala. I got my suit all laid out. All you have to do is put on your prettiest frock and get ready in time."

Her prettiest dress. Now, she couldn't wear that. She wished she could, but even for a gala, it was a bit too much.

"What is wrong?" Sam asked

Darn, she got caught. "Who says anything is wrong?" she said, trying to sound as casual as possible.

"The dazed look in your eyes. You have been acting strange all week. First I thought it was the break-up, but you seemed more relieved than sad about it. So it must be something else."

There was no use denying it anymore, he knew her too well. "I'll show you, it's in the back of my wardrobe." She turned down the heat under the pans so nothing could happen. Dinner would have to wait a bit longer.

"You're coming out of the closet?" he joked.

No, but something else was.

She felt a sense of dread creeping upon her as they entered her bedroom. He wasn't gonna like it. Opening the doors of her wardrobe, she flinched, like it was going to jump out and attack her. There it was, in all its beauty. But she doubted he was going to see it that way.

He was quiet for a long time. When he finally spoke, he seemed mostly surprised. "Is that a wedding dress? You didn't tell me you were engaged to that jerk."

"That's because we weren't." She bit her bottom lip. Maybe she should just have lied. But then again, this was Sam. Hard as she might try, in time he would have found out.

"So what is that thing doing in here?"

She shrugged "I couldn't stop myself. It's perfect."

He looked at her with disbelief, just as she had expected. "It's just a dress. And not even a dress you can wear regularly."

"You don't get it. It's everything I ever been dreaming of."

"You have been dreaming of a dress?"

"I saw the picture a of it a while ago. I cut it out, I saved it. Looked at it from time to time. Then I saw it for real. And I couldn't resist," she said by way of an apology.

"Have you lost your mind?"

"Maybe. . . probably." Most likely.

"How much did it cost?"

"$6500." It didn't sound so bad when you said it fast.

Sam, however, did not agree."$6500? How? Why? I don't even have that much money in Lily's college fund. You should return it, this is ridiculous."

"Hey, it's my money. I can do what I like with it. I was saving it for a new car but I guess that just will have to wait. The car is still fine, anyways."

"A dress instead of a car? You are supposed to be the sensible one here, Iz."

"Well, for once I was not. I saw this, and . . . I just had to. I'm not returning it. I never felt more beautiful."

"Okay. Put it on. Make me understand." He plucked the dress from his closet, and handed it to her.

"Now?" she asked confused. She had expected a lot of reactions, but this wasn't one of them.

"Yes."

"What about dinner?"

"It can wait a little bit longer."

She started to take the dress of the hook. "You will have to help me. The corset is laced at the back, and it is hard to get on all by myself."

"Fine. Just show me what makes this dress so bloody special." He sounded bitter.

"Don't be so negative. Please." She was used to such a tone from John

– when Sam did it, it hurt.

"I'm sorry. I'm sorry. I shouldn't step on your dreams. Please forgive me." He put her arms around her for a hug.

"It's alright. You really want me to put it on?"

He nodded and headed for the door to give her some privacy. She undressed and got into the skirt. It got easier with each time she tried. Then the top – she unlaced it and held it in place.

"Sam, I could use a hand." He came back in. "Can you lace it from top to bottom? It's easier to get out of that way. And then pull it tight."

"How tight?"

"Well, tight so it can't slip, but not so much that I become one of those fainting ladies from Victorian times. It's easiest to pull them when the cord is in. Like shoe laces."

Sam sighed deeply as he set to work.

"What?"

"The things I do for you."

She giggled. "See it as good practice . . . for when you have to lace up Lily's corsets."

"She is never wearing those, and if she is, you can help her in." He pulled hard.

"Oi! I gotta breathe remember?"

"Sorry." Loosening it a little, he tied it up.

She turned around, giving a little curtsy and smiled. The princess feeling was all there.

He inhaled deeply. "Alright, you look breathtaking. Glowing . . . But then again, you always look breathtaking, no matter what you wear."

"Thank you. But I think the dress just gives it a little extra, don't you?" She twirled, skirts rustling.

"Yes, surely – but when are you gonna wear it though?" he asked.

That was the only problem. "I don't know . . . I'll guess I will need to find a guy. And marry him. Somebody other than John," she thought out loud.

Sam's face dropped. "You are gonna get married just so you can wear a dress? Please Izzy, you are joking, right? . . ."

She . . . wasn't sure. Maybe she was. On the other hand, maybe that was the solution.

There was a small knock on the door before Lily sneaked in. "I'm hungry . . . Oooh Aunt Izzy, you look pretty!"

Izzy looked at Sam and smirked, "See, she gets it."

"Get what exactly?"

"The need to wear pretty things occasionally just because they are pretty, right sweetie?"

Lily nodded in agreement.

"And the fact that a four-year-old gets you tells us what, exactly?"

She gave him a look and enclosed Lily in her arms. "That Lily has good taste, right girl?"

Lily nodded. She patted the dress just like Izzy had done in the shop, and seemed just as entranced by it. It was such a pity Sam couldn't understand. But then again, he was a man.

"Now let me get out of this, and I'll finish making dinner."

"You can keep it on!" Lily suggested.

"Not while chopping tomatoes, sweetie. It might stain."

Lily nodded, understanding. Grabbing her father's hand she led him out of the room.

Izzy quickly got out of the dress and left it on the bed. Getting back to the kitchen, Sam had turned up the heat under the pans again and was stirring in them.

"Hey, it's your night off. Sit down and relax."

"It's fine, really."

"Sit down or I will see it as a personal offense against my cooking skills," she said pretending to be angry. She knew perfectly well though that if she didn't chase him off he would finish it completely and never get a break. And he was working too hard already.

He went to the living room to play with Lily, and she watched them sit together. What she wouldn't do to have Lily as her own daughter. How could her mother ever have chosen to step away from that?

Dinner was quickly on the table after that. It had turned out alright – Izzy guessed Sam had added some spices while she was getting dressed again. Lily wanted to know more about the dress, and if having it now meant that Izzy was a princess.

"Nope, but I feel like one when I wear it," she confided.

"Now your dream prince will come." Lily stated as if that was completely logical.

It was a nice idea. Unfortunately, real life wasn't that simple. Izzy didn't want to crush the girl's hopes and dreams just yet. Life would do that soon enough as she grew up. So she said "Who knows?" and gave Lily a wink.

Sam grumbled quietly, but kept quiet, and remained so during the rest of dinner. They went back to his place to put Lily to bed.

"So how many times have you worn that dress?" he started again afterwards. Both of them sat down on the couch.

"Well, three times now. Once in the shop. . .Once at home with no one around, though it was quite difficult to lace up. And tonight." And it made her happy every time, even now, even when he disapproved.

"And seriously, how many times do you think you will wear it? I mean you can hardly go outside wearing it. What do you wanna do, have dress up parties with it? Or go on a hunt for Mr. Right?"

Well, that was not such a bad idea. It was high time that Mr. Right came along, especially after being with Mr. Wrong for so long. "And what if I do? The dress is magnificent and makes me happy."

"You are right, I don't understand."

"Hey, don't get cross with me. I'm a grown woman and I can make my own decisions. I can afford this dress, so there is nothing to worry about."

"Except the fact that you have lost your mind. And I am not cross – just worried about you."

"I'm not lost – I found myself again. You should be happy – With John, I almost lost my sense of self. He was chipping away at everything that I am. The dress made me find the courage to see him for what he truly was and to stand up to him. Yes, he dumped me – it was like he sensed it coming – but I would have done so myself if he had not."

"All because of that dress."

"No of course not – the dress just gave the spark. It gave me my old self back. Do you have any idea how much of that John took away?"

"Yes, unfortunately."

"So why didn't you say anything? I could have dumped him a long time ago."

"Because . . . I was afraid you'd resent me for it. That you'd think I was after you and because of that I'd lose you all together. Anyways, he looked okay at first."

Yes, John was the perfect match on paper. Tall, dark, handsome, good prospects and already quite wealthy. It was a pity his personality was mean and petty. He had hid it well behind a wall of amicability. Sam was the opposite. Izzy she knew he could sometimes across as a bit reserved to people who did not know him – the divorce had been a big factor in that. But she knew he was warm and loving, and forever there when she needed him. "I'd never think that you'd have an ulterior motive. You are my best friend. I rely on your honesty." She put her arms around him and hugged him.

He smirked. "And if I tell you you're crazy for buying that dress?"

"Then I'll tell you that you are probably right, but I have never been happier."

"All because of a dress?" He still had a hard time understanding it, and she didn't know what else to say to convince him.

"Yes."

"That is sad."

"I'm sorry but that is how it is. Don't I deserve something that makes me happy?" She felt a bit hurt that he would say that. And sad that she had not managed to make him understand. Getting his approval had meant more to her than she had realized.

"Of course you do, you deserve everything. But I just wished . . . oh never mind, as long as it makes you happy," Sam replied, defeated, realizing that she would not change her mind.

She wanted him to know that she had not completely lost it and joined the club of airheads "I know what you think, it's outrageously expensive. I have thought about that. I wish it wasn't that expensive. But I think the way the dress makes me feel outweighs the price. And if you look at the detail, the amount of work that must have gone into making it, it is a fair price. This is a one-time thing. I'm not gonna go all shallow and spend like crazy on designer clothes all of a sudden. I just need to remind myself I am worth . . . something. To bring back joy to my life."

"It's alright. I just wish that it was something else that made you this happy. It seems so . . . frivolous."

"Sometimes frivolous can be good. It takes your mind off things. I need that right now. And before you say anything, no I don't think I will be sorry about it later on."

"Alright. You know I love you, right?" He put an arm around her and squeezed her extra tight.

She rested her on his shoulder. "Yes, I love you too, dear. Say, wanna get married? I got this dress . . ."

"Get married? Again?" His face was filled with quasi-shock.

"So you do remember!"

This confused Sam. "What?"

"Playing wedding as kids. I think you were four. You made the cutest groom." She would love to go back to that time.

"Hmmm, I do have the vaguest recollection of an itchy suit and a cake. I meant my own wedding though, to . . . you know. She put me off of getting married for the rest of my life. I don't think I will find I will find somebody any day soon. You, me, and Lily – that is enough for me."

She could feel the pain in those words. Sam was such a lovely guy – he deserved all the love and happiness in the world. "Sam, that sounds mighty bitter, you know?"

He agreed. "I do. But that's how it is."

A wicked smile spread across Izzy´s face as she thought of something. "Shall I buy you a dress too? See if it does it for you too. It wouldn't be your first time in a dress."

They both burst out in laughter. "I only wore them because you two put me in them . . . and took pictures! I was too young to know what you were doing. Besides, you'll go bankrupt."

"Aw, but you're worth it." And much more, to see him happy. Besides it would be worth it for the sheer hilarity.

CHAPTER SEVEN

It was gala night – she was not looking forward to it, but she had put on her makeup anyways and was ready to go. John would not have liked the dress she had chosen to wear. It was made of soft shiny satin, a deep shade of emerald, and strapless, which he would consider tacky, like anything else that showed a bit too much skin. She wore an elaborate bohemian style necklace on it, with large stones. It was fake. The stones were nothing more than glass, but the necklace looked fabulous. Again, John would have disapproved and would probably have insisted on wearing those damn pearls. Well, they had been pawned, along with the rest of the jewelry. John may not have had taste, but it had not been cheap tack. Even secondhand, it had earned her $700 back for her car fund.

Checking her makeup one last time, it was time to leave. It was so nice not to be rushed and to do things at her own tempo.

Sam was ready and waiting for her. He opened the door all dressed up in his tux. "Hello gorgeous, you look absolutely beautiful," he said with a broad smile.

Now, that was what a girl wanted to hear. "Mmmmm, you are looking quite alright yourself, mister." She kissed his cheek. His usually messy mop of curls had been tamed into almost orderly ringlets. He smelled good too – musk and spice. "Have you gotten broader? You look broader."

"It's a new tux."

"What? You didn't have to go to all that trouble for me."

"The old one was getting worn, it had to be replaced. So, I needed a new one anyways." It was a lie, and she knew it. Sam hardly had any reasons to wear a tux, besides when he tagged along to her engagements. Well, maybe this was his dress. "I actually bought it a while back. Do you think it looks good?"

"Great . . . Though you might want to get the tag off your sleeve." Izzy went the kitchen drawer for scissors. "Allow me."

"Sorry, should have checked."

"No worries, it happens." Especially to men. She couldn't help noticing the tag – $300. She would have to make it up to him, somehow. Of course, him being Sam, she would have to be sneaky about it. He'd never accept it if she just handed him the money for it up front. Something for Lily it would have to be. "Where is Lily?"

"Hi Aunty!" A little girl attached herself to Izzy's leg. "Can't I come tonight? Please? I dressed up pretty too!" She was wearing her fairy dress, little flower pins in her hair, looking absolutely angelic.

Sam picked Lily up and gave his daughter a cuddle. "She insisted on asking you."

Izzy gave her a wry smile. "Sweetie, even I don't wanna go. If it was up to me, I'd stay here with you tonight."

"Then don't go." Child's logic. If only it was that simple.

"I have to, and you get to play games with Mrs. Halford all night. That's nice, right?"

Lily nodded but her face did not seem to agree. "I have to, and you get to play games with Mrs. Halford all night. That's nice, right?"

Lily nodded but her face did not seem to agree.

There was a knock on the door. "There she'll be," Sam said opening the door.

Mrs. Halford was like an adopted granny to Lily. She lived in the same building and, having no children or grandchildren of her own, she simply doted on Lily. Once in a while when Sam needed a sitter, and Izzy was not available, she would step in and look after Lily, spoiling her rotten.

"Oh don't you two make a lovely couple," she cooed, "That dress looks beautiful on you Izzy, and Sam looking all dapper in his suit."

"You should see her other dress!" Lily cheered. Oh dear. Izzy swallowed. Now Mrs. Halford would know her secret as well.

"Really? Well you can tell me all about it. Now I think it's time for your daddy and Izzy to go."

Lily gave them both a big hug, and then it was time to leave. "Have a lovely time you two," Mrs. Halford said, waving them goodbye. Izzy and Sam chatted on the way over. Traffic was a bit busy so for the first time in over a year – she was going to be late. Izzy liked it. As they found their parking space, she remembered something.

"Sam, is it okay if I call you John tonight?"

"What??" It was good that she hadn't asked earlier when he was driving – they might have gotten into an accident. Sam looked startled and irritated at the mere mention of John's name.

"Well, the reason I wanted a man at my side tonight so badly was because the client of tonight's party keeps hitting on me, and does not take no for an answer. I told him I already had a boyfriend . . ."

"John." Sam's face looked sour.

"Exactly – which was true at the time." Of course the objection was gone now, she could just . . . no. She was not going to kiss toads willingly, and this one was slicker than an eel.

"So you need me as a stand-in boyfriend?"

"Yeah, sorta. Sorry. If you are not comfortable with it, then just come along as yourself. Just . . . calling you John would save a lot of explaining. I think that if I tell him you are Sam, he'll start asking questions and see it as opportunity to be worse than ever."

"And your colleagues who know the real John? Won't they tell on you?"

"They already know how bad this client is – I doubt if they will be any trouble. But I'll try and give them a heads-up . . . I'll text them."

"Alright . . . if it helps, I will be the best John ever."

She raised an eyebrow. "I'm not that kinda girl, dear." He looked confused. "I'll go on a date with you, but no hankypanky."

"What?"

"I might have lovers, but I do not have Johns." She did her best to keep a straight face but it was hard.

Sam rolled his eyes at her. "Sheesh. You're the one with the dirty mind, not me. When you said you were going back to the old Izzy, I didn't know you meant the sixteen-year-old Izzy."

She giggled, and patted his shoulder. "Poor dear, having to put up with me all these years."

"Well I kinda got used it by now . . . You're ok, kiddo. So do you expect me to behave like John too? I bet if I try hard enough, I can make a great pompous ass."

The mere idea sent a shiver down her spine "Please no!"

"Gotcha," he grinned.

"On the other hand, if you want to mimic John's jealousy and act possessive, that might help."

"He sounds like a lovely character. Tell me more . . . So what is this guy's name?"

"Roger Taylor."

"And what should I look out for?"

"Any time he comes too close. He keeps trying to touch me. When he's next to me, he puts his hand on my leg, and if I walk by or get in a lift with him, he tries to slap my ass. Even when there are people there."

"That sounds an awful lot like sexual harassment."

"It probably is, but if I would take it to court it would just mean a lot of hassle and me looking like a silly prude. I told him off as gently as I could, but he just won't quit. The only other option is slapping him, but he's a client. I have thought about it though."

"You thought about just not going tonight? There is a girl on my couch that would love to spend time with you, even dressed like that. Heck, you could even put the wedding dress on – she can't stop talking about it."

That made her smile, "I told you it's a special dress."

"I'll take your word for it," Sam replied, not wanting to waste any more words on it.

"Anyways, I have to go. Roger might be a pig but he is a very well paying pig, and right now we can't afford to lose him. But luckily, I have you as my bodyguard," she explained

Sam spread open his arms. "And I-I-I-I-I-I-I-I-I will always loooove yooouuuuu," he sang.

She laughed. "Yeah, Kevin Costner, keep that up, and I might have to fire you. Come on, let's go inside before I freeze."

"You escort a girl to a party, vow to protect her, and that's the thanks you get," he complained with a wicked smile as he opened the door for her.

Roger Taylor greeted her the moment she came in, hugging her like she was his long lost friend. He looked a bit disappointed when he saw Sam put an arm round her though and introduced himself as "John Wakefield." When he even kissed her cheek and called her "his gorgeous girlfriend," she thought Roger went a shade paler. John would certainly never have done that for her – he'd be moping by the bar by now, or spotting potential clients. Roger quickly excused himself to greet other guests, and it left her wondering what the night would have been like if Sam had not been by her side. All in all, Sam was doing much better than John. Public displays of affection were not John's thing.

"Alright, I am gonna give a few colleagues a personal heads-up in case they haven't checked their phones. You get yourself a glass of champagne, and I'll be back soon as I can," she whispered in Sam's ear. She was able to forewarn two colleagues before Roger jumped her again like a starved hyena. She just hoped the other three got the text or had been informed by her colleagues.

"Has your boyfriend left you, dear?"

"No Roger, I needed to leave him for a few seconds to make sure everything tonight runs smoothly. That is my job after all, what you are paying me far." She was trying to move away from him, but each time she took a step back, he did a step forward.

"You are so dedicated, always looking out for my needs." He was driving her into a corner, and out of sight from the other guests. Help!

"Really, I'd do the same for any other client."

"And modest too, that is what I like about you." Oh god, please let somebody save her now.

Suddenly from behind an arm slipped round her waist that wasn't Roger's. "Here you are dear, is everything alright?"

Sam – she could kiss him . . . In fact, that was a great idea. She turned his face toward her and gave him a passionate kiss on the mouth. He froze at first, but then he kissed her back. Gently, lovingly, but then slowly building up in passion until she lost herself in the kiss. Oh boy. This was Sam. Where had he learned to kiss that way?

When he finally broke the kiss, she looked around and Roger was gone completely. In fact they were completely alone. "That worked well," she said, trying to regain her bearings, and forget what had just happened. After all, it was just to chase Roger off, not a real kiss.

"Hmm, yes. Yes, indeed," Sam replied, equally dazed. The air between them was suddenly a bit uncomfortable.

"Sorry about that, I didn't know what else to do," she apologized.

""It's alright . . . Really, it's fine." He cleared his throat. "That Roger is really persistent, isn't he? I leave you alone for five minutes and he pounces on you. Is he always like this?"

"Yes. And worse."

He nodded. "I see. I will have to keep a much better eye on you so he doesn't get a chance. Come on, let's go out there."

The rest of the evening he clung to her like a shadow, which seemed to work perfectly. Roger kept his distance and stayed on the other side of the room.

Until dinner that was. Roger had placed her right next to him at his side. It was probably something that was prearranged. Sam however did some quick thinking and changed his seat with hers. It broke up the boy-girl-boy-girl set up, but at least she was safe from Roger's hands and not going to jail for stabbing him with a fork.

Not that having a man between them stopped Roger. Having kept his distance for the evening he seemed to have the need to make up for it. Everything he said was full of innuendo. Some of it was downright rude.

"Lovely sausage don't you think, Izzy?"

She had started with politely answering him but had now come to the point where plainly ignoring him was a lot easier. "Izzy loves a sausage, I can tell. Well you can have my sausage any time you like, love."

Dinner had been lovely so far, the food was delicious, but she just lost her appetite. She got up from the table. "Excuse me, I need to powder my nose for a second." And throw up.

She tried to recompose herself in the ladies bathroom, taking deep breaths and splashing some water over her wrists. Maybe she should have stayed at home. Tell her boss she had become ill and could not possibly attend. It was too late for regrets, though. Another hour max, and then she would slip out of here with Sam. For now, she just had to get through dessert without getting sick.

As soon as she opened the door, Sam was standing there, though.

"What are you doing here?" she asked confused. It was nice he was concerned, but she wasn't feeling that bad.

Sam explained, though. "Mr. Taylor followed you as soon as you got up, so I decided to do so as well. He was standing here like he wanted to go in. Until he saw me that was. Then he scarpered off like a stray dog."

This was getting scary – it was like Roger was deliberately was trying to corner her to do heaven knows what. Why couldn't he just leave her be? She could not make it any clearer that she wasn't interested, not while staying polite and professional, anyways. "We are leaving the second we can, alright?"

"Hey you won't get any objections from me. Leaving soon is probably the only thing that can prevent me from punching him in the face."

"Since when have you gotten so violent?" she laughed.

"Since these losers keep following you around. I gotta protect my girl." That made her blush.

She needed to find some composure – he was probably just saying this in case Roger was still near. "Well, if he tries anything again, I'm not stopping you. At this point, I don't know what else to do to make him back off." This was getting more out of hand by the minute – she just hoped that Roger would rein it in for the time remaining.

Of course, he did not. The next hour crawled by excruciatingly slowly. More crude jokes and humiliation at her expense. She could see that the other dinner guests at the table felt as embarrassed as she did. How did this guy run a multimillion dollar company and still get clients when he was this annoying? Well, she kind of knew the answer to that: he didn't. He was the son of the man that started the company, and his role was very limited. The running of the business was left to more capable men.

Somehow she got through it though, and Roger remained unharmed. From time to time, Sam would take her hand under the table and squeeze it. His looks spoke a thousand words, and she knew exactly how he felt. As soon as dinner was over, she and Sam snuck out to get their coats. It was early, but she was sure her colleagues would not object. In fact, Susan had practically suggested it.

Outside, it had started snowing. The flakes melted as soon as they hit the pavement, leaving slushy puddles. An icy wind hit them full in the face as they opened the door. "You wait here – that dress is no match for this weather. I'll get the car. We don't both need to freeze," Sam suggested.

"My knight in shining armor."

"Homeward we are bound, as soon as I get my rusty steed."

"Thank you, kind sir." She curtsied and he left with a silly smile on his face. She was so relieved that the night was over. Or maybe she had spoken too soon. Roger was heading for her, and Sam was not there to protect her anymore.

"Leaving so soon?" he asked.

"Yes, dinner did not quite agree with me, so I am heading home." Technically that was true. The sausages in particular had been awful.

"I'm sorry to hear that."

"Sahh – John will be right her with the car." Close call, she had almost slipped up, and that so close to the finishing line. She would have waited outside if that hadn't meant freezing into a popsicle. Well, it could only last a few more seconds, and then Sam would be there. What was the worst Roger could do? Plus, there was a guard sitting at reception.

"Your boyfriend was a bit overprotective of you tonight." Roger suggested.

"I hadn't noticed." Not protective enough it seemed, for Roger was still here, bothering her.

"Honestly dear, you can do much better than him."

"Really?" With him? Sam was ten times the man he was. Even John was less annoying.

"Dump him." The nerve of that man was astounding. He just wouldn't give up.

"Sorry, no can do. I love him." She looked out into the street. Where was Sam? She didn't know how much longer she could keep this up."

"What does he have that I don't? I am rich, affluent, powerful." And pompous, egocentric, irritating . . .

"A kind heart," Izzy answered curtly. She wanted to smack Roger, even though it would probably only make things worse.

"And I don't?" He was blocking her path now.

She should be tactful – this could potentially cost her her job. "No." She turned around and walked out. The old Izzy might have rolled over, but she had had it. Losing her job would be worth it, though she hoped it would not come to that. Besides she had not kicked him in the balls like she wanted to.

CHAPTER EIGHT

It was Saturday, and Izzy still had a job. In fact, she still hadn't heard anything from Roger, which probably was a good thing. The bill had been paid, and there was a new event in the planning. One she did not have meet Roger for. Her colleagues had seen how horrible he treated her, so from now on Susan would handle him. She was an iron lady – real nice if you knew her and she liked you, but if she didn't . . . well, you were better off staying clear of her. Fortunately, she liked Izzy a lot, and the feeling was mutual.

So, today was the day – she was going to ring the bartender. For the last hour, Izzy had been trying to calm the butterflies in her stomach –even a whole packet of chocolate chip cookies had not done the trick. It had nothing to do with the guy she was calling – it was fear, plain and simple. Dating again, just the mere thought of it, filled her with dread.

There was only one way to get over it though, and that was by just calling him. She was a grown woman that handled dozens of calls every day on a professional basis. This was a personal call though, which involved flirting – and she was crap at flirting, especially on commando, with a guy that was actually cute . . . even if he was a bit older. Well, the only fortunate thing was that he could not see her. Alright, she needed to just get over it, unless she wanted to spend the whole day staring at the phone. Worst case scenario, she could always hang up. She had the number in one hand and the phone in the other. Here went nothing . . .

Dingdong. Saved by the bell. Or not. Now she would have even more time to get nervous. She went to the door. "Sophie! What are you doing here?" The girls hugged tightly. She was about the last person Izzy had expected to see. Then she saw Sam hiding in the shadows, with Lily in his arms. "Is this your doing?"

"I thought you could use a friend after the week you had. So I called Sophie."

That was so sweet of him. "Thank you."

Sophie made herself at home and sat down on the couch. "So what is this dress Lily told me about?"

Maybe telling Lily had not been the best idea. Soon the whole world would know that she had a wedding dress hiding in the back of her closet, and Izzy doubted if many people would understand. "Ah that . . . remember that picture I sent you of what I called the best dress in the world?"

Sophie started digging in her memory. "Ummmm, no. . . Oh wait –you mean that dress that was totally over the top? With the corset, huge skirt and tons of lace? Looked like it half-belonged in another century."

"Yes. . ." Izzy whispered quietly. She felt as if the air had been knocked out of her. Sophie's opinion was important to her – maybe even more important than Sam's on this matter. She had expected him not to like the dress, but Sophie . . .

"That thing was fantastic!" Sophie squealed in a pitch so high that only dogs could hear.

Izzy sighed with relief. "Thanks for the heart attack. For a moment there I thought you hated it. Come with me, and I'll show you."

Lily stretched out her arms and tried to wiggle out of her father's grip. "Me too."

She landed in Sophie's arms. "Come along, squirt. So, this dress is as good as that one?"

"It is that dress."

Sophie's mouth fell open. "What? But that must have cost a fortune!"

Izzy felt guilty . . . Sam did not say anything, but she knew how much he disapproved. Right now, she felt anything but sure of Sophie's reaction. "Let's just say I'll have to put off buying a new car any day soon."

"You go, girl. So you dumped John and decided it was time to go for it?" Sam had obviously informed her well.

But he had not told everything "Not exactly," Izzy explained. "I saw the dress, bought it. And then John dumped me somehow. All in the same day."

Sophie scrunched up her face. "Ouch. Did he see the dress or something?"

"Nope. I just . . . had enough of his behavior, so I didn't give in like I usually do. I confronted him. And for a moment it looked like he was gonna change, but it turned out that was only for the worst. I had just made my mind up to dump him when he beat me to it . . . which was so unfair. I so was ready to do so myself. I was planning it out already."

"Some guys have a dump radar. And they dump you before you get the chance, so they can come out on top."

"No. . . I think he thought threatening to dump me would shock me in submission. He did not know how badly I wanted to get rid of him though."

"Are you gonna put on the dress?" They were still standing in front of the closet, and the little girl decided to remind them of their priorities.

"Yes Iz, I gotta see this jewel," Sophie said all excited.

"Alright. Ready?"

Sophie and Lily nodded in unison.

Izzy slowly opened the closet. She picked the dress off the hanger, and laid it out on the bed. Sophie was completely quiet, as Lily stroked it like it was a puppy. "Put it on, Aunt Izzy!" she said impatiently.

"Alright." Izzy undressed and put on the skirt. "Sophie, can I get some help with the top?" No reaction. "Sophie . . . Earth to Sophie?"

For the past few minutes, Sophie had been in a trance. "It's perfect. Even better than the picture . . . I think I want one too."

"Your brother will love that." Sarcasm dripped from Izzy's voice. She could already hear his comments in her mind about corrupting his sister. Usually it was the other way round, though. "Now, could you lace up the back for me, please?"

"Oh yes, of course. Say, how do you do that by yourself?"

"With a lot of difficulty, believe me. I near dislocated my shoulder trying it the first time. I had Sam helped me out the other day."

"Oh I bet he just loved that."

"Yeah, enormously. I don't think he likes the dress – he thinks it's frivolous."

"He's a guy, what do you expect? We buy pretty stuff for us, not for them. They don't care what we look like as long as they can fuck it."

"Sophie!" Izzy hissed. "Lily is in the room." And Sam was probably one of the few guys that weren't like that.

"Sorry, I'm not used to having kids around." Sophie turned to Lily. "Pretend you didn't hear that, sweetie – aunty said something bad."

"What?" Lily asked confused. For one, she didn't seem sure which aunt she wasn't supposed to have heard.

Sophie patted her on the head. "Good girl."

Izzy would need to have a talk about this with Sophie later – you couldn't say everything around a little girl like that. And you certainly couldn't fix it by telling her to forget about it.

"Aunt Izzy, I can tie my shoe laces – I even got a diploma. I could tie up your dress." Was it bad to consider help from a four-year-old? She would mope a lot less than Sam, that was for sure.

"I completely get that you love the dress, but how did you end up buying it?" Sophie asked reaching the top. "It is spectacular by the way – I could look at it for hours."

"I could not resist. I was just passing by the shop. But the temptation was too great – I had to see it up close, you know. I mean I have no business in a bridal shop. And then they offered to let me to try it on – it all happened before I knew it. The feeling when I put it on . . . indescribable. I just felt like . . ." There were no words that could express it.

"A princess!" Lily cheered.

From the mouth of babes. "Yes, that's it."

"So you bought it?"

"Well, I tried not to, I tried to convince myself it was not sensible. But then they offered a heavy discount, and that clinched it."

"Pfff, being sensible is overrated." Izzy was dreading the example they were setting for Lily when she heard her friend talk like this. "How much was it?"

"$6500." Izzy whispered, knowing what Sam's reaction had been.

Of course hers was the polar opposite. "That's a bargain! You should have bought two. One for me."

"You should hear what your brother had to say about that."

"Yeah well, I won't repeat what I said earlier but that goes double for him."

"I don't think your brother is as shallow as you think he is, Sophie. He's matured a lot. And he is a great guy."

"You should marry him them – you got the dress. It will be just like old times, with him just doing it for the cake . . . And running off at the *moment suprême*."

They laughed hard.

"Tea is ready if you would like some," Sam shouted from the kitchen. "And cake." It made Izzy smile. The princess got her tea served after all. They walked back to the living room as Sam was pouring out the tea.

"Sam Beauforde, do you take this woman Isabelle Rose Stanton to be your awful wedded wife . . ."

"Lawful." Izzy corrected.

"Hey. I know what I am saying. So, do you take Izzy to be your awful wedded wife, to nag and to scold till death do you part?"

Sam looked at Izzy. "Are you still going on about that nonsense?"

"Don't look at me, I didn't even remind her of it. She came up with it all by herself."

"And he still can't manage to say I do after nearly . . . twenty-five years. God, we are getting old. That's a quarter of a century." Sophie's face filled with horror.

"Get used to it . . . Still happy you bought the magical dress, Iz?" he asked handing her a cup of tea.

"Yes. When I wear this dress I remind myself of who I am and what I want."

"And what are you?" he asked critically.

"I'm worth it. That sounds really stupid and generic, I know, but John constantly made me feel inadequate. I have had enough of that. Next guy I fall in love with is gonna take me as I am or he can go to . . . take a hike." No foul language in front of Lily – the conversation was too mature for her as it was.

"This dress is made to be worn at a wedding." Sophie said.

"Yes well, man first, I think. Kinda crucial for such an event, don't you think?" Weddings without grooms tended to end disastrously.

"So you are getting yourself out there again?"

"I guess I am. Bag me a hubby." It sounded stupid, and Izzy had to laugh.

Sophie took it more seriously though. "I don't think it's a bad idea – buying that dress as a sort of a promise to yourself. Sometimes to reach a goal, it is good to have a physical reminder. In fact I might start recommending it to a few of my clients."

That was not quite how Izzy saw it, but Sophie had a point. To be honest, any reason that justified her buying that dress had her vote.

Sam frowned. "Have you both gone mad? Are you gonna start a cult or something with some loopy belief propagation that you need a wedding dress to be perfectly happy? Really I thought you'd talk some sense into her, not make it worse. I should have remembered that you two think exactly alike."

Sophie ruffled his curls. "Oh come on, little brother, it's not that bad."

"I think just remembered why I am never gonna marry again. You're gonna turn women into bridezillas even before they get the guy!"

"You are overreacting, Sam." Izzy tried to calm him down. She couldn't stand seeing him so aggravated.

"I'm not the one buying dresses that cost as much as my car."

Sophie put an arm around her brother's shoulder and squeezed. "You know he was happy kid when he was little – you'd never have thought he'd turn into such a cynical man."

"I know, I remember. Never a care in the world. And just look at him now. You think it's because I dropped him on his head as a baby?" She shouldn't make it worse, but maybe if they made light of it, he'd lighten up as well. It was only a joke.

"If you are just gonna make fun of me, I am leaving." He picked up Lily's vest, which was draped over the armrest.

"Good, we need a girly chat. See you later, brother dearest." Sophie blew him a kiss.

"Lily, we're leaving!"

Izzy wanted to stop him, but didn't know what to say.

"But I wanna stay with Aunty Sophie and look at the dress!"

"Well you can look at the dress later – it's not going anywhere, evidently," Sam sighed.

"Sam! Be nice" Izzy chided him

Sophie hugged Lily. "I'll come by a bit later, and we will all go out, alright Lily? But first me and Izzy are gonna chat a bit."

"Will Aunt Izzy come with us too?"

Izzy looked at Sam, who shrugged and mouthed "Sorry."

"Yes sweetie, I will," she promised the girl.

"Yay!" she cheered as her father carted her off. "Daddy, are you mad at Aunt Izzy? I heard you shouting," she asked as they headed out.

"No, I am not mad. I just disagree with some of the choices she is making."

"But then you shouldn't shout. People don't listen to shouty people you always say . . . Lily turned around. "Bye!"

"Later sweetie!" Sophie and Izzy said in unison, waving goodbye to Lily.

As soon as the door closed, they burst into laughter. "She told him off, alright."

Izzy was just so proud of Lily. Although she wasn't happy with how Sam had left. "You should really come by more. She is such an amazing girl. I just love her to bits."

"I will, I miss you all. I mean, I like my job back home, but I miss you like crazy. And I wanna be here for you when things like this happen. As best friend, I am supposed to support you when you lose the love of your life. And you haven't even told me!"

"John? The love of my life? Hardly. More the mistake of my life that I failed to get rid of in time. If he was the love of my life, shoot me now."

"Now you sound like Sam."

"Well, we do hang out a lot, I guess he is starting to rub off. Sophie, do you have any idea why the dress upsets him so much? I mean, even by Sam's standards, he has been pretty grouchy about the whole thing. I get he isn't happy, but I thought he would get over it. And now he enlisted you."

"Well, that backfired. I think it's terrific what you have done. True Izzy-spirit, just going for it! Who cares what others might think?" Sophie put an arm around her. "He'll come around, he always does. We are family, he has to."

"You are. I'm not."

"Sure you are. You couldn't be more related if it was through blood. We chose you. And I know for a fact that he can't live without you. Nor can Lily." Izzy was being cuddled to death at this point.

"So what is up with him?" she asked.

"It has to do with *her*." That meant the ex. Nobody ever mentioned her by name. "She was a complete bridezilla. It was horrible, she tried to control everything. That was why you weren't even invited for the wedding – I think – though the reason was not exactly clear. It might have been to spite me. I wasn't a good little slave like her other bridesmaids."

That was enlightening for Izzy. "Really? I've always wondered about that. I mean I wasn't exactly his best friend at the time, but I thought at least they'd invite me."

"I think Sam blames himself for not seeing her true character back then. He was so in love and they got married so fast that he hardly knew what she was like."

Poor Sam. "That's so sad. But if had dumped her, then he would never have had Lily – so maybe it worked out for the best."

"He knows that, but still . . ." Sophie shrugged. "He's Sam. He handles things on his own. Not too well usually, but he prefers it that way, keeping things bottled up. At least he has you to talk to. Believe me, we're all very grateful for that, my mom especially. She said he started to sound more cheerful again when you arrived."

"You know he hasn't talked about *her* since they split up. And even before that, I never heard anything about their past or how they met. Just what was happening in the here-and-now."

"Back to you though. You are sitting here in a fabulous dress but what are your plans?" This was personal coach Sophie talking.

Izzy wasn't ready yet for that question. "Be extremely happy?"

"Seriously now."

Why couldn't that be enough? She thought about what she wanted. There was only one thing that was clear. "I don't wanna grow old alone. So I guess that means dating."

"You'll never grow old alone dear. You have got me and Sam to keep you company right through till the afterlife. I promise you this now, when we are old and gray, we will find an old folks home where we can all stay together. Problem solved?"

Izzy hugged her. "Thanks, but what if you find a husband, or Sam remarries?"

"Then our spouses can come too. By the way, I don't see Sam remarrying yet, do you?"

"He deserves somebody fabulous that loves him, he really does. He has so much love to give."

"Well he has you, doesn't he?"

"That's not the same, is it? I'm just his friend. Somehow Thursday's kiss sprang to mind and Izzy felt herself blushing slightly.

Sophie was pouring herself another cup of tea, "But you should date again, you know. Get back on the horse, plenty more fish in the sea, and all that crap."

Yeah right … that sounded convincing … *not.* Even if Sophie had a point. "Hmm, yeah . . .you know, I actually got a number on the night John dumped me? From a bartender who took pity on me when he saw how John treated me. He actually suggested that I dump John on the spot. He was quite charming, too."

"Cute?"

"Quite – although he's probably about ten years older than me. But he still has this boyish charm, if you know what I mean."

Sophie picked up the phone and gave it to Izzy. "Then call him. Now."

"With you here?" And no time to worry, um. . . prepare?

"Why not?"

"Just that would make it very juvenile. I feel flashbacks coming on already."

"Then you better call him before I start making squealing noises and comments on the background." She knew that Sophie would make good on that promise. The numbers were already in the phone – all she needed to do was press the call button. Maybe she was in luck and she'd get voicemail.

"Hi. Robert speaking."

Izzy's nerves hit a new peak – she really felt like she was sixteen again. Well, at least she knew it was the right guy – his Irish accent was unmistakable. "Hi – it's Izzy, I don't know if you remember me, but I was in your bar last week with my now ex-boyfriend. You asked me out. And I would like to take you up on your offer."

It was quiet at the other side of the line. He had forgotten who she was. Or he had remembered, but was not interested after all. "So you dumped him?" he finally asked.

"Sorta." The whole truth was far too complicated. "Let's just say we're over."

"Nothing to do with me, I hope?"

"Nope. It was a long time coming."

"So, I guess then it is time to ask you out again. Properly this time. Now let me think how to do this, I might be a wee bit rusty. It was a long time since I asked a lady out."

That was comforting – at least he did not take a girl out every week. Or he was an enormous charmer. "Take your time."

"There is one problem though." His wife and kids, most likely. "My only night off is Monday. The rest of the week I am in the pub."

"But Bobby, I could not possibly go out on a school night!" Izzy laughed hysterically.

"Well you could come to the pub on the weekend, but that's not really a date."

"I was just kidding, Monday is fine. Just don't make it too late."

"No, of course not. I'll pick you up at 6:30 and have you home by 10:00 so your folks won't get angry. How does that sound?" he replied, joking in the same way she had just done.

"Perfect." She gave him her address where he could pick her up. As she put down the, phone she cheered. She had a date! And it had been far less painful than she had feared.

CHAPTER NINE

The weekend had been filled with giggling, laughter and juvenile behavior. By the end of it, Sam seemed to have accepted the dress, or at least his mood had lightened, and he did not cloud over every time it was mentioned. Izzy was happy for it. She couldn't stand to upset him.

Now it was Monday evening, and Robert could be here any minute. She had no idea what to wear because she had no idea where they were going to – he hadn't said anything about it. So the only option was cute but safe. A little black dress with warm tights, boots, and a colorful scarf to jazz the whole thing up a little. Dressed up enough to be let in to a club or a high class restaurant, dressed down and warm enough to eat hot dogs in the park. She hoped he was a hot dogs kind of guy. With John she'd had more than her fill of haute cuisine. Time for something completely different. She was actually starting to look forward to it, to go out with a complete stranger she knew nothing about. Who could be a complete ax mur . . . Oh stop it, now she was getting herself into a state of fright without any reason. He was not a complete stranger – she had seen him before – Robert was a nice guy. Probably. Well, he had tried to rescue her from John, that had to mean something. And he had been very charming.

And besides, Sophie was totally right – it was time to dip her toes back in the water and get herself out there. Robert was the perfect guy for that, being cute and kind. He had sent her a few texts over the weekend that had made her smile. There was nothing to worry about, really. Except that now the downstairs buzzer notified her that he was there, and she pressed the button so he could come up.

She brushed her hair one last time. The wind would probably mess it up as soon as she got out, but at least it looked ok now. Then he knocked.

She opened the door, and there he was, dressed casually in jeans and a leather jacket. He looked good, with sophistically graying sideburns and a magical twinkle in his smile that she had noticed the last time they met. Instead of saying hello though, he remained quiet and stared at her. This was nerve wracking.

"Disappointed? Not the girl you though I was?" she asked worried. Maybe he was changing his mind after all now he saw her again. Or he asked so many girls out that he could not tell them apart anymore, and she wasn't the one he expected.

Robert smiled. "Not at all, dear. Just enjoying the view. You look radiant just standing there. Even more beautiful than the last time I saw you. It's like a weight has been lifted off your shoulders."

She smirked. That was exactly how she felt, but it was a bit unnerving that he could see that. "I do feel a lot freer without John. Getting rid of him was probably the best decision I have made in my life, and one I should have taken a long time ago, Thanks for the pity date."

"No lass, no pity at all. Unless it is you, pitying an old fool, that is. I'm honored that you'd even considered going out with me. It's not too late to change your mind."

"Of course not." That came out wrong. "I mean of course I am going out with you. I called you, remember? I wouldn't have done that if I hadn't liked you. Besides, you are not that old . . . are you?" Maybe it was a bit rude to ask, but she was very curious. And this was probably the best opportunity she was going to get.

"First flash of youth. After all I am planning to become 350 years old at least, so at fifty, I would say the best is yet to come," he joked, with a refreshing sense of humor.

The number came as a bit of a shock, though. "You are fifty?" Fifteen years older . . . that was more than she had expected. Such an age difference came with consequences. He probably would not want kids anymore – he'd be a pensioner by the time they went off to college. Still, it wasn't something to consider right now. This was a date with a very nice man, and whatever might or might not happen in the future, she was not gonna let that ruin the evening.

"Fifty-one even. Yes I am an old geezer, I know – sorry," he agreed.

Now she had made him feel bad. That was not her intention He wasn't old. Not to look at. She felt kind of guilty for even thinking so. Age shouldn't matter if a person was nice – it was just a number. "Not at all. I was just about to say you look fantastic."

"For my age." he added

"No! For any age."

"It's okay deary, I'm just teasing you. Thank you for the compliment. And these are for you." He pulled out a bouquet of beautiful red roses from behind his back. "I haven't forgotten all the rules of dating just yet."

"Oh thank you, they are lovely! Come in, I'll put them in water," she said getting out of the doorway.

He looked around. "Lovely place you got. Very stylish and elegant, but still cozy."

"Thanks." She got a vase and quickly arranged the flowers in it.

"What would you like to do tonight?" he asked settling down on the couch.

So he had not arranged anything yet. Instead she could what she wanted for a change. Freedom, spontaneity, not to mention a good sense of humor – she was starting to like this guy more and more by the minute. "How about doing something you never done before?" Izzy suggested.

"Oh well, that's a long list. I don't get out much . . . out of the bar, that is. That didn't sound too good, did it?"

"It's alright." She did not exactly get out much herself, if you didn't count the parties she had to attend for work. "How about the ice skating rink?" She hadn't been there for years, but it seemed like the perfect weather for it, seeing it had become colder and colder the past few days. Lily probably would love to learn to skate, so it had been something she had been meaning to check out anyways.

"Yeah, why not? I haven't been skating since I was a wee lad. And never in a skating rink."

"I'm sure it's like riding a bike," she assured him.

"Have I mentioned that I am not too good at that either? We were poor growing up, so I never properly learned."

"If you don't want to do it, we can find something else . . ." They both needed to enjoy this date, not just her, or she'd be as bad as John.

"Hell, no! It will be fun, I'm sure. And at least when I go flat on my face, it will be literally, rather than figuratively."

"Really, if you would rather do something else, that's fine."

"No – my lady's heart is set on ice skating, so that is what we will do. It will be my pleasure."

"I'm sure you'll be fine, and I promise I'll nurse you back to health if you break a leg."

"That's almost worth a broken leg . . . if it wouldn't put me out of business."

"The bar I went to when I met you is yours?"

"Lock, stock, and beer barrels. After all, it carries my name."

She hadn't realized. Then again, she still did not know his last name. "So you are Robert O'Keeffe?"

"Yes . . . sorry, I should have mentioned that when we spoke on the phone, shouldn't I? Now you were probably wondering if you were going out with some psychopath."

"Well, not really." Worry was just her middle name. She had forgotten it might have been handy to ask his last name.

"Anyways, I'm very proud of the bar. Started it eight years ago when I came back to the States – we almost didn't survive. But it's a homey place, and that attracted the customers. The clientele are very loyal – most of them are like friends. So when you and Mr. Suit walked in, you pretty much stood out like a sore thumb. Well him anyways – you looked fine."

"Mr. Suit? Oh you mean John. Yeah, he is not the kinda guy you would find in a place like yours. I don't know who recommended it to him, but I don't think he ever went there before."

"No, he had not, I would have remembered a sour face like his. His face looked as if he had stepped into something dirty when he walked." Robert bristled – and rightly so.

"John likes his bars high class and uptown. They are also not called bars, but lounges, and they have furniture on which it is impossible to sit. I hate them. But I am not one of those people who wants to talk about their ex all night. Too glad to be rid of him. We have an ice rink to go to."

"Yes – yes we do. Want to grab some dinner on the way? I know this great greasy spoon, run by a mate of mine."

"Maybe on the way back? They always say you shouldn't exercise on a full stomach. I don't know how hard skating will be . . . it's been a while for me too. But I don't think we need the extra weight of a full belly to throw us off balance, do you?"

He laughed, "You're probably right. We don't have to go there either – we could go somewhere else, if you like . . ."

"No, the diner sounds great. John used to take me to these fancy-schmancy restaurants where the food was horrible . . . wait, we were not gonna talk about him anymore."

"It's fine. Comparisons are allowed . . . as long as they are in my favor."

"That won't be a problem, I think. You are doing much better than he did so far. But honestly, he is not worth talking about. But I will tell you one thing – just because it's an extremely expensive, three-Michelin-star restaurant does not mean they can cook."

"Really? Well I am glad – I'm not a three-star-restaurant kinda guy anyways. I don't think they would even consider letting me in with me looking like this, to be honest."

"You look fine." Izzy picked up her coat. "Shall we go?"

On the way there, Robert told her all kind of funny anecdotes about things that had happened to him when he had been tending the bar. It was a cold night – the wind had really picked up and was making it feel like it was below zero, so the skating rink actually felt warm in comparison. The lights however, were very bright – and not flattering in the least, Izzy noticed. There was nothing like fluorescent lighting to bring out wrinkles and harsh lines. This was no way to impress a first date. Nevertheless, here they were, and she was looking forward to it. Robert did not seem to mind.

After renting their skates, they sat side by side on a bench to put them on.

"It's been a long time since I have done this," Izzy said. "I wonder if I can still do a pirouette?"

"Well, only one way to find out," Robert said, getting up and immediately going all wibbly-wobbly. Izzy reached out to steady him, as he was about to fall over.

"Are you ok?" she asked after he had balanced himself somewhat.

"Yes. I wanted to do the gentlemanly thing and help you up. I am afraid we might both end up on the floor if we do that, though."

"Don't worry, I'll be fine." As she got up however her stomach growled loudly.

"Perhaps we should have eaten after all?" Robert asked.

Izzy felt herself go red from embarrassment.

"No worries, deary. It happens to the best of us. It shows that you're human. And that is how I like my women."

She laughed. "Not alien stick insects?"

"Oh no – definitely not those. I'd be too afraid they might accidentally break, and then what?"

Fortunately, the ice rink had a lovely soup stand. Making their way over there was difficult, though – Izzy had forgotten just how slippery artificial ice was. Poor Robert had never been on artificial ice at all and looked much like Bambi in the cartoon, with limbs all over the place. She felt a bit sorry for even having suggested coming here. But they made it. Buying a mug of soup each, they leaned against the wall.

"Sorry about it being a weekday – nobody dates on a Monday. People sit at home . . . wash their hair . . . I'm just always working at the weekend."

"Stop apologizing! I think it's great you own your own bar. And it's nice that the rink is almost empty. Much safer on the whole."

"Oh, you mean that my skating might endanger the safety of others?"

"And your own, from what I saw," she giggled.

"Just a bit rusty. Must be because I was famished. I should be fine now."

She wasn't very convinced about that. "Are you sure?"

"Yes I am," he assured her. "Let's go for a walk along the boards. I mean skate."

With one hand on the railing and the hand other holding onto Izzy, Robert somehow completed a lap.

"Now that wasn't too bad, was it?"

"I have to say it exceeded my expectations by far," she agreed

"Thank heavens then for low expectations. Now let me see you do that pirouette."

"Oh dear, I don't know if I still can." She couldn't even remember the last time she had tried.

"A skate around the rink then. I know you want to. Don't let this old man stop you."

"Hey, you are not old, remember?"

"That was before I skated – right now I feel like a hundred . . . and eighty. Now come on, let's see you really go for it."

She did as he asked, gaining speed and swirling over the floor, darting between the few people that were actually there. She had forgotten how much fun it was to feel this carefree, but now she enjoyed every second. Skating back to Robert, she even managed a little jump.

"Wow, you are amazing."

She blushed. "Naw, that's nothing – you should see the real ice skaters."

"Now, now, no selling yourself short. When I say it's amazing, it's amazing. So would you be up for another turn around the railing with grandpa? I might even let go of the railing this time."

He made her laugh. "Sure. You know, the trick is to get some speed to steady yourself." She started pulling him along, and before long, he was almost skating.

"You are a pretty good teacher, miss. But I think I am better off tending bar."

"Is bartending everything you always wanted to do?"

"Not exactly. I must have had a thousand professions before I finally landed here. But it is the thing I ended up liking the most in the end. When you are behind the bar, people tell you about their lives. I like that. Tell me about yours."

"That was smooth," she laughed, "Gee, let me think. Well there isn't much to tell. I work as an event planner . . ." And what else? Was her life that boring? Maybe she had to add that to her to-do list too: Get a life.

"Do you like it?"

"Yes, I love it. Organizing all the little details that make a party perfect. Making people happy as you bring their dream to life. But I also like the actual process. You get to see so many lovely things, it's perfect. Arrange flowers, decorations, party favors, food. And of course there is the sampling – that is one of the best things."

"So you are the life of the party?"

"Yeah, I guess you could say that. Me and my colleagues. Without us, no party."

"Do you organize a lot of parties at home?"

"No, not really . . . I guess I don't need to. I get to do all that stuff at work. Last thing I organized was Lily's birthday."

"Lily? Who is that?"

"A four-year-old girl that I am aunt to. Well, sort of. I have known her daddy forever. His sister and I have been best friends since before kindergarten. She now lives on the other side of the country, but he lives across the hall. He's like family."

"You can never have enough of that. I miss mine sometimes. My dad died a while ago, and most of my cousins still live in Ireland. My mum, she left when I was little. I don't even know if she is still alive. She ran out on my dad to be with another man and that was the last we heard of her."

"I'm sorry. That's very sad. Lily's mom left too. Sam, her dad, takes really good care of her, though."

"I'm over her abandonment. The person I really miss is my dad. But I have the bar, and the people that come to it are like family. Some of the patrons drop by every day, telling me how their day was. They are friends as well as guests."

She wondered if his mother's abandonment had to do with the fact he was still single. At this point she didn't dare ask though. "Tell me about your dad?" she asked instead.

"Oh, he was a lovely man. Kind, loving, loyal. A real gent. Always there when somebody needed him."

That sounded just like the kind of man Sam was.

"I miss him most around this time of year, when it starts getting colder. He always went out of his way to make something special of Christmas. I think it was because he was trying to make up for me not having a mum. He did not want me to miss out."

"That's so sweet."

"The best thing was decorating the tree. On top would go this glass angel. I still have her – she comes out every year to look over the bar. Actually I have a collection these days – had to get some more to keep her company. They remind me of my dad. It's a pity I can't keep them out all year round."

"Why not? I doubt anyone would object, especially if they hear the story behind it." It was so touching.

"Well, I guess I could. But there is something special about pulling them out on the first of December. I would not want to lose that ritual."

"I understand completely."

His stomach now growled instead of hers. "Time for dinner?"

She nodded. "I think so."

The diner he took her to was lovely. Quaint, with good food and lovely staff. Well, maybe the last wasn't very surprising, since they all seemed to know Robert. The food, however, was so lovely that she ate more than she had ever done before in a restaurant.

"I'm glad we did this last – I think you will have to roll me out," Izzy said, patting her stomach.

All in all, it had been a lovely date. He had made her laugh and she hadn't even thought about John. Something was missing, though, something she could not put her finger on. She liked Robert a lot – he was terrific to be with – but the romantic connection just wasn't there.

CHAPTER TEN

Izzy hung out a lot with Robert over the next few weeks. His bar was about the coziest place in the world, and all the patrons were very friendly. It was truly like a family, and they had welcomed her with open arms. But as much as she wanted to be, she wasn't in love with Robert. He was an absolutely terrific guy – funny, kindhearted – but somehow there just weren't any sparks between them. She liked him, but she wasn't in love. She was going to have to tell him. Stringing him along wasn't fair, not on either of them. She and John had been doing that for years.

If only she had realized sooner that she didn't like John, then she might have found somebody else by now. Somebody that loved her, that understood her. At almost thirty-five, Izzy felt a sense of urgency. All the good guys were already taken – and most of the bad ones as well. There was a biological clock that was not exactly quiet either, especially not when she looked at Lily. To have a kid like her, with a man like Sam . . . What woman would be stupid enough to walk away from that? She would never understand it. In fact, she would have gladly traded places.

But she did not want a man just for the sake of having kids. There were sperm banks and test tubes if she ever got that desperate. What she wanted was a partner for life. Someone to share the good, the bad, and the ugly with, and who would be there through it all. But also somebody that she could love with all her heart. She wanted it all.

And then there was that spectacular dress in her closet to remind her of the other thing she had been dreaming of since she was little – a wedding. Women her age – most were married, and some had even gotten divorced and then remarried – twice! Izzy had yet to be married even for the first time. It was high time she got serious about it, just like Sophie had said. Which meant being honest with her feelings.

However, she did not want to break Robert's heart either. He was too nice for that. So she would have to do it now, before they got too involved. It was the kindest way. She was already on her way to the bar.

Looking at the clock, Izzy realized she'd better hurry up, for she had promised Lily that she would spend the afternoon with her, and get her clothes for Christmas. First, though, she had to bite the bullet and get it out of the way. With a heavy heart, she went in. Robert waved cheerily at her, and she felt like a monster.

Maybe it wasn't the best idea to do this during lunchtime. Robert was rushed of his feet, and she tried to help where she could, taking orders and bringing drinks round to customers. Hopefully, she'd get a chance later.

"Have I told you yet that you are absolutely amazing," he told her as she scooted past him with a full tray of drinks. "At this rate I will need to start paying you . . . or marry you."

It was as if he plunged a dagger in her heart – Izzy nearly dropped the tray.

"Easy there, it was just a joke," he said, taking the tray out of her hands. Seeing something was wrong, he pulled her aside. "What's the matter, dearie?"

It was now or never. "Robert, I really like you a lot, you are a wonderful guy . . ."

He seemed to have heard that before. "Why do I feel there is a 'but' coming?"

"Sorry. It just isn't there. I think you are an amazing guy, but not for me. Not like that, at least. I really like hanging out with you, though." She couldn't even look at him.

"Ouch, you know how to hurt a guy," he said, clutching his chest with a grin.

She felt close to crying. "I'm sorry, but I can't feel what I don't feel."

He put an arm around her. "It's okay, it's okay. You are probably right, you feel like a best friend, not a partner. After all, if that were so, wouldn't we at least have kissed by now?"

She hadn't even thought about that, but he was so right. "I love spending time with you though. And the pub is so much fun. I can't believe I learned how to tap a beer correctly."

"Maybe I am trying too hard. Getting old, not wanting to end up alone. I mean, I have the bar, but it ain't the same."

"That I can relate to. There is a point you start wondering if you'll be left up on the shelf."

"Naw, you are far too young for that. And too pretty. I promise you, if it comes to that, come back and I'll marry you in a heartbeat. After all there is nothing like free labor," he joked.

Finally she could laugh again. "Ah, so that is why you seduce women?"

"Damn, now you know my secret." He put an arm around her. "You know, I really like having you around, kid. You remind me of somebody I knew a long time ago."

"Somebody special?"

His eyes misted over. "Very. The one that got away."

That sounded serious. "Oh dear, what happened?"

"I was living over here at the time. She was somebody I'd never thought I'd fall for, a "good girl," and a rival even. I was a bit of a bad boy back then. But she turned out to be everything I ever wanted – sweet, sassy, funny. Fate got between us though. My dad got ill, and I had to go back home. So we broke up. I could not let her wait all that time whilst I was looking after my pa. It was the hardest choice I ever had to make."

"And you didn't look her up when you got back?"

"I tried to, but I couldn't find her. Well, she is probably happily married by now, so it's too late anyways."

"That's so sad." Izzy felt all disappointed. Stories like that needed to end in "And they lived happily ever after." Not in "And they never saw each other ever again."

"Och well . . . maybe it just wasn't meant to be. How about if you and me stick to what we are good at, and just stay friends? You can come by the pub once in a while for a chat. I wouldn't want to lose sight of you forever."

"I'd like that." She was so relieved she wouldn't be cast aside completely.

"And I get a free barmaid, of course. Are you sticking around today?"

"Nope. Sorry, I got a very important date. In fact, I should get going."

"I'm being replaced already?"

"Well, not really. Unless you can't handle the competition from a four-year-old."

"Of course I can't. They have a cuteness factor I could never compete with. Taking Lily out?" he asked, knowing exactly who she meant.

"Yes, for a little shopping . . . I promised that I'd buy her a new dress."

"A girl can never have too many of those. Alright, run along. Leave me. Break my heart." He said so with a twinkle in his eye, so Izzy knew he did not quite mean it. Still, she was a bit worried.

"Will you be alright?"

"I'll live. I'm happy we are still friends. I'm gonna keep you to your promise about coming back."

"I will, cross my heart and hope to die." And thus he got his first kiss after all. On the cheek, but still. "See you soon!"

That had gone far better than she had hoped. She was running late though, and tried to get home as fast as she could. The last thing she wanted to do was disappoint Lily. Sam was already waiting for her as she arrived, looking not quite happy.

She quickly apologized. "I'm so sorry, I had to go to the bar."

"Still seeing this Robert?" he asked. It did not exactly sound like an accusation, but it certainly came close.

"Yes, but I don't think we are anything more than friends. I told him so today, and he feels the same, so that is good. I promised I'd drop again soon, though."

Sam nearly fell over himself with surprise. She couldn't understand why he was so upset over this. It was almost like he was a bit jealous. "You've broken up with him, but you are still gonna see him again? Why?"

"Because he is not like John. He makes a very good friend. A girl can't have too many of those, can she?"

"I guess." Sam did not sound quite convinced.

Maybe she should introduce him to Robert – they were so alike that they would probably get along quite well. "Plus he runs a lovely bar. You'd like it. Come with me some day."

"Sure." That sounded more like a no. Oh well, she'd work on him. In the end, he usually gave in.

She went into the living room where a little girl was watching TV. "Lily, are you ready to go shopping with me?"

"Yes!" Lily got up and hugged her. "Is daddy coming with us?"

"No this is a girl's day out, sweetie. No men allowed. But you can show daddy what you have bought when we get back, is that ok?"

Lilly nodded.

"Go get your coat then."

The little girl ran off, and Sam pulled her aside. "Thanks for doing this."

"Are you kidding me? It's my pleasure! I get to spend time with my favorite girl. And have you any idea how cute clothes for four-year-olds are? I would put them on myself if they'd fit. But I can't. So I can at least buy them for Lily. Don't worry, I won't pressure her into anything."

"And nothing too outrageous or expensive," he said trying to tuck some money into her hand.

She wouldn't allow it. This was her chance to thank him for always being there for her. "Hey, I am paying. That way I can be as outrageous as I like."

"But . . ." he protested.

"No buts, this is MY treat. This is my niece, sorta . . . I will spoil her rotten as I see fit."

"Don't let her become too spoiled though, please. If she becomes a diva, I am blaming you."

"Lily? Impossible! She is far too kindhearted for that. She takes after her father there." She kissed his cheek.

"I'm ready, Aunt Izzy." Lily came around the corner.

"What time will you be back?" Sam wanted to know.

Izzy thought about it. “Around seven? I thought of going to a movie with her afterwards.”

“That’s fine. Will I be expecting you for dinner?”

“Um . . . yes, please?” She could take Lily to a diner or get something to eat at the cinema, but Sam’s cooking was so much better. Plus, otherwise he’d be eating here all by himself.

“You as well? You won’t be seeing Robert?”

“No, I wasn’t planning to go by there today. I think that needs to rest a bit.” She didn’t want to get into it too much in front of Lily.

“So I am just expected to feed you?” he now started grinning.

“Pleeeaaaase?” she begged. “Lily, pout at your daddy for me, please, my begging does not seem to work.”

“Please daddy?” the girl backed her up, throwing in all of her adorableness.

“God, you two are incorrigible. Alright, I’ll relent. See you two later.” He kissed his daughter on the cheek, and Izzy stuck out her cheek too. “Alright,” he grumbled, kissing it.

“See you later, you big softie,” she said waving goodbye.

“Hey, I can still change my mind – I need to feed her but not you,” he cheerfully bickered. She knew he didn’t mean it for a second.

Lily waved as well. “Bye daddy.”

And off they went, hitting the shops. Lily was such a joy to go out with, and very patient for her age – she had yet to throw a tantrum.

“Can I have a dress like yours, aunty?” was the first question she asked.

It was her own fault . . . At Lily’s age, she’d have done absolutely anything for a dress like that. Correction: clearly, she still would – after all, she had just spent $6500 to buy one. “I don’t think they make them in your size, sweetie. But we’ll see what we can do later, okay? Maybe something pretty for Christmas?”

“It’s okay, I don’t want a prince yet anyways. Boys are icky.” The disgust with which that last bit was uttered made it very hard for Izzy not to laugh, but she managed somehow.

“But we don’t buy pretty things for them – we buy them for ourselves, so we feel pretty. I promise we’ll find something. First you need a few practical things, though. You are growing far too fast – practically nothing fits anymore.”

Lily, having inherited her father’s practical side, asked, “Should I stop growing?”

To have a small girl forever was tempting. Izzy shook her head, though. “No dear, not at all. This just gives me a reason to take you out shopping, which I love.”

One pair of jeans, three tops, two leggings, a skirt, a sweater, and a coat later, they were finally at the dress department . . . which was having a sale – three for two. Izzy knew she shouldn't. Knowing Sam, he'd just about manage one dress, two maybe . . . but three? That would be a ridiculous expense. It was Izzy's money though, and she couldn't resist. Lily was a kid in a candy shop and wanted to try on everything at once. It was playing dress up with hundreds of dresses.

One of the first dresses Lily wanted to try on was a red dress with frills and a belt of roses. She looked absolutely delightful, and Izzy was pretty sure this was one of the dresses they would end up taking. "Daddy always sighs when I wanna try on many dresses," Lily sighed as she twirled round in front of the mirror.

"That's typical for men, sweetie. They huff and puff, and don't understand the fun of it. But that's why I'm here. I'll be happy to take you out shopping any day."

"Even when I am all grown up?" Lily looked unsure.

"Yes, even then. By the way, your daddy needs a new sweater. Shall we pick one out for him later?" Getting Sam to shop – you nearly had to drag him there. Having bought clothes for him before, she knew his sizes like the back of her hand. Sam almost never bought something new, saving all his money to spend on his daughter. Well, except for the tux – that had really surprised her. His favorite sweater, however, was showing signs of wear and tear. If she let Lily pick out a new one, he could not possibly object to it being bought.

"I also wanna buy him a present for Christmas," Lily said, trying on a blue dress. This wasn't the one, they quickly agreed.

She was amazed Lily would already think of this, seeing Christmas was still a month away. "Of course. What do you wanna get him?"

"Gloves! His hands are always cold when he comes and picks me up from school."

"Great idea!" Izzy encouraged her. Sam wasn't a man who ever wore ties, so buying those would be a waste. Gloves, however, would be perfect, and it showed how thoughtful Lily was.

"Auntie, this dress is gold, just like yours." It was a princess dress, a costume. The fabric was from far inferior quality, but Izzy completely understood the attraction. As a little girl, she would have wanted exactly the same. At $90, it was a bit extravagant, but maybe just this once . . . Who was she kidding – if Lily liked it, she'd buy it.

"It is! Do you want to try it on?"

Lily nodded so hard it looked like her head was about to fall off. As Lily put the dress on and then looked in the mirror, Izzy recognized her expression – it was the same as Izzy'd had when she had put on her dress. At not even 2% of the price of her dress, she could not begrudge the girl this. And there was lots of stretch in the fabric, so Lily would be able to enjoy it and play with it for a long time.

Then she thought of something. "You can have it, on one condition. You are not getting it straight away. I want to do something to it to make it extra special." If she bought some extra lace and silk flowers, she could make it even more like her dress. Lily would love that, and then she would get it with Christmas. That way, she could also hide the fact that she had bought three dresses a little longer.

"Alright," Lily agreed.

That was it. Three dresses were bought – one Christmas red, the golden one which Sam was almost certainly going to disapprove of, and one bright and flowery that could be worn any season and was slightly oversized so Lily could hopefully still fit into it when spring came. Then they moved on to the men's department to buy Sam a sweater.

"I like this one," Lily said, picking out a bright red one.

"Me too, but red is not something your daddy wears a lot," Izzy tried to guide her.

"Maybe you should knit him one." Lily suggested. Izzy had done so before, and also for Lily.

"I'd love to, but I think he needs this one a bit sooner." Knitting him a vest would take most of a month. It was an idea for Christmas, though.

"Auntie, this one looks just like the one he has, but much softer." It was indeed almost identical, but ever so soft.

"Yes, indeed! You'll be wanting to cuddle him all day when he wears this." She picked out Sam's size. "Now for the gloves."

They moved over to the counter where a clerk stepped up to help them. "Picking out gloves for your husband, ma'am?"

"For my daddy. For Christmas." Lily piped up. Well, that saved her from having to answer that question.

"And do you know his size?"

"Umm . . ." That was probably the one size she did not know. He had large hands, but how large was large?

"This size." Lily pulled a drawing out of her pocket where she and Sam had drawn outlines around their hands.

"You clever little thing! You have planned ahead," Izzy said, full of amazement.

Lily proudly nodded.

"That size," Izzy said, handing over the drawing. "Leather, supple as possible. He works outside a lot as a cameraman, so he needs optimal mobility in his fingers."

"They don't come cheap, ma'am. About $70 and more."

She would have paid double – this was the perfect gift. Useful and stylish. And the fact Lily was giving them meant he could not object, which was even better. "That's alright. As long as they are very easy to work with."

"Our customers say they are like a second skin. As long as they are the right size, that is. Looking at your daughter's drawing, I think this should be it. If not, you can exchange them after Christmas for the right pair, as long as you keep the receipt."

Should she say something? Lily seemed fine with being called her daughter – in fact she felt the girl cling to her leg. "Thank you."

The gloves got put in a box and beautifully gift wrapped. The clerk seemed to put in extra effort, seeing it was for Lily, using extra colorful ribbons.

"Shall I hang on to them, so you can surprise daddy at Christmas?" If Lily hid them, Sam was bound to find them clearing up. Or they would be so well hidden that on Christmas Day, they'd be forgotten. "You can make a lovely card to go with it, and I'll make sure it ends up under the tree on Christmas Eve."

Done. Now it was time to go see a movie.

CHAPTER ELEVEN

Izzy felt furious, like she could blow up any second. Really, she was ready to strangle somebody. Unfortunately, getting in contact with the guy that was responsible for these feelings was probably the last thing she should do. Well, besides strangling him then. He wasn't worth going to jail for. When she had said no contact, she had meant it.

Of course, John could care less about this, the jerk. This morning, there had been a message on her voicemail from him. She couldn't believe it. He wanted to take her out. There was a do at his work, and . . . yadayadayada, as if nothing was the matter. She was just supposed to drop everything and come running. Somewhere in it, he even managed to accuse her of ruining his career if she did not come. Well, she hoped she would, because there was no way in hell she was gonna attend this social gathering of his. Honestly, the nerve of this guy was unbelievable.

She spent the morning preoccupied with looking for a solution to shut him up. She felt anxious and agitated, and her work was suffering with it. How dare he do this to her? They were no longer together – why couldn't he just understand that? Did he honestly expect her to come running when he asked? It was all about his stupid precious work again. But it had been over two months since they had broken up – surely someone at his work would have noticed that by now.

She tried to remember if she had told Claire yet. Their last meeting had been so full of things that needed to be decided, details that needed to be arranged, that she had forgotten to mention it. Ringing Claire about it now would though would seem strange. Unless it was hidden in a work-related question perhaps . . . Izzy couldn't think of any good questions though, and lots of other projects needed to be finished before Christmas. It would be completely unprofessional. Claire was a client before she was a friend, however much Izzy might like her. She could try and bring it up next time they spoke, but for now it was useless. And even then, it did not seem fair to saddle Claire with the problem.

Of course, the other alternative was going to John at his workplace and kicking up such a storm that he would never even dare to contact her again. That wasn't her style though, and she did not feel like making a spectacle of herself just to get rid of him. An email would probably not do the trick though, unless she sent it to all his colleagues as well. Which would seem more like the act of a desperate woman trying to win him back. And all she was desperate for was getting rid of him, not getting him back.

Karin was going on and on about the arrangements for a Christmas party they were arranging, nagging about all the little details. "Are we going with red or gold?"

"Red."

"And from whom are we ordering?"

Izzy snapped. "Just decide for yourself, will you!?" Immediately she regretted it. Obnoxious as it might be, this was a work meeting where these things were discussed. She would have to explain. "Sorry, I didn't mean it that way. John called me today. I thought he would have gotten it through his thick skull by now that we have broken up, but no. He wants me to go to a party with him."

"You dumped John?" Other people now looked up to.

Great now she needed to tell everyone. "Yes."

"I thought you two were solid. He was so good looking . . ." She could have him if she liked, Izzy thought. "I mean he was a bit of a prick, but you never seemed to mind." Karin was a bit dim, and probably the colleague Izzy liked least.

"Well, *I* started to mind." Izzy retorted. Like she would willingly stay with a prick. Well, she had . . . for far too long.

Luckily, not all reactions were that bad. "Good on you," Susan congratulated her. "So that's why Sam pretended to be John at the Taylor event?"

"Yes – not that I think John would have come if we had been together. I'm so glad to be rid of him. Now if he could just stay away, I'd be pleased as punch."

Francesca was the gossip girl and matchmaker of the bunch. She was also really nice. "I've got a cousin in town this week who would be perfect for you. I could set you up on a date."

"I don't know." Izzy wanted a date, but she wasn't sure if this was the best way to go about it. Somewhere in the back of her mind, alarm bells started ringing. She had not, however, met another man since Robert, and if she were really serious about trying to find somebody . . . well, it didn't happen all by itself.

"Come on, it'll be fun. Plus, you need to start dating again. Get your toes back in the water. I'll call him now." Exactly what Sophie had said.

Maybe it was a sign.

Francesca disappeared from the room to arrange it before Izzy could protest. Karin went back to her own work and stopped bothering Izzy.

"Do you want me to have a talk with John? I'm notorious when it comes to driving men away," Susan offered.

"Thanks, but this is one I need to handle myself. By the way, you are not so bad. Only when you want to be. Otherwise, you are the sweetest woman I know."

Francesca came cheering. "You have a date tonight!"

"What? So soon?" That gave her no time to prepare . . . or to get nervous. Maybe it was a good thing.

"Why not? Did you wanna go out with John tonight? This way you can tell him you had a prior engagement and throw it back in his face."

"The party isn't until next Friday."

"Well I am sure I can get you a date for that too, if you like. So are you going? Xander is really very nice, and he said he was looking forward to it. You can't let him down now."

It seemed Izzy had no choice – everything had been already arranged. "Yeah, alright."

"Fantastic, you'll love him, I promise." Francesca seemed more excited about it than Izzy felt. Of course, Fran knew who she was meeting, while Izzy had no clue.

Not going home after work meant she needed to make a call, and so she slipped out. "Sam, I'm not coming home for dinner tonight. I got a date, apparently."

"Apparently?" he asked surprised.

"Well Francesca called her cousin and set me up for tonight. It all happened so quickly, it was arranged before I could protest."

She heard Sam starting to laugh rather fiendishly. "Well, good luck with that."

"What? She means well."

"Yeah, and the road to hell is paved with good intentions. Have you ever been on a blind date?"

"No. But how bad can it be?"

"Bad, trust me. Did you at least see a picture of this guy?"

"No. It's a blind date, isn't it?"

"Well then you'd better keep a blindfold on throughout. Listen, get that picture so you know what to expect. And if you are on the date and he turns out to be a dud, call me. I'll call back with some sort of emergency and get you out, okay?"

"I'm sure that won't be necessary."

"Well, just know you have that option, alright?"

The call had made her nervous after all it seemed. Quickly she asked Francesca for a picture. Xander was nothing special, a regular guy – nothing to repulse her but nothing to attract her either at first sight. That was okay though – Francesca he had said he was terrific, so hopefully his personality would make up for his dull appearance. Throughout the day, Francesca kept singing his praises, making Xander sound like Wonder Man. She arranged everything, like one would expect of a good party planner, although maybe she went a bit overboard on the whole. Restaurant, taxi – all was arranged. On her lunch break, Fran even bought a dress for Izzy to wear.

"Thank you, but I could have just gone home and changed, Fran," Izzy said, feeling slightly stunned.

"It's my treat. Break-ups are hard, and you need things to cheer you up. Come on, try it on!"

Izzy had to agree, the green velvet dress looked stunning. Classy, without looking stiff. Francesca helped her with her makeup as if they were a couple of teenagers. Then she brought her to the taxi that was waiting. For a moment Izzy wondered if Francesca were going to chaperone the date as well. Fran waved goodbye however, and off Izzy went.

The restaurant was a three-star one, with a half-year waiting list. Izzy wondered how Francesca had managed to pull it off, and made a mental note to thank her for this. Whatever the night might bring, she had obviously put a lot of effort into it, and that with so little time.

Xander met her at the bar as they waited for their table to become available. He was a fair bit heavier than the picture had suggested, but Izzy was not going to let that put her off.

"Here," he said, putting a small package in her hand.

"Chocolates? Oh thank you, they're my favorite brand! How did you know?"

"Franny had them sent over to the apartment today with a note that I should give them to you." He sounded rather disappointed about that.

Well, she shouldn't judge him just yet, just because he seemed to be slightly boorish. Maybe it was just a way to cover up his shyness. "Your cousin is very nice to arrange all this for us."

"Oh I don't know, I would have just as well stayed at home, really. This posh stuff really isn't my style, all those stuck-up waiters and tiny bites that never seem to be able to fill you up."

"We could go somewhere else if you like?" It would be an insult to Fran to walk away from such a fine restaurant, but if he didn't want to be here, Izzy wasn't going to force him.

"Naw, that's alright, Fran is paying for it. So you can order what you like. I know I will," he said, patting his tummy.

She was? This was really too much. It was a very kind gesture and of course Xander was her cousin, but it hardly seemed fair to set up a date and pay for it as well. Xander should have been the one paying, but that did not seem likely. "I'll pay," Izzy offered.

"Huh? Well alright – whatever floats your boat. What is taking so long though? I'm hungry and this is a restaurant. Shouldn't that be against the law or something . . . say, what about opening that box of chocolates and trying some."

He was already making a go for the box, when the maître d' came to tell them their table was ready. "I can hold ze box of chocolat pour vous till you leave, sir. You will get it back with your coats," the waiter suggested strongly. The French accent was clearly fake, but his tone was undeniable.

Xander started to protest. "Hey this is a restaurant, can't I eat when I wanna, you arro. . ."

Oh my god, they were gonna be kicked out at this rate. Izzy quickly intervened. "They are mine, and yes please!" Of course technically they were Fran's . . . Like everything else about this date.

"Can you believe the arrogance of that jerk?" Xander said embarrassingly loudly after they had been seated.

"He was just doing his job. Let's enjoy dinner."

"Yes." He quickly ordered the most expensive items on the menu. . . and now she had promised to pay. Great. "My girlfriend . . . my ex-girlfriend used to take us to places like this. I was a lot thinner back then."

She wondered how long ago he got dumped. "Oh really?"

"Yeah . . . I don't like to talk about her though."

Ten full minutes passed without conversation – Xander was busy surfing the net on his phone. Luckily, the appetizers came, so Izzy had something to do, but the date did not improve. Xander ate like a pig, and Izzy noticed that he drank quite heavily too. She had to admit the food itself was quite good, though she still preferred Sam's cooking. Something was missing though, and she couldn't put her finger on it.

"So this is a pity date. Fran said you recently broke up," Xander said, with his mouth full.

The nerve! If this was indeed a pity date, it was her pitying him. "No, I'm happily single at the moment. My relationship had ended a long time ago, we just hadn't officially broken up." She didn't want to tell him more than she absolutely had to, but she was not going to let him make her sound like some pathetic cast off.

"I was led to believe you were all broken up over him. That's the only reason I agreed. And because Fran practically made me."

Fran had done what? He would have said no, and she could have been enjoying a quiet night in with Sam instead of this torture. Several more minutes were spent in silence. The second course arrived – he had ordered the biggest sirloin steak there was. Well, he could certainly not complain about portions here. Just the sight of watching him eat made Izzy lose her appetite. Her salmon was practically untouched by the time they were serving desert.

"You know, I am sorry about my earlier behavior." He was? Well, that was at least something. "My ex – I really miss her. She was a classy chick, always looking her best. She was always so good to me. I can't believe we broke up." He started sobbing, quietly at first, but soon getting louder. It was a good thing the waiter had put them in the quietest corner of the restaurant, but people were still watching.

Great – now he was blubbering. She'd have preferred the silence. "There there, it's ok. Break-ups are never easy. It'll get better in time."

"It's been a year!" Xander blew his nose in the napkin rather disgustingly. "One day she said she just didn't want me anymore, and the next day she moved out."

"That's too bad, but you'll find somebody else eventually."

"You wouldn't do that to a guy, would you? You wouldn't leave me," he slurred, grabbing her hand and pulling it toward him. His palm felt greasy and sweaty.

She quickly pulled hers back. "Look, you seem like a n-nice guy." The word had trouble forming in her mouth. "But I don't think you are over your ex yet. And I don't think we'd be good together. So before you get any wrong ideas . . ."

"You're just like her!" It wasn't clear if that was an accusation or a compliment.

"I think it's best if I leave . . . Check please!"

"No miss, it is on the house. It's all taken care of." The French accent was gone – even the maître d' seemed to have had enough of Xander's antics and just wanted the situation to be over.

She followed him. "Let me at least give you a tip for putting up with him."

The maître d' smiled at her. "No need – you were a delight to have. The cook is a friend of Miss Pascarella and owed her a favor – a huge one, by the looks of it. To be honest, that is the only reason we even served him – we usually don't tolerate such behavior from our guests."

"I'm sorry," she apologized.

"It is not your fault. Your cab is waiting. You can safely escape, and we'll take care of him."

"Thank you ever so much. What will you do with him?"

"We'll get him home, don't worry." he assured her.

She was hardly in the cab when her phone rang. "How was it?" Fran asked . Either Xander or the restaurant had obviously contacted her,

"Awful! Hell! How could you do this to me?" This was by far the worst date Izzy had ever been on. Some days it didn't pay to get out of bed, really. The whole day had been an absolute disaster.

"I'm sorry! I'll make it up to you. Xander used to be really nice, a really upbeat sweetheart of a guy. Until his ex broke up with him. Since then he changed into . . . well, what you saw. I thought if anybody could turn him back into his old self, it was you. I guess I was wrong. I'll make it up to you, alright? I know this guy . . ."

"No! No more blind dates. I can't believe I went through with this one, especially after Sam warned me. I should have taken him up on his offer and had him call me to get out of there. Sorry Fran, I hope we are still friends, but no more of this. Please."

"I am the one that's really sorry. I shouldn't have put you through that. Forgive me?"

Despite today, Fran was actually very nice. "You're forgiven. But I am going home now. Goodnight." With that she hung up the phone. She couldn't wait to close the door behind her and take a long warm soak to wash the worries of the day away. She decided to ignore John for what it was worth. Let him sweat until he realized she wasn't coming. He could just stick it where the sun didn't shine, for all she cared. It would be a useful lesson for him.

CHAPTER TWELVE

So, Robert wasn't the one. Xander certainly wasn't the one. That guy had so many issues it was hard to know where to start. Francesca had said that he had wanted to take her out on a second date. Izzy had quickly declined, and Fran couldn't blame her.

Two guys down, and still she hadn't found somebody that was boyfriend material, let alone husband material. Maybe it was asking too much. She hadn't really been trying. Plenty of fish in the sea, but some of these fish were slimy customers. Besides, Robert was lovely, he just wasn't the right guy for her. She wished him all the luck in the world with finding somebody.

These first dates had been easy to find – they had offered themselves up, practically. Maybe that was why they had not worked out. The next one she would choose herself. That would require her going out there and looking, though. It wasn't something she was looking forward to, and probably for good reason. She called Sophie for support and advice.

"Hey girl, have you found that man yet?" was the first question. Trust Sophie to always be forward.

Izzy sighed. "Not really."

"Robert wasn't your kind of guy? He sounded very nice."

She wondered if she had made the wrong decision there. He was kind, and she could definitely be herself around him, just like Sam. No. "He was . . . he just wasn't THE guy. We make great friends, and he is great to hang out with, but there is no chemistry, not like that. He taught me some great bartending skills though."

Sophie cooed. "Oh, great. Next party I'm throwing, you're soooo coming and giving me a lesson."

"Next party I'm throwing, you mean? Or are you coming over here? I am a busy girl these days, especially if you consider that I have to start dating again as well. Actually, I was wondering what I should do next, though."

"Internet dating, of course." Sophie replied, as if that was most natural choice in the world.

Izzy wasn't sure. Those dating sites seem to have such a stigma around it. "Isn't that for desperate people?" she asked carefully.

"Nooo, everybody does it nowadays. I got a profile – would you consider me desperate?" Sophie answered indignantly.

Some things were best not to comment on. Sophie wasn't desperate per se but she was a hopeless romantic, with the accent on the hopeless part. But Sophie was far too nice to ever let her know that. "Of course not," Izzy said instead.

"Get online. I'll talk you through it. Better yet, make it video call. I'll be there in a minute, and then we can do it together."

"Alright. . . and thank you, Sophie."

"What are best friends for? And don't thank me yet, I haven't done anything so far."

Izzy laid down the phone and got her laptop. Retreating to the comforts of her own bedroom, she sat down on the bed and turned on the computer, waiting till it was completely on. What would they want to know from her, she wondered? She didn't really like talking about herself, and filling in a profile was like water torture. Trying to sound perfect in a few words, even though she wasn't. It was absolutely horrid.

She looked at the dress, hanging in the corner looking fabulously beautiful. "Don't mock me, I'm doing this for you, so you can be worn."

The dress simply sparkled as if it was saying "Yeah, keep telling yourself that missy, we both know it isn't true. You just don't want to end up alone."

Or maybe she was just imagining that. Her laptop started making noises, Sophie was calling her . . . with video. Izzy quickly ran her fingers through her hair to make herself look semi-decent. Sophie wouldn't care what she looked like but still . . . one should always make an effort to look their best. And not like something that the cat had just dragged in.

"Hiya . . ." Sophie waved at her. "Follow the link I am sending you so you can make a profile."

"Is this site any good?" Izzy asked feeling a bit weary. It looked very sappy, that was for sure. Pink hearts and couples holding hands. But that was what she wanted, right?

"I dated some really cute guys that I met on this site, don't worry." Sophie assured her.

"You're on this site??" That came out wrong and she knew her facial expression was probably even worse. She didn't mean to make it sound like she was accusing Sophie of something. Whatever that something might be.

"Izzy, grow up. It's the twenty-first century, everybody does it. If you are gonna wait for a knight to climb your castle wall, you are gonna be very disappointed."

That certainly sounded very ambiguous. "Um, alright" Okay, she clicked on "Make a Profile." Immediately, they started asking her the dreaded questions.

"What's wrong. I can see in your face something is the matter." Sophie commented from the other side. That woman knew her far too well

"It's asking me what I want in a guy." If she knew that, she wouldn't have ended up with John. She had a bad track record when it came to picking guys. John just was the last one in a string of them. And the one she had stayed the longest with. Maybe she was destined to end up alone after all?

"Well what do you want?"

"Someone sweet, loyal, with a quirky sense of humor. Somebody I can rely on when I need him, and who is not completely self-obsessed. Somebody I can trust and tell anything."

"You know you are describing my brother, don't you?" Damn, she had a point. It wasn't an option though. No way. Sam was Sam. He was far too familiar . . . and too young.

"What? No, not Sam . . . Well, anyways, he isn't so bad. I'd definitely want a guy like him if I could be so lucky." She quickly wrote down her key points and moved on to the next question. "What's next? Describe yourself. Ugh, I hate that bit. Now I know why I never did this before. I hate selling myself like that."

"But who wouldn't want to buy you?" Sophie smiled and thought with her about what to write. "Ok, how about 'Cute but crazy party girl is looking for sweet and funny guy to date.'"

"I love organizing parties, but not necessarily going to them. Put it like this they might think I am some sort of blond bimbo party girl, which I am NOT. God knows what kind of guys will react. I want men that will be interested in me for me, not looking for an airhead. Else I don't even want to bother." She was done with pretense for good after John.

"Alright, alright. You don't have to bite my head off, I get the point. You are far prettier than those kinds of Barbie dolls anyways. How about 'Sweet but crazy girl that loves to stay at home and knit seeks ditto boy, knitting skills not required. Is a wiz at organizing parties.'" There was a mean grin on Sophie's face.

Problem was, that described Izzy quite well. It was true, she loved knitting, and nowadays she was more often at home than out. Well at home across the hall, playing with Lily. In terms of being exciting, her life had to be at the bottom of the list. "Great, now I sound like a granny. Maybe I should just give up. Unless grandpa wants to date me."

"Well, you dated Robert, how old was he again?" Another sly grin.

"That's mean, he's an absolute terrific guy, just . . ."

" . . . not for you." Sophie completed the sentence for her. "I know, I was kidding. If he is anything like you described him, than he seemed like a pretty good guy. Take a picture next time you meet him. I'm very curious what he looks like. You make him sound so charming. AND he has his own bar."

"Wanna date him yourself? You would have my blessing." Especially since it would mean she'd have to move here if they got serious. That really had possibilities. Video calls were fun of course, but it wasn't like a chat in a tea room after you had spent the whole day shopping together.

"Well, maybe. Now back to the subject. You want to meet somebody, right? This is the opportunity to get to meet dozens of men, and all from the comfort of your own home. No dressing up and going to bars and sweaty clubs. You can stay in your pj's if you like."

That was tempting enough to make her continue. Getting to meet guys while you were curled up in a blanket. It still did not solve the problem at hand, though. "Yeah but what do I write down in the profile? I can't leave it blank, can I?"

"You could. It doesn't matter much Iz. Most guys just look at your picture. And you can always change it later anyways."

"They want a picture as well?" Ugh. Of course they did – how could she ever think they would not? It was the internet – visual stimuli everywhere. She hated looking at pictures of herself, though. And to know that it was the only thing guys looking at her profile were interested in gave it the feel of a meat market.

"Yeah, that's the next step. Use the one Sam made of you last Christmas. You look great there."

She remembered those. "I was a bit tipsy there."

"Don't worry it doesn't show. Or you could use the one he made of you sleeping last month, you look angelic," Sophie suggested.

"You saw those pictures? Sam hasn't shown them to me yet."

"He was working on them while I was there. I'm sure he'll show them to you once he is done."

Izzy hoped so – she was curious to see what they looked like. It was strange – usually Sam would have shown them by now. "I looked good though, right?"

"As if you had just dropped from heaven."

"Good." So all she had to do to look great was get drunk or hungover. Well, wasn't that great? Anyways, she'd better get on with it. "Alright, picture uploaded, profile completed. It's asking me if I want to answer more questions to get better matches."

"You can do that another time. It does help a bit, but for now I want to take you to the chat room, so you can just meet some guys who are online now. It's fun, I promise. My screen name LittleRed20, so you can just PM me as well."

"PM?" Izzy felt really stupid right now. She was no stranger to the internet, but had never been in a chat room.

"Personal Message. Who are you? Wait, Izzy273? Come on Iz, couldn't you have chosen something more creative?"

"I didn't know it was a requirement." She was getting a little bit annoyed now that Sophie seemed to think she was doing everything wrong.

"Well, it'll do. Just wait around and see if somebody speaks to you for now." "Like this" Izzy's computer messaged. So this was a PM? That wasn't too hard. Several more popped up. She was popular, or so it seemed.

A question popped up which she did not know how to answer. All those damn letter combinations these days. They made her feel old. "Sophie, what does a/s/l mean?"

"Age, sex, location. Lie about your age. Everyone does." Sophie was typing as well – obviously someone had messaged her too.

"But I was truthful in my profile about it. Anyways, why should I lie that I'm younger? So that they can think 'Well she looks old for her age'?"

"Men think in numbers – they get a kick out of it no matter what you look like. It's the same with breast sizes – they wanna hear it's double D even if they have no clue what that means or looks like."

"I have a B cup, and I am not ashamed of that. I want a guy to take me as I am, not tell him a bunch of lies."

"Everybody lies in the beginning of a relationship. We try to make ourselves look better than we are. So we take off a few years or dress sizes."

"Yeah that is how I ended up with John, he looked so nice. Well, I am not gonna do that again. If guys can't be honest about who they are, they can go to hell."

"Enjoy the rest of your life with my brother, 'cause you are never gonna find a guy with an attitude like that."

"Fine . . . oh my god . . . he is asking what kind of panties I am wearing." She felt embarrassed, even though she had done nothing to encourage this behavior.

"Tell him his momma told him not to go on the internet anymore without her supervision and then close the conversation."

"Done . . . argh . . . now he is asking if I'm his mom, because that would make him a motherfucker."

"Ignore, the guy is trolling you."

Izzy rubbed her temples. "I don't think this stuff is for me Sophie."

"Don't give up just yet. The chat room can get a bit raunchy. Just hang in there alright. What's the perv's name? We can report him to the moderators if you like. That's what they are there for."

"Now some other bloke is asking me if I wanna cam."

"Don't! Never cam. You'll see things that can't be unseen. Those guys are always trouble."

"Well I wasn't planning to. I think I will log off the chat, ok? Before I feel too dirty."

"Fine. Sorry, maybe it's because it's early, all the trolls seem to be out to play. Half of them are probably fourteen, here on a false profile. I always look to make sure the pictures aren't from a celebrity. If you think that the looks like a young Brad Pitt or Johnny Depp, than it probably is, and the actual guy is 300 pounds or still in diapers."

"Really, you are not making this internet dating sound very attractive. Trolls, fakers, pervs."

"Well, you'll find all those people in a bar too, only then they are drunk and standing right next to you. This is in the safety of your own home, with a computer screen between you two. Come online tonight, alright? I'll be there too, I promise and there will be a lot more normal people."

"Alright. I don't know if this is for me though."

"Don't give up on the internet dating thing just yet. There are plenty of good guys on there too – you just need a little patience and let them come forward. The more shy guys will usually send you an email notification that they like you and then you can start talking to them."

"So why go to the chat straight away? This is dreadful." Dreadful emails were a lot easier to ignore.

"I thought it would be a good way to show you the options – the rest is pretty self-explanatory. By the way, you can pick out guys yourself too and send them a notification that you like them . . . And NO Izzy, that is not being too forward. This is the internet – you don't need to wait till the guy comes to you."

"I wasn't gonna say anything."

"But you thought it."

Izzy smirked. "What, are you a mind reader now?"

"When it comes to your mind, I am." And she was right – when it came to dating, Izzy tended to be on the side of old-fashioned. But that was just because old-fashioned men were gentlemen, weren't they? On the other hand, only this morning she was complaining that she did not have any choice in the matter. Well, now she could choose out of thousands of men.

CHAPTER THIRTEEN

So far so good. Izzy had been talking to Brad for about a week now. He was very intelligent and a joy to talk to. He certainly made her laugh a lot with his silly observations, and it didn't hurt that on his picture he was quite good looking either. Frankly, at thirty-five, she was surprised no one had snapped him up yet. But then again, no one had snapped her up either. Every night so far they had talked in the chatroom right until they had to go to bed, and seeing as he only lived on the other side of town, he suggested they meet up. The time and place was up to her. She thought about it. Sophie had imprinted on her to be careful – the internet was full of loons. So she decided to have her date in the safest public place she knew: Robert's bar. She just needed to ask him if he was alright with that. If she invited Brad to meet her this Saturday, and all worked out, she might have a man in her life by the time the holidays came up. That would save from an awful lot of nagging comments by her mother over Christmas.

So Friday after work, she dropped by Robert's bar to ask him. She had already told Brad to meet her there tomorrow, but of course she could always tell him there had been a change of plans. She hoped not, though. Holiday cheer was starting to spread everywhere and had even found its way to the bar. Garlands of green were decorated with red and gold baubles. But the masterpiece was hanging just behind Robert.

Izzy stepped closer to admire them. "You've got the angels out. They're lovely." They were all different in style, but each one was beautiful and charming in its own right. As the light hit them, they sparkled.

"This one is my pa's," Robert said proudly, pointing at the one in the middle. It was a simple, humble-looking angel with golden wings, and the loveliest expression on her face. "I always feel like he's watching me when I put it up."

"I'm sure he is." Izzy turned back to face Robert. "Maybe she can watch over me too. I've got a question, and it's a bit embarrassing."

"Sounds intriguing. What's the problem?

"I met someone online. And I kinda invited him over to the bar already.

Is it alright? I mean in case he is a psychopath ax murderer, I'd like some witnesses who know me and, you know . . ." She was blushing. Maybe this was the wrong idea. They had gone out after all, and now she was confronting him with someone who could potentially become her boyfriend.

"You want a chaperone? I can ask Rhonda." Rhonda was the busybody of the bar, prying into everybody's lives. She would have loved to stick her nose in something like this, given half the chance.

Fear was written on Izzy's face "No that won't be necessary. But . . ."

Robert chuckled. He had just wanted to see her cringe "Bring him! I don't want to be the cause of your untimely death. Heaven forbid something happens to you and I could have prevented it."

"See you tomorrow around three," she smiled.

"He better be nice to you or else . . ." Robert jokingly made a slit neck gesture around his throat. "The patrons will not stand for abuse of their favorite barmaid." She had been right – that was exactly why she wanted it here. And she was glad Robert did not object.

Saturday morning was spent at Sam's apartment. Sam needed to do some special "Christmas Shopping" meaning Lily couldn't come along. So Izzy happily stepped in to babysit her. The card for the gloves still needed to be made, and Lily got her paper and crayons. Chatting away cheerily, they made it into a masterpiece.

"We gotta use lots of glitter, so it will be pretty," Lily said, all serious.

"Oh, I am sure daddy will love that." Though maybe not grandma, with all the glitter that was falling on the floor already. She needed to make sure she'd vacuum before Sam got back, or the surprise would be spoiled. Although . . . granny, gramps, and Aunt Sophie needed cards as well. She could always blame it on that. As soon as Lily was done, she hid Sam's card in her purse. "To put with the present. Want to make some more?"

Lily nodded and started to work on the next one. It kept her busy all morning and even after lunch. She was still working on them as it neared two but Sam still wasn't in sight. Izzy started to worry. He should have been here by now. Of course she needed to leave soon, but that wasn't as important as Sam getting back home safely. She decided to call.

"Sorry Iz, it's madness out here. You'd think the world was gonna end. I spent the last twenty minutes in line for checkout and I am nearly there, okay?" he replied before she could even say anything."

"It's ok, you just had me worried. Come home soon, okay?"

"Your date!" he remembered.

"Don't worry about that. I'll try and call to tell him that I am running late. Just be careful. Don't get trampled by a stampede of angry moms and such." She immediately tried calling Brad, but he did not pick up. Oh well, time to vacuum. Glitter was everywhere, including in Lily's hair. However there were three beautiful cards on the table and one in her purse, and that was the important bit. Izzy would not have minded getting one of those herself.

"Daddy coming home yet?" Lily asked.

"Soon as he can, sweetie, soon as he can."

At a quarter to three, Sam finally entered the door. "I dropped a few parcels off in your apartment," he whispered in Izzy's ear. Lily's presents, of course . . . Izzy nodded.

Well, she was never gonna make it now, and Brad still had not picked up. All she could do was leave now and hope for the best. If he had left, it just wasn't meant to be. A quick change into a dark blue crushed velvet dress that was more date-like than jeans covered in glitter, and she was out of there. Traffic was actually not bad, but of course, whenever you are running late, Murphy's law comes in action. There wasn't a single parking spot to be found in front of the pub, however much she looked. She knew Robert would not mind if she parked in the private alley and so managed to find a spot there. He was just out himself, and she slipped in with him through the back.

"Take a breath dearie, you look all flustered," he said in deep calming tones, putting his hands on her shoulders. It helped.

"Sam came home late from buying Lily her presents, so I'm late," she explained. She tore off her shawl and coat – the pub was warm, and all the hurrying made her feel like she was boiling.

"Well, you are more than worth the wait." He gave her a glass of water, which she gulped down. "Better?"

She nodded. "Much. Thank you."

"There is an unfamiliar young man sitting by the window looking absolutely bored – is that one yours?" Robert pointed her in the right direction.

"Yes, that's him." At least he looked like his picture. A good-looking, well-dressed man in his thirties, with a shock of blond hair, perfectly coiffured. In fact his hair looked better than hers, which looked far from smooth and had been hastily turned into a bun. He could have been a model in his younger years, though now age was slightly starting to show.

"Well, good luck."

"That bodes well. That exactly was what Sam said when I went on my blind date, and that one was horrendous."

"Well, I could say break a leg, but I suggest you make it his when he turns out to be an absolute prick, okay?"

Izzy giggled. "I'll keep that in mind.

He moved a little closer until he was in whispering distance, making sure that only she could hear it. "Listen dear, I thought about what you said, and you are precious to me. So if anything goes wrong, anything at all and you need back up, you order a White Russian, OK? I'll make sure he leaves ASAP. Even if I have to grab him by the scruff and drag him out."

She thought about it. "And if I want an actual White Russian?"

"Izzy, be honest. Did you really like that?"

No but it was the only cocktail she knew. "Well, it's very useful if you want to get drunk really fast. Sometimes that can be really good. I hope that won't be the case this time though. He sounded good over the internet."

"Let's hope he is. Well, don't leave your gentleman waiting. I'll come over there in a minute to take your order. And if you wanna get drunk, I have plenty of other options besides a White Russian."

Well, that was something for later. For now she'd better get over there, before the guy left. "Hi," she said, as friendly as possible and sticking out her hand. "Sorry.."

"You're late," Brad immediately snarked. He shook her hand but looked utterly repulsed when he took it. At least John had been able to feign politeness on their first date

"Yes, sorry – I was babysitting, and the dad came back a little bit later than expected. I tried to call . . ."

It would have been nice if he had actually let her finish a sentence. However, she hardly got a word in edgewise. "You are a babysitter? At your age? I thought you planned parties." There was disdain in his voice.

"No, I mean, yes, I am a party planner . . . an event planner. This was a favor for a friend." She only then noticed that her hands were still full of glitter, and she tried to wipe them off on her dress – which only resulted in her getting glitter on her dress. She also noticed there was some on his hands from when she shook them.

"That must have been some favor. I hate kids, they are loud, annoying, and stupid. And they always make a mess. Don't you think so?"

So he was not the one. Next, please. Couldn't he have said this online? It would have saved her a lot of time, and she could have just stayed with Lily instead of running around like a headless chicken. She guessed she would at least have to stick it out for the date though. And who knew, maybe he wasn't that bad and she'd make another friend at least. She wasn't holding her breath, though.

"But Lily is an absolute delight – I love spending time with her."

"Who?"

"Lily . . . the girl I spent the morning with babysitting." Duh. She thought he was smart. Princeton graduate. But maybe he had lied. It was easier to pretend in chat. After all, you had time to think about words as you wrote them down. Or maybe they just still needed to break the ice.

"Right, her . . . Don't you just hate it when parents give their kids flower names? Just because they are called Rose doesn't mean they smell as sweet."

"My middle name is Rose." If looks could kill, he would have dropped dead on the spot.

"Really? That's funny" No apology. "Well I bet little Lily is delightful right until she throws a temper tantrum. You know kids are just so . . ." It continued into an ongoing monologue about what was wrong with kids, ranging from how annoying they could be to how they constantly craved attention. He even accused them of making him sick all the time. She was just about to cut him off when Robert came for their order.

A friendly face at last . . . She had only been here for fifteen minutes but it felt like hours. Maybe she should order that White Russian now. No, this was her own mess, and she should sit this one out. He had not yet showed any signs of being mentally unstable, other than being a prick. "A cream tea with all the trimmings, please," she ordered.

"And does the gent want the same?" he asked turning to Brad.

"Oh no, I hate tea, especially that stuff you English people call tea."

She could hear Robert sizzle. You could not insult him more than by calling him English. "Would sir like a coffee then, with a slice of All-American Apple Pie?" he said through gritted teeth.

"Yes that would be lovely, old man." Old man? To be honest, in this light Robert looked younger than Brad, or at least better. He at least had something of a youthful twinkle in his eyes, while Brad looked all washed out. Of course, the youthful twinkle was in murder mode at the moment.

"Thank you," she whispered. For not murdering him, she wanted to add. Poor Robert – even John had not been been this rude.

"Can you believe how rude that waiter was," Brad immediately complained as Robert left.

"Well, first of all he is the owner. Second of all, this is an Irish pub and he is Irish, so to suggest he is English is an insult."

"Well, how should I know?" Perhaps from the sign on the door? "Some people are just so easily insulted. It's petty, really."

Ok, so it was definitely not gonna be friends either. She was going to have to grin and bear it and hope that the date would be over quickly. Soon there would be food to distract her. Brad, unlike Xander, was not a guy that liked long gaps in the conversation. Instead he seemed to fill every pause with more nagging. He complained about the weather, accused his colleagues of ignoring him something for which she couldn't blame them, had some gripe about fat people which she did not fully understand, then went into a racist slur against Blacks, Muslims, Italians, and god knows who else . . . Actually, he protested against God too. In between, he boasted about himself, having gone to Princeton and being so far superior to anyone else. And that every five minutes. She swore that if he mentioned Princeton one more time, she was gonna shove that last scone up his nose.

She didn't though. It was five o'clock now. She had made it through an entire hour without uttering a word. She hadn't even gotten a chance. He had spent all that time complaining about everything and anything under the sun, without her even getting in a word edgewise. In the chatroom, he had grumbled too but it had been so over the top that she had thought it was some kind of dark humor. She had actually had laughed about it. But now, face to face with him she realized he was dead serious about it. All that was left from the cream tea was crumbs. She needed something stronger.

She got up. "I'm gonna get a drink." It wasn't a question, it wasn't even meant to be polite. She just hoped he would see it as a hint and buzz off.

Of course he did not. "I'll have a vodka."

What? She might work here as a barmaid sometimes, but she wasn't here to serve him. Although, seeing how he had reacted to her being a babysitter, being a waitress might send him over the edge. Alright, let's get this show on the road – the sooner this was over the better. And at the bar, she would at least get to see some friendly faces.

She sighed and dragged herself to the bar to get his "order." "Please don't tell me I told you so," she begged Robert.

"Never. He isn't your type, is he?"

"I think I'd favor taking John back before I went out with him again to be honest. I have been considering ordering a White Russian for the last half hour now."

"Do you want me to throw him out? We don't have that sign for nothing, you know" He pointed at the Refuse Custom sign. "I've been dying to use it for years. My regular patrons are far too nice, though."

Izzy giggled. "I think I can handle him. I would love a drink though. And he wants a vodka."

"I'll get him the strongest I got – maybe he'll be a bit more tolerable then."

"Make it a double. He certainly can't get any worse."

"And for you . . .." He poured in vodka, cranberry juice, raspberry cordial, and elderflower cordial, shook it, and then poured. "I think you will like this."

She took a sip. "It's delicious! I think I might want two."

"La Bohème." he said.

La Bohème was the name of a famous opera. "Fits perfectly," Izzy agreed.

"I'll bring you another one later, alright? And kick him out if he's still not gone."

She giggled again. "Don't worry, if he isn't gone by then, I'll do the honors myself. But I'll definitely be wanting more of these." Taking a big sip of her cocktail, she went back to her table.

Brad was sitting with his arms crossed. "You were awfully chummy with the staff just now." The look of disapproval was all over his face. It was a look she was all too familiar with

Alright, this was it, she had reached her limit. "Because he is a friend. Which you are not. You are just the biggest, most arrogant, pompous ass I ever met, and believe me, I've met quite a few."

"I have never been so insulted in my life!"

"Well, some people are just so easily insulted . . ." she said, sugary sweet. There was a sly smile on her face.

"I'm leaving!" The high-pitched shriek Brad let out made people throughout the bar turn their heads turned in his direction.

Strangely enough, Izzy did not feel embarrassed. In fact it made her feel bold and empowered. "Thank goodness. I can't stand men that behave like spoiled little children. They are so stupid and annoying," she said, throwing more of his earlier rhetoric back in his face.

Brad huffed, and puffed, and then stormed out of there with his tail between his legs. The collective bar got on their feet to applause her. "You go Izzy!" she heard someone shout.

Robert went to her to put an arm around her. "Are you alright?"

"Never been better. I finally got the guts to stand up to that kind of bullies." She gave Robert a hug. "Thanks for looking out for me though."

"Now, are you staying to have some dinner?"

"Yeah, but let me first pay for the tea and drinks." She took out the wallet from her purse along with a cloud of glitter.

He laughed. "You got fairy dust in there, dear?"

"No, just a card for Sam, made by Lily to go with his present."

He snorted. "Put your money away, you already put in the hours. Besides, you are messing up my bar." He got a cloth and wiped the glitter away.

Alright, so this internet dating thing hadn't worked out. Or maybe she was no good at picking men. She'd talk it over with Sophie over the holidays, though. For now she just was gonna enjoy the rest of the evening.

"Another La Bohème, please."

CHAPTER FOURTEEN

It was almost Christmas, and it looked like it was going to be a white one. There would certainly be snow where they were heading – Izzy had already gotten a string of warnings and friendly advice from her mother, imploring her to dress up warmly. As if she hadn't grown up there all those years ago. "Yes, but it's up to three degrees warmer in the city due to all those buildings radiating heat," her mother had said. That still had not made her forget what cold felt like, though. However, she was looking forward to seeing that picture postcard winter wonderland again. Snow just wasn't as pretty in the city as it was out there.

Izzy had packed her bags ready to go home, together with all the presents. Sam's gloves and card were hidden in a suitcase. In a few hours, Sam, Lily and she would be leaving to spend Christmas with their families. She was looking forward to it, even though her mom was undoubtedly going to nag about her boyfriend-less status. But first, she had another errand to make before they could leave.

"Can you pick me up at Rob's bar? I have a gift for him that I still need to deliver." She had carefully picked out a present that she knew he would appreciate. If she took the bus there, then Sam could finish up getting ready, and maybe she could entice him to take a last little break before the big drive. Plus, he'd be forced to finally meet Robert. Not that she thought he would hate it.

"You are awfully chummy with him, aren't you?" Did still she detect a slight bit of jealousy? Surely not. Robert was such a nice guy, Sam couldn't possibly have any objections.

"He is just a friend. A good friend. Very reliable. Like you. And he doesn't have any family here, so I thought I'd at least get him a present to cheer him up a bit this time of year."

"Alright. I'll pick you up there. How are you gonna get there though?"

"Public transport?"

"At this time of year? Your mom won't forgive me if I bring you home with a cold. Give us fifteen minutes, and I'll drop you off as well. I need to go that way anyways. In fact if you wouldn't mind taking Lily along, that would save me a whole lot of time. Which might mean we arrive home before midnight this year." It was a long drive, an extremely long drive. But it was worth it to be home for the holidays. And at least they did not have to make it alone, which made it bearable.

"I'm sure that won't be a problem." The fifteen minutes spent waiting for Lily and Sam in a warm and cozy apartment would beat waiting out in the cold for the bus any day. "Do you want to come with me, Lily?"

"Yes!" she answered, jumping into her arms. Izzy helped her into her coat and put on her shawl.

"All your bags are waiting in your hallway?" Sam asked.

Izzy nodded to confirm.

He grabbed his jacket and car keys. "Alright. I'll drop you two off, get last minute provisions, pack the car and pick you up."

"You sure you don't need help packing? Maybe if we would just take a few bags already and put them in the boot?" She feared it would all be too much for him. He was going to do the first stretch of the drive until they got out of town. Then she would drive until it got dark, after which Sam would take over again. Izzy wasn't a very good driver in the dark. Night blindness, just like her mom.

"I don't want to leave too much in the car. That's asking for trouble. I'll manage, don't worry. I'll be there before you know it."

It was early, so the bar was still closed when she arrived. Robert was already there setting up though, sweeping the floor before customers arrived. He did not mind getting interrupted – when she knocked on the window, he waved and let her in.

"Izzy, what a surprise. I thought you would be on your way home by now."

"Almost. There was something I needed to do first, though."

Then he noticed the little girl she had in tow. He sank through his knees to be at eye level with her. "Ahh, you must be the lovely Lily. I heard all about you. I'm Robert. Do you want a chocolate?"

Lily nodded. Climbing up on the barstool, she picked out a chocolate from the large jar on the counter.

"Don't worry, they are without alcohol." he whispered to Izzy. "Do you perhaps want two, Lily?"

"Thank you!" Lily beamed at him.

He sighed. "Girls like that make me wish I had made the time to have kids."

Had she been mistaken in him? He was practically everything she wanted in a man. Except for the spark. He had become very dear to her in these few months, but more like a father or an uncle. No, she had made the right decision. Love was the most important thing of all, and she owed it to herself to find that. Plus, thirty-four wasn't that old. Lots of women started having kids at that age these days. Some of them even had them at fifty. There was plenty of time left.

"Are you staying for long?" Robert wanted to know.

"Until Sam picks us up again in an hour or so. I have a present for you," she said, getting a small box from her purse. Carefully, she placed it on the bar.

"You shouldn't. I have nothing for you!"

"Well, that is not the point of presents, is it? Besides, she looked at me and told me she wanted a home. So I told her I knew just the place."

"That really makes me curious." He pulled off the bow. "An angel! With a cheeky glint in her eye. She's wonderful. I see this is one I will need to look out for. I might need to keep her apart from the others before she infects them with her wicked ways."

"But she'll be lonely," Lily said quietly with a sad little voice. The big eyes were impossible to disagree with.

"Ah, yes. We can't have that, of course. Well then, let's put her up with the rest. Will you do the honors?" He picked the girl up so she could reach it. "Where shall we put her?"

"There." Lily pointed to an open spot next to Robert's angel.

"Perfect. If anyone can keep a naughty angel in check, it's her. She's my dad's angel. All the way from Ireland."

"She's beautiful," Lily whispered.

"Yes she is. As a little boy I used to pretend she was my mom watching over me."

"You don't have a mommy either?" Lily asked immediately understanding. It was like watching twin souls.

Izzy saw that got to Robert. His eyes misted over, and he stumbled for a second, even though Lily was still firmly in his grip. The girl grabbed the wreath, trying to tie on the angel. "Careful, they are made of glass. They can break," she warned them as all the angels dangled from the sudden extra pressure. She hated to think anything would happen to them.

"We're alright, they are tied on extra secure." Robert assured her. Then he answered Lily's question. "My mom left us when I was a little boy. I have very few memories of her."

"I don't remember my mom at all," Lily said matter of factly. "It's okay though. I got Izzy. She is better than a mom."

Now Izzy misted over. She had to turn away for a second to recompose herself. A tear rolled from her cheek.

Robert noticed and kept the little girl busy. "There, now my dad's angel can take little Izzy's under her wing. Shall we get ourselves a cup of cocoa?"

Lily nodded. "Do they have names?"

"Who?"

"The angels."

"No . . . I guess they do, but they have never told me. Maybe they will tell you."

Lily looked at the angels and then listened.

"What are they telling you?"

"That they have no names, but they would like if we gave them some."

"Well then, we must think of some. Let me get a pen and a piece of paper. I'm a bit old, and I might forget if we don't all write it down. It's a good thing I was nearly done setting up."

Izzy took a deep breath. "Can I help you get ready?" she said, finally regaining her composure.

"No, sit down with us, I'll do it in a minute. The coffee machine needs to be started up but it is always a bit temperamental in the morning before its first brew."

One by one, each angel got her name. Robert's became Moira, and Izzy's was called Belle. They were just about done as Izzy's phone vibrated. Sam.

"Is it always this busy here? I can't find anywhere to park."

"Yeah, sorry – you can park in the back alley behind the bar. Robert will let you in."

"It's alright, I found one." The phone call disconnected, and Sam appeared in the window a minute later. Izzy smiled and waved back.

Robert noticed. "Now I know why we didn't work out. You never looked at me that way. You are in love with him."

"With Sam? No! He is just my best friend."

"The eyes never lie, dear."

She felt confused and wanted to tell him he was wrong, but Sam came in already. Quickly she tried to pretend if nothing happened. Sam was Sam. The status he had in her life was far beyond any boyfriend or husband. Nothing was worth risking that.

"I found a spot. But I think we should better hurry. It's getting busy out there."

"Sit down, catch your breath. It's not even noon yet, and you have been running around all morning," Izzy argued. As she said it, she realized they sounded like an old married couple. Maybe that was what Robert saw.

"Sam, nice to finally meet you." Robert stuck out his hand. "Your daughter is a credit to you."

They shook hands. "Nice to meet you too. So you are the Robert I have been hearing about?"

"One and the same. Can I get you a beer perhaps?"

"Well, I still have a long drive ahead . . ."

"Oh yes, my fault. Should have known. Going home for the holidays. Cup of Christmas coffee then? It's a special recipe from somebody I knew a long time ago. Don't worry, there's no booze hidden in it, just spice." He started tinkering with the espresso machine which coughed like an old man getting out of bed. It was interesting to see how it wasn't just people that needed a cup of java in the morning to get them going.

"Lovely place you got here," Sam commented, "Very cozy. I can see why Izzy likes hanging out here." Izzy knew he'd understand once he had been here.

"Thank you, it is all mine. A lot of hard graft went into it, but it was all worth it."

"This is the bestest bar I have ever been in." Lily happily agreed.

Sam and Izzy laughed – they couldn't help it. Sam put his arms around his daughter and kissed her forehead. "It's also the only bar she has ever been in, isn't it princess?"

She nodded in a way that said, "Yes, so what?" which nearly made them laugh again.

"Well, obviously the lady has good taste. It's the nicest compliment I have ever had, miss." Robert made a bow for Lily. "That calls for an extra cocoa with whipped cream, don't you think?"

Lily nodded and jumped up on her seat. "Thank you."

"One for the other lady too? Or would she rather have the coffee?"

"Hmmm, coffee please. With whipped cream if you can."

"Greedy. Well, alright then. Your wish is my command," Robert sighed.

Sam chuckled. "Women! They have you wrapped around their finger before you notice it." Maybe the two of them getting along was not Izzy's best idea ever. They had a very similar taste in humor. Before she knew it, they'd be plotting against her.

"Yeah, but we tend to love them for it," Robert agreed.

Sam hugged his daughter a little tighter and looked at Izzy. "True. Very true. Had this pub for long?"

"About eight years now. I acquired it not long after I got back from Ireland, where I had just buried my dad. It's a pity he did not get to see it."

"I bet he'd been proud. Don't you miss your family? The rest of them I mean."

"He was my family. My mother left when I was four, much like . . ." Robert paused and looked at Lily, who was now drawing pictures of angels next to the names they had written down, oblivious to the conversation overhead. "Much like your situation. At least that is what I gather from Izzy. I greatly admire what you are doing – it is not easy raising a kid by yourself. My dad did everything for me, but it's still hard being a mom and dad at the same time."

"Well I have great help." Sam looked at Izzy again. He took the last sip from his cup. "That was lovely coffee. I'm afraid it is time to go now though if we want to get there this side of Christmas. It's a really long drive."

"Of course. Be safe, all of you. I hope to see you all again after the holidays." Robert said.

"You will. I'll drag him along if I have to," Izzy confirmed.

"Don't worry, I'd love to come," Sam agreed.

Lily wiggled on her chair. "I need to go potty."

"I'll take her. Maybe it is best we all go before we leave," Izzy suggested, before steering the little girl toward the ladies room.

Sam nodded. He was just about to get up and go to the gents as Robert grabbed him by the shoulder.

"Alright mate, I know it is none of my business. But as a bartender, you learn a lot about people. And I can see in the way that you look at Izzy that you are in love with her. And she's in love with you, even if for some reason she does not want to admit that. You are always first in her mind. You and Lily. So do me a favor . . . do her a favor. Act on it now, before she ends up with some other prick. I have never seen a couple share so much love without being together. Please?"

Sam was completely startled by this piece of news. Robert, of course, had hit the nail on head, and this threw things into new perspective for Sam. It was written all over his face. "I got to . . . I need to . . . Thank you. I'll be right back," he said stumbling off.

Izzy, who had just reemerged, saw something was the matter but could not put her finger on it, so she decided to let it slide. "Have a lovely Christmas, Robert."

"You too. And a Happy New Year." After they left Robert smiled and looked at the angel with a tear in his eye. "Merry Christmas, Dad."

CHAPTER FIFTEEN

Christmas morning, everybody was at the Beauforde house. They were all sitting on the couch, watching Izzy's favorite – Santa Claus, The Movie. It was the movie she had grown up with, and Christmas wasn't quite Christmas without watching it at least once, even though she could practically recite the script in her sleep. The Yuletide spirit had finally got to her, with family all around her. She was wearing the most comfortable clothes she owned, aside from her pajamas, and the only reason she wasn't wearing her pajamas was because she had needed to go outside to get from her house to the Beaufordes' house – although she had considered doing that in her dressing gown and slippers. Dressing up was for later, for dinner. Lily was curled up in her arms as Sam brought round cups of warm cocoa. Izzy's parents were there and, of course, the Beaufordes as well. It was their house after all, where they just had their Christmas breakfast. Sophie was groaning that this must be the hundredth time they were watching this movie, but Izzy did not mind. It got to her every time she watched it, especially the part where the little girl took care of the beggar boy. She grabbed a profiterole from the dish on the table.

"They're still frozen!" Ann, her mom, cried out.

It had already disappeared in her mouth, though. "Yaash, annnd?" Take a sip of cocoa, and it was heaven as the whipped cream innards melted in her mouth.

"You just had your breakfast." her mother said disapproving.

Izzy grinned and went back to watching the movie. Yesterday, they had picked out trees together for both homes and decorated them. She had been completely covered in tinsel at one point, but it had been a blast. Today they would spend the day together, with more family coming later. The Beaufordes and Stantons had been spending Christmas together for years now, because they lived on the same street, and well, since they were little, Izzy and Sophie would be over at each other's house for half the time anyway. Somewhere along the line, their parents had decided to give in and spend the time together as one big happy family. It made more sense that way. Besides, their moms got along great as well. At Izzy's and Sophie's expense, of course.

"Can you believe not one of them is married! We put such beautiful kids on this planet, and nobody's snapped them up yet," Sylvie Beauforde lamented.

Izzy's own mom shrugged. "Well, at least one of yours gave you a grandkid. Mine still hasn't even started. Maybe we should let them hook up together so we can share Lily."

Sylvie nodded. "Yes, they practically live together anyways. Whenever I call Sam, Izzy is over there."

"Can you two knock off the comedy routine please," Sam intervened grumpily. "Nobody is marrying anybody."

For some reason, the words and Sam's reaction got to Izzy. The idea of them together was obviously preposterous to him. And why shouldn't it be? They were practically brother and sister. Well, minus the bickering. Sophie and Sam always bickered, even if they loved each other dearly. Izzy, on the other hand, trusted him like a confidant.

Anyway, like Sophie, Izzy was six years older than Sam. She could remember the day that he was born vividly. She had held him before his sister had, seeing as Sophie did not want to have anything to do with the "squirmy worm." And she had loved him since that day. That wasn't romantic love – that was the kind of love you had for family. He was probably looking for somebody his own age. If he was looking at all that was. Why was she even having these thoughts?

The mothers looked at him as if he was no more than ten years old. "He is bit of a grouch, your boy," Ann observed.

"Yeah, he is. I don't know why. I raised him better than that. And he can be so lovely if he wants to be."

Lily got up and padded over to Ann. "You can be my gran too if you like."

"Good move, Lily. More presents!" Sophie cheered. It was nonsense – Izzy's parents always got a present for Lily anyways and spoiled her as if she was their own. So, technically, she had two sets of grandparents already, even though her maternal grandparents were as elusive as her mother.

"Don't say that, Sophie!" Sam chided her. "I don't want her head to be filled with materialistic nonsense. Christmas is not all about presents."

Sophie stuck out her tongue. To her, Sam would always be the little brother she did not have to listen to.

Lily, however, intervened. "I don't need presents. I just like Nana Ann."

"That's my girl," Sam said, mostly to his sister.

Tears were welling in Ann's eyes. "Oh honey, that is so sweet of you," she said hugging the girl.

Sophie giggled. "It looks like you will have to marry my brother now for sure, Izzy!"

Again the words sent a strange shiver through Izzy. Quickly she threw a pillow at Sophie, so she wouldn't notice her reaction. Otherwise, Izzy would never hear the end of it.

"Pillow fight! Now it really is Christmas!" Sophie cheered, chucking back a pillow that just barely missed the cup of cocoa in Izzy's hands.

"Well, technically, a pillow needs to rip so all the feathers come out to make it a real pillow fight," Sam said, taking the pillow from Izzy's lap and tossing it back again, momentarily forgetting his daddy status.

Sylvie got in between them. "Nobody is ripping anything. Stay away from my scatter cushions."

"You're no fun, mom," Sophie complained.

"Honestly, I thought I was dealing with grown-ups by now. Lily is better behaved than you lot put together."

"Well, that has much to do with the fact Sam raises her so well, Aunt Sylvie." Izzy said. Yes, it had become "Aunt" over the years, just like she was "Aunt" Izzy. Mrs. Beauforde was too formal, and to call her mom . . . Well, Izzy already had one of those.

Sophie was getting impatient. "When are we gonna open the presents?"

Her mom shook her head and sighed deeply. "Dear God, where did I go wrong?"

"The movie is almost over, alright? After that, we open presents. If my little girl has some patience," Jim, her father replied.

"Bah humbug." Sophie moped.

"Hey missy, it is not too late for Santa to decide to turn your presents into coal," Jim warned her.

Izzy had to giggle at this. Some things would never change, or so it seemed. Taking another sip of her cocoa, she sat back. Sam was now sitting with Lily in his arms, and Izzy wished . . . well what did she wish? She wanted that – a husband and a daughter – more than anything, but . . . why did Robert have to say that she was in love with Sam? It had filled her with doubt. She loved her friendship with Sam as it was. It gave her everything she wanted . . . well, except for sex. If she could do without that for the rest of her life, they were practically married already. Suddenly, Izzy thought of that kiss she had shared with Sam at the Taylor party. That had felt like nothing she had ever experienced. But that had been just make-believe to get rid of Roger.

It made her feel sad. She had to shake this gloomy feeling. This was Christmas, she was surrounded by people that loved her, and she had nothing to complain about.

"Izzy? Izzy? Are you coming?" Sam was standing in front of her, and stuck out a hand to help her up. "You seemed to have zoned out for a minute there . . . Come on. If we don't get there fast, Sophie will open them all." He had his camera ready in his hand to take pictures.

Lily was standing by with two gifts in her hands. They weren't for her but from her. That was so typical of Lily, thinking of others before herself. She was bursting with excitement to know what they thought of her presents. "Mine first!" she said, handing them to Izzy and Sam.

"You first, daddy," Izzy said. Lily had obviously done well keeping it a secret, for Sam seemed genuinely seemed surprised.

"For me? Let's see what we got here . . .What a pretty card!"

"Open it! There is a present too!!" The little girl could hardly contain herself, and the bigger girl . . . she anxiously hoped he would like it too.

Sam tore off the bow. "Leather gloves! Wow!"

"So you'll have warm hands," Lily chirped.

"They are extra supple so you can wear them while you are working, and they should be your size, seeing you have such a smart daughter who brought a drawing of both your hands."

"Ah . . . that explains why she insisted on that, and the next day the drawing was gone."

"Try them on!" Lily insisted.

Izzy picked up Sam's camera and snapped a photo of him wearing the gloves. As he was always the photographer, there were almost no pictures of him. Izzy's would not be a masterpiece, but at least there would be one photo of Sam from this year's Christmas. He quickly grabbed back the camera and focused it on her.

"Gotta test those gloves, right? Open your present. Before my daughter gets beside herself. She has been keeping it a secret since November."

Now Izzy was really impressed. "Really Lily? Well done!" Quickly, she opened the box. The card, with a drawing of what looked like her and Lily was maybe even more precious, but that could wait. Something shimmered inside, "What a gorgeous necklace," she said pushing back the tissue paper. And it was. Delicate flowers of white and gold.

"To go with your princess dress. See I drew it on the card," Lily explained.

It was perfect – both the card and the necklace. Hugging Lily tight, she whispered a thank you to Sam.

"What princess dress?' her mother wanted to know.

"Oh just a dress I bought that Lily loves very much. It's very beautiful," she said, hoping neither Sam nor Sophie would rat her out. Fortunately, they did not.

"Well, if it is that special, I will have to see it next time I visit. On your birthday, perhaps. We are coming, of course – we could not miss this one.

Thirty-five." Great, another reminder of how old she was becoming. Well at least her mom let more questions about the dress rest for now. Maybe Izzy could find something else to show her mom by that point. God knew how Ann Stanton would react to the idea of her daughter buying a wedding dress. Izzy would end up in a mental institution for sure. What sane woman bought a dress without having a fiancé? Just because Sophie had embraced the idea and Sam had grudgingly accepted it did not mean her mother would. And her mother would certainly not understand why Izzy had bought it. Izzy had trouble understanding it herself, sometimes. All she knew was that she could not return it. It was too late for that now, anyway.

"Thank you so much for the necklace, sweetie. It'll match perfectly."

"Daddy saw it first. He said it would look pretty on you." That maybe was the best present yet. She had hated falling out with him over the dress. That he would buy this for her meant he had fully accepted it.

"Now let's open your gifts," she said to Lily. The little girl searched under the Christmas tree to find her gifts, and, of course, she got spoiled. Neither her grandparents, nor Sophie, nor Izzy's parents would miss this opportunity, and that was on top of the gifts Sam had already bought her. And Izzy's gifts, of course. Suddenly Izzy realized that one of the gifts was the golden dress that looked like hers, especially now that it had the roses and beads on it. Oh well, she couldn't take the gift back now. She had promised Lily it would be there, and the girl was so looking forward to it. So her mother would have to see the bridal gown at some point. Hello, insane asylum.

The dress was in a golden hat box, which had been adorned with more roses and was waiting to be opened. Lily picked it last, opening it after all her other gifts had been unwrapped. Everybody was waiting to see what was in it. As Lily opened the box, her face lit up. "You made it even prettier!"

"Oh Izzy, it's just like your dress." Thanks, Sophie. Izzy saw her mother's ear prick up.

"Can I try it on now?" Lily wanted to know.

Izzy was eager to leave the room, and this gave her the perfect opportunity. "Of course you can," she replied, following Lily to her bedroom.

Sam followed her as well. "She knew you had bought that?"

"Yes – we bought it when we went shopping for the dress she has on now. It wasn't that expensive, I promise, and they had a three-for-one sale, so the total cost works out to be maybe . . . one percent of my dress," Izzy said, trying to defend herself and feeling guilty again.

Sam's face darkened for a minute. Then all of a sudden he started laughing. "One percent? Don't you wish you were four again and could fit into that dress instead of the expensive version?"

Izzy had to laugh too. "Yes definitely. It would have been a lot easier on my bank account."

Lily had managed to get in the dress by herself, not waiting for the grown-ups that were talking.

Izzy saw Sam's face go tender as he looked at his daughter. "You look beautiful, my princess."

"Thank you, daddy. Will you do my hair, Aunt Izzy?"

"After we are done opening presents. I think if we make Aunt Sophie wait any longer to open her presents, she'll burst. But you can wear my necklace if you like. My dress is at home, and you are wearing yours, so you should have it on." Taking the necklace off, Izzy put it around Lily's neck. Perfect.

Sam was smiling. "When we get home I want a picture of the both of you in your dresses." She could kiss him for such a sweet remark.

Sophie's impatience had indeed gotten the better of her, and she had started opening her gifts. Izzy had gotten her a set of illustrated tarot cards that she knew Sophie had been coveting for a while now and Sophie was over the moon with them, wanting to read everyone's fortune. It was hard buying gifts for people when they got older. It was even harder trying to think of what gifts you wanted. Izzy already had almost everything she wanted, and what she still wanted . . . well, money could not buy that. So she got books and knitting yarn as presents. Which made her very happy, nonetheless. Sam had even gotten her the special knitting needles she had been wanting.

For him, she had bought special camera equipment that he had been drooling over for months now.

"Izzy, that is far too expensive!" was the first thing he said as he opened the box. He had been trying to save up for it, she knew, but with a young girl to take care of, other priorities always got in the way.

"Don't worry, I scoured the internet till I found the cheapest one." Which was true. It had not been cheap, though. But she could afford it. And he had earned it.

"But it was like $500."

"It wasn't that much. Just use it well alright?"

Sophie said next to her. "Liar," she whispered in her ear. "I can tell by your eyes."

"Don't tell him or he'll want me to send it back."

"You never give me such big presents."

"You don't give me dinner several times a week without asking for anything. Honestly, I gotta find some way to pay him back for that, seeing as he never lets me do anything in return. Christmas and spoiling Lily are the only chances I get."

"That's my brother's pride for you. Proud and stubborn, always wanting to do everything himself. It's good he has you."

With their parents also opening their gifts, that concluded this part of the holiday. Lily was twirling around the room in her new dress, telling her new doll all about herself and her family. It was sweet to watch.

"If only she had some siblings or cousins to play with. It would be so much nicer for her," Sylvie sighed.

"Sorry, mom. As soon as I meet Mr. Right I'll let you know." Sophie waved the tarot cards. "But we can always ask them?"

Sam disappeared out of the room for a minute. When he came back he had a brown cardboard box in his hands. "This only just arrived right before we left, so I had no time to wrap it. I opened it to see if it was in one piece though. So um . . . sorry for the lack of wrapping, but this is for you."

"You didn't have to get me anything else!" Izzy said surprised, before looking in the box. "My plate! You found it! Thanks Sam." She flung her arms around him and hugged him. Sam always listened to her . . . and cared. His presents had meaning behind them, unlike . . . well, that was why the plate had been shattered in the first place.

"A set of them actually . . . in case you get any more suitors that need to be chased out of the house." His eyes twinkled as he grinned.

Izzy rolled her eyes. "I hope not. Although I have to say my dating life is not exactly going well. Those dates were a disaster. They are not worth throwing beautiful plates at, though. In fact, John wasn't either – I was just a bit desperate at the time. I'll keep these ones safe."

Her mother entered the room and had obviously heard part of the conversation. "Yes, about that. I have invited André this afternoon. He has a steady job in insurance . . ."

Fear struck Izzy. "No mom, you are not setting me up. I'm not having it. No more blind dates."

"But you know him. He was one year ahead of you in school," her mother protested.

"No more half-blind or even full-sighted dates, either. I had enough. I'm declaring Christmas date free!"

"But I can't uninvite him," her more said apologetic.

That was true. "Fine. I'll talk to him, but one word from you about 'how lovely we'd be together' and I am not speaking to you for a year. Understood?"

Her mother mumbled. "I didn't know you would get this defensive. I am doing it in your best interest."

Izzy was being a bitch, and she knew it. After all it was Christmas, and in her own way her mother had meant well. "Sorry mom, I should not have reacted that way. But my dates so far turned out far from great and I don't want any more dates for now. I'm done."

She looked at Sam, who was very happy for some reason. "Hey, I can pretend to be your boyfriend again. Though I doubt he'll believe I'm John. His sister and me went out once, a long, long time ago." If only Sam were a few years older . . . and not her best friend . . .

CHAPTER SIXTEEN

It was the last day of the year, and the sun was going down. Izzy was sitting outside on the swinging bench on the porch, watching the snow fall, wrapped in thick blankets. It was beautiful and gave her a sense of inner peace. She had to think, and the house was too crowded. Besides, the cold might help clear her head. It all felt so muddled right now. Each time she looked at Sam, she felt a longing that she could not place. Well, that wasn't true – she knew what it was, she just didn't want to own up to it. The risk was too great. And was she doing it for the right reasons, or was she just getting desperate?

She loved Sam – she couldn't remember not loving him, and these days they were so close, he usually knew what she was thinking before she did. They got along so well together, and she had to admit that she had been comparing every man to him, so far. Nobody had been able to match.

But was that love? She had never seen Sam in a sexual way. Well, besides that kiss at the Taylor party. Every time she thought of that, she could feel it burning on her lips, like it had just happened. Dammit, why did Robert have to say something? She had never felt this insecure in her life. And she couldn't tell Sophie, either.

The door opened. "What are you doing out here in the cold? . . . oh hang on, what a gorgeous sunset! Move over and make some room for me under those blankets." Sam sat beside her on the bench, slightly rocking it. He immediately put an arm around her, and she snuggled up against him. He was nice and warm, and she felt so comfy sitting with him. "So what are you up to?"

"The house is so stuffy, and I wanted to clear my head."

"Making New Year's resolutions, eh?"

"Sorta."

"And what have you come up with? No diet plans, I hope? You look absolutely gorgeous just as you are, and any man who says otherwise, I will personally punch his lights out." He kissed the top of her head.

"Don't worry, no diet plans. I was just thinking. I'll be thirty-five next year. I always thought I would be married by now, have kids. And it doesn't seem like that is gonna happen. All I got is the dress."

"And that is making you sad?"

"Well the dress is not. I still feel a flutter every time I look at it. The fact that I am still alone, however, and it doesn't seem like that is gonna change any day soon . . . kinda, yes."

"Well you could take our mothers up on their offer and marry me?'

Izzy was quiet, and it was a shock to her that the first reaction her heart gave was "Yes." Sam was obviously only joking, it wasn't a serious proposal. So why was she longing for it so much?

"Hey Izzy, smile a little! I was only kidding. But it wouldn't be such a horror to be married to me, would it?"

Oh god, now she had offended him as well. "No, of course not! You are quite a catch, toy boy."

That at least put a grin back on his face. "Toy boy? Me?"

"Of course!" That was stupid. Why did she have to emphasize their age difference? Maybe if she changed the subject . . . "I don't know. Maybe I should give up on this dating malarkey. I never seem to pick the right guy anyways."

"Well . . ." He couldn't say that wasn't true, and she knew it. She seemed to pick guys who felt themselves to be superior and who, in time, would treat her like she was worthless. She liked smart guys, but why did they always have to have such a damn chip on their shoulder? Sam was smart, but he did not have that. "Maybe you are trying too hard. That can't be any good. And you always seem to be going for those types your mother would approve of, but they never treat you right."

When Sam spoke the truth, he did not do it by half. He was so right that it shocked her. The types she had gone after were guys with money and careers. They looked good to bring home – her mother had loved John, for instance. But had she really ever been in love with any of them? Had they been in love with her? Also, she had pretty much gone from boyfriend to boyfriend as if she would be lost without one. Yet, she claimed to be an independent woman. Suddenly she realized she had pretty much been stuck in a Victorian novel in which the ladies tried to catch a man with good prospects to secure their future. A wealthy husband to look after her and her offspring. Of good genetic structure to breed with. Of course it was not exactly the same, but her dating life could have pretty much come directly out of a Jane Austin novel. Had she really been that shallow? She had dreamed of romance and had never been able to find it. No wonder.

"Izzy? Izzy? Is something wrong?" Sam was shaking her.

"Other than wasting the last twenty-odd years of my life on losers with good prospects? Just fine. I think you are right. No more desperate dating.

If that perfect guy comes along, he will have to woo me. I am just gonna focus on myself this year."

"That sounds like a good idea," he said relieved.

She put her head on his shoulder. "Oh Sam, I think I have been a fool. I have been telling myself I am a strong, smart, single-minded career woman, but underneath it, all I want is a husband and a family. I'm a farce."

"No, you are not a farce. You are the strong, smart, single-minded career woman you speak of, and a great role model for Lily. You love your job, right?"

"Yes. I do . . . but I think I would give them up for a husband and a baby any day if that was asked from me. So really, in my heart I'm as old-fashioned as my mom is. Isn't that pathetic?"

"The right guy would never ask such a thing of you. He would want you to live your dreams – all of them."

"You know, John seemed to think my job was just some trivial play activity to fill the time. He would never take it seriously. I would have turned into a Stepford wife if I had married him."

"Izzy – are you happy with your life as it is?" Sam suddenly asked.

"I . . . I . . . I never thought about that, do you know?"

"Yes, I do. You aren't a party planner for nothing – you have a tendency to live in the future. But look at the now for a moment. What do you see?" Gosh, he was telling it like it was. And he knew her like no other.

"Alright, let me think. What did I do to deserve a great friend like you?"

"You just missed dropping me on the head as a baby. Unlike my sister. That entitled you to eternal loyalty."

She laughed. "That easy, eh? Okay, my life as it is now. Great job, terrific friends . . . that I love dearly." She placed a hand on his shoulder. "By the way, your sister did not drop you on the head."

"Yes, she did. On holiday, when I was five. I had a concussion and had to stay in bed the entire holiday.

"Oh really?" Izzy searched her memory. "Oh yeah! That's where you got the scar on your forehead." She traced the line that was ever so vague now.

"So – what do you still want out of life?"

"A Lily . . ." That was the best way to describe it. "Well, a son, a daughter, it really doesn't matter. I just really want to be a mother. Always have wanted that. And I don't want to do it alone, so I want a husband too."

"Well, you got a Lily . . ." he offered.

"But she is yours, not mine. I'm her aunt."

"You are all the mother she knows. And you got me too." His arm went round her shoulder.

"True. So what are you saying?"

Silence encompassed them. Sam looked deep into her eyes, and the rest of the world seemed to melt away. They got closer . . .

"Izzy! Daddy! Time to make the punch! Granny says you need to watch me, else I can't stir." Lily dove in between them, and the moment was lost.

"Lily! Your coat!" Izzy said immediately wrapping the blanket around the girl. "We don't go outside without being dressed warmly."

"It was only for a second. I needed to call you."

They quickly got up and went inside, Sam holding his daughter in his arms, keeping her warm. "Even then. Else you get ill and we don't want that, " he said.

"Am I gonna be sick now?" Lily asked concerned.

"Let's hope not, else we can't play in the snow tomorrow and make angels. Next time you put your coat on, ok?" Izzy said, tickling the little girl, who giggled.

"Yes, aunty."

It was true – she did have a daughter – maybe not biological, and not in name, but Izzy would do absolutely anything for this child. There was nothing to complain about. She needed to let go of this perfect image and enjoy the now. Love would come when she was ready. She needed to enjoy the moment.

The "Making of the Punch" was one of the New Year's traditions. As were the bells that were already polished up to a sheen and waiting on the table to ring in the new year. A cooking pot was set on a hot plate. With apple juice, oranges, elderflower cordial, cinnamon sticks, spices, and raisins, together they created the perfect mulled apple cider. No alcohol, though there was a little flask of rum at hand for those who wanted a drop or two. The recipe had been perfected over generations.

Lily loved to stir the punch and stood on a stool as Sam kept an eye on her. One by one, all the ingredients went in, making the whole room smell lovely. This batch would probably not last till midnight, but luckily more was at hand. "My little brewing witch," Sophie said, giving her niece a hug.

"But I'm not evil!"

"Well, there are good witches too. You are a white witch, a brewer of magic elixirs that spread peace and happiness."

Lily nodded and continued stirring. "And love."

"Yes, may next year be full of love," Sophie agreed.

"You are trying to turn her into a witch like yourself?" Izzy whispered softly to Sophie.

"Yes, the world needs more of us. Give back the meaning to all this pagan rituals we are doing."

And Sophie definitely had a point. Sylvie, who was originally from the South, was now busy making her lucky bean soup to bring prosperity in the new year, while Ann was working on her apple strudel to bring love and sweetness. These rituals were the tradition in their households, with all the superstitions that came with them.

Izzy picked up an apple and started peeling it, thinking more about the things Sam had just told her. Was he right? Was she always focusing on the future instead of the here-and-now? Well, that was the first thing she was gonna change next year. Then there was that moment on the porch, just before Lily had come. Had she imagined that? Or had something really been about to happen? Izzy didn't know what to do. If she were wrong, it would ruin their whole friendship. Even if she were right, but they turned out to be incompatible, it would ruin them. She would lose both him and Lily. Was that worth it?

Argh, she was doing it again – living in the future. Imagining things that might well never happen. Let it go, Izzy, she told herself. No use worrying about it now.

"Izzy, you haven't said a word since you got in the kitchen. Are you still mad at me that I invited André at Christmas?" her mother asked.

"What? Oh no, mom." She had forgotten all about him. André hadn't even paid attention to her, and vice versa. He seemed more enamored with Sophie, who wasn't interested either. She had mostly been talking to Sam. "Just last-day-of-the-year thoughts. What do I want to do with my life next year. New Year's resolutions."

"And what are those, dear? Finding a husband perhaps?" her mother asked.

So that was where Izzy herself got it from. Years of conditioning had brought her to this point. Well, no more. "To be honest, mother, I thought of giving up dating all together."

"What?!?" her mother and Sophie simultaneously said.

"Come on, Izzy, that internet date can't have been that bad?"

"No . . . it was worse! He was worse than John and all my exes put together. This desperate charade – I am sick of it. I was just talking to Sam . . ."

"No wonder you are giving up, talking to "The Monk" himself. Last time he had sex, Lily was made."

"Keep your voice down – she might hear you. I'm not giving up, and that wasn't what we talked about. Sam made me realize something . . . I always live with this vision of what will be, instead of in the now. Well, that stops now. I refuse to go on a useless quest for the right guy. If he is out there, he can find me."

"That never happens. Men are too stupid for that. Do you think I would be with your father if I had let it all up to him?" her mother spoke up.

Sylvia also put in her two cents. "Really, dear. My Sam is a smart boy, but when it comes to affairs of the heart, he's not that smart."

Izzy had to stand up for herself now, or she'd never do it. "But this isn't about love – this is about me. I have always seen myself as an independent woman. So why would I let my value hang on the opinion of a man, and whether he likes me or not? Yes, I still want a husband, I still want children. But this desperate search is bringing me nothing but grief."

"But what about the dress?" Sophie. Great, now there really was there no way of avoiding it.

"What is it about this dress that you keep talking about it?" her mother immediately wanted to know.

Izzy shrugged "I bought a wedding dress, okay?"

"To find your dream man," Sophie added.

"No! I bought that dress because it was the most gorgeous thing I have ever seen and – unlike the men I dated so far – it made me feel absolutely beautiful, without question." Then she turned to her mother. "So before you have me declared insane: yes, I bought a dress that cost a ton of money, to make me feel good. In fact it made me feel better about myself than any guy I ever dated did. So excuse me, but I am not gonna rush into the next relationship just because I am turning thirty-five and the clock has started ticking. The next guy I go out with had better be worth my time, or he can go to hell for all I care. Is that understood?"

All the women in the kitchen were quiet – none of them dared to say anything after Izzy's tirade. Izzy hadn't even known herself that this was how she was feeling until she had said it out loud. But it was true. The hunt for a man was making her feel as inadequate as John had done. It was crazy and only brought her misery. No more. Next year, she was gonna be happy with who she was, man or no man. And if she did meet somebody, he'd better appreciate her as she was.

Sam entered the kitchen. "Everything alright? I thought I heard voices being raised."

Everyone nodded. "Yes, brother, don't worry. Izzy was just telling us she was swearing off men so she can join you in the convent," Sophie sneered. "That was not what I said!"

"Alright, alright. I was just joking. You probably have a point too. Most guys barely manage to make you feel good for five minutes, and the rest of the time you are stuck with them. Say, is there room in the convent for me? Though, I am bringing my toys. They are better at satisfying my needs anyways."

Izzy tried not to laugh at her friend's shocking revelation. Sylvie was standing with a wooden spoon in her hand. "Sophie. I swear, neither of us is too old to have you put over my knee and wash your mouth with soap."

"Kinky."

Sylvie took a deep breath, but Sam jumped in between them. "Please mom, don't encourage her. You know she'll only get worse. Alright? Can I leave you alone without all hell breaking loose? I have a daughter stirring a large pot of cider in the next room."

"We'll be alright." Izzy ensured him.

'You too?' he mouthed, and she simply nodded. To be honest, New Year's resolutions made, she felt more peaceful than she done in years. Even the fact that her mother now knew about the dress didn't matter. This coming year, she would just be Izzy, and they could take it or leave it. She was gonna be happy with herself . . .

Though perhaps she should change her underwear, just in case. Sophie had said it was a South American custom to bring luck in love for the coming year. And surely it could do no harm.

"Sophie, did you have another pair of pink panties?" she quietly whispered.

Sophie grinned from ear to ear and hugged her. "I knew you hadn't completely given up!"

CHAPTER SEVENTEEN

The new year had been rung in with bells and whistles, literally. They said that the first person that you kissed in the new year was the one you were going to be with for the whole year. That was good – at least it meant Lily wasn't going anywhere. At twelve o'clock, the girl had jumped into Izzy's arms and given her a cuddle, which was followed by a kiss on her forehead from Sam. So her two favorite people in the world would be with her for the new year. That was all Izzy wished for.

Now the year had begun, though, and she was trying to keep up with her resolution to enjoy the present. With so much to plan, that was a tall order, though. It was back to work, and there was a lot of it. This was one of the busiest times of the year. And besides being flooded with new clients for office parties, it was now time to plan Claire's opening in earnest. At the end of next month, they would need to throw a party that the high-class uptowners would remember for a long time. It was coming down to the details now. At the end of next week, Izzy would have a meeting with Claire, so she needed to get all her plans together. Party favors needed to be chosen, and Izzy was going from place to place to get the samples together. The next place was only blocks away from Robert's bar, so she couldn't resist popping over. It was the end of the day, anyways.

He greeted her with a warm smile. "Izzy, you are looking lovely. How was Christmas?"

"Fine! Lots of time with the family. Time to relax a little. Unlike now. My feet hurt from all the errands I had to run," she said kicking off her pumps. "How about you?"

"Same old, same old. Spent the day with lots of patrons, most of whom don't have anybody to spend the day with either. Some of the others even brought their family along. It was nice."

"Still, it means you were working on Christmas. Next year I'll take you with us, alright?"

"No, I couldn't leave them high and dry. They have nowhere else to go."

He was right, and, if she was honest, a Christmas at the bar sounded lovely. Going home for the holidays was a tradition though, one she could not see breaking any time soon. "I see the angels are still hanging?"

"Yeah, I decided to let them spread their good cheer around for another week and then it's back to the box until next year. What about you and Sam? Did anything happen between you two??" Robert said with an expectant look in his eyes.

"Oh please! It's bad enough that my mother questioned my single status every five seconds – not you too! Nothing happened. I have decided to dedicate this year to me and what I want. Not some besotted manhunt. Sam inspired me, in fact. He said I was living in the future too much. So I am living for the now."

Robert rubbed his forehead. "That's a pity. Not your resolution of course, but I really thought . . . well, never mind, even I get it wrong sometimes."

"You thought what?"

"Nothing . . . really. It's not worth mentioning."

Suddenly somebody put a hand on her shoulder. "Izzy! I thought I heard your voice."

She turned around. Behind her was a real surprise. "Mike, what are you doing here?" He was looking quite the dandy in a well-tailored, dark blue suit.

"Well this was my local, till I moved last year. Haven't been here since. But I was in the area, so I thought I would drop by. How delightful to see you here! How are you? And why is John never bringing you to any of the office parties anymore? They are terribly dull without you."

"Well, me and John broke up. For months now, really. Why? Hasn't he told anybody? Still?" Surely he had to by now.

Mike shook his head, "Nope. He's been making excuses that you were ill, or busy, and so on. Stomach bugs, prior engagements, you name it. I thought something wasn't right, though. When did you break up?"

"The same night that you last saw me. Claire knows, so I don't know who he thinks he is fooling. I would have thought he would have told everybody by now. What is he playing at? I'm not planning to get back together with him. EVER." She wasn't angry anymore, but she was annoyed. Maybe she should have sent out that email to everyone after all. Then she would not have had to deal with this nonsense.

"His promotion is still pending. Which, I had to say, surprised me – he did everything they asked of him. Even got that account."

"He still did not become partner? Oh, I bet he is blaming me for that, knowing him." It served him right, though. He had always put his career above everything. This sounded like sweet revenge, and she hadn't needed to do anything for it.

"They are stalling it. It makes sense now. Serves him right after what he did to you."

"Oh, that wasn't so bad. We were gonna break up anyways. I just had not expected it that night, but I definitely not sorry it happened. He was a jerk, but it's my own fault for staying with him that long."

"So you didn't mind that he cheated on you?"

"What?!?" The shriek Izzy let out was so loud, everyone around them stared in their direction. Yes, John had said there was somebody else, but she hadn't believed him for a second.

Robert even came in their direction. "Everything alright Izzy? I would ask if he was bothering you, but with Mike, there's really not a big chance of that."

"Yes I'm alright. Mike just told me something that shocked me." She couldn't process it, she just couldn't.

"What, that Mike is gay?" Robert said laughing.

The words did not connect with her brain at first as her mind was still on John. But then . . . "He's gay?" The shock was less, but she did not know how many more revelations she could handle.

That surprised Robert. "You hadn't noticed?"

"Robbie, it's okay. I try to lay low at work. So people treat me in accordance with my merits, rather than my . . .. other merits."

"Yeah, you're a fruitcake alright." Robert said cheerily. Izzy felt confused. Robert wasn't bigot, as far as she knew. Had she just landed in an alternative universe or something?

Mike didn't mind, though. In fact, he gave Robert a hug. "With extra nuts, and you know it! Oh, how I missed our bantering!" So this was normal, an inside joke between the two of them. Phew. Robert being a jerk was not something Izzy could handle right now.

"So why are you making the lady cry? She has become a very good friend of mine, you know, so you are not allowed to do that." Robert put his hands on Izzy's shoulders.

"You two are together? You dark horse, you." The way Mike pointed at them was certainly a bit camp, Izzy realized.

"Friends. Good friends, I hope, but nothing more," Robert said. Izzy nodded in agreement. "So why is Izzy upset?"

"Something I said about John." Mike confessed.

Robert's face darkened, much like Sam's would whenever John was mentioned. "That ponce?"

"That cheating ponce, you mean." Izzy added. "So Mike, what happened, when did it happen, and why didn't you tell me sooner?" She wanted answers, and she wanted them now.

"I figured he had told you and that was why you weren't coming to the parties anymore. You dumped his ass." Mike looked troubled. "The night of the party I wanted to tell you myself, but John kept pulling you away. Finally I said to him that if he didn't tell you, I would. And then you disappeared before the night was over."

"But I still don't get it. What happened?" How bad was it? That was what she really wanted to know. A kiss, even if he had fallen in love, that she could handle. After all, it was good riddance. Let him be somebody else's problem. But if he was in love, why would he still insist at work that they were together? "He isn't gay too, is he?" By this point, that would not have surprised her. In fact it would explain it. Whether he was gay or not, she had kinda functioned as a beard anyways – just being there to prove to others that he had a girlfriend.

"No! Noooooo!" She could see how the idea repulsed Mike, which was kind of funny. "It definitely was a woman! I was working late one night, and I needed a report that I had given to John earlier that day. With no light on in his office, I figured he had gone home, so I just went in. Only he had not gone home – he was . . .er . . . being very intimate with somebody on his desk. Which wasn't you. I don't know who it was. I tried not to look and got out of there fast as I could, but it was some blond woman that he was making . . . whoopee with. And you're not blond." Mike was looking as uncomfortable as she was feeling.

"He was fucking somebody else?" Her world collapsed. She felt dirty and used.

"Yes. And I don't know for sure, but according to the janitor that wasn't the first time. I bumped into him as I practically ran out of there and he said John had been "working late," so to speak, for weeks.

She tried to remember when John had started working late. "It must be true. Maybe even longer than that. It started after the summer holidays. Suddenly, he hardly had time anymore to see me. So you think it started back then?"

"Your guess is as good as mine. I'm sorry Izzy."

"Hey, it's not your fault I was dating a two-timing dick." She thought about the last time she and John had had sex. If this affair had started sometime before the autumn, she and John would have had sex several times before they broke up – and some of it unprotected. Who knew what she could have caught. "I think I need to get checked for STDs – who knows what kind of woman he has been doing it with."

Mike stroked her hand. "I know a clinic if you like that is open right now. I'll even drive you there, you don't want to be alone right now, believe me. It's best to get these things over with as quick as possible. Unless you want to go to your own gynecologist?"

Izzy had none at the moment, as hers was on maternity leave. "Let's just go to that clinic. I'd rather know today." She could kill John right now. Why hadn't he just broken up with her? All because of his stupid career?

Robert put an arm around her. "You're probably fine."

"You don't know that," she whispered.

"Well, best thing is to get tested. These people are fast – they should have the results in a couple of days."

And so they left. The clinic looked . . . well, clinical. Top of the line though – crisp and clean. Filling in the insurance forms, they were led to a little waiting room where two other people were waiting. She felt sick to her stomach with worry – and absolutely furious with John.

Mike held her hand. "They are very nice, don't worry. I've been here before."

She gave a faint smile.

"And yes, I was scared too. But for all we know, John was having safe sex."

Izzy rolled her eyes.

"Yeah, okay it didn't look like it. They were rather going at it . . . but you don't wanna know all this."

"Me and John used condoms most of the time, but not always. He was kinda OCD when it came to sex. Wanted everything his way." And last time they had sex the condom had broken though. John had gotten mad, told her she had done on purpose, that she wanted to trap him by having kids. It had made no sense. Well it made sense now.

"That sounds like John, yes. I am sorry that you ever dated him. I swear if I wasn't gay I'd have asked you out myself a long time ago. You are the nicest woman I have ever met."

Izzy's name was called. She had chosen for a blood test and swab to be absolutely sure, which meant stripping down. Well, at least she got a female doctor, who reassured her she had nothing to fear. The blood was drawn first. Then she needed to lie down in the stirrups. A thousands thoughts went on in her head. Mostly murderous ones toward John. If he had found another girlfriend she would have had no problem with that. But to have sex with somebody behind her back. She wondered how she would have felt if they had broken up last summer. Would she have been sad? Or had they already drifted apart so much that it would have been a relief? Well, it didn't matter much – he hadn't, and had been carrying on behind her back instead. If any of these tests turned out positive she was gonna . . .

"And we are done. The test results will be mailed to you within three working days, tops. You'll get a phone call once they are available."

"Thank you," she said, getting dressed again as quick as she could. Mike was outside waiting for her.

'Do you want to go out for dinner? Or TP John's house or something?" he offered.

"No, I just wanna go home. The TPing sounds tempting but John lives in a flat. So the only one we will burden is the concierge. And right now I just wanna crawl into a blanket and drown my sorrow. I didn't mind breaking up with John, but this . . ."

"I fully understand. I have been there too. Men are completely unreliable dear, but we still fall in love with them." Mike placed a hand over hers.

Again the question arose. Had she been in love with John? Right now all she felt was pure hate. "Maybe I should turn lesbian."

"Well, if you become butch enough, I'll go out with you, ok?" Izzy had to laugh at that, and felt a little better. "Are you sure you want to go home?" Mike said. "You shouldn't be alone right now."

"I won't be. Sam will be there."

"Oh . . . Sam . . . and who is that, pray tell?"

"My best friend."

"A guy?

"Yes."

"So why aren't you together? Is he gay? Married?"

"No, and divorced. I've known him since birth."

"Older, younger?"

"Younger. Six years."

"Oh a toy boy . . . You know, being a cougar is awfully fashionable these days."

"He's like a brother."

"Poor thing, he's been friendzoned. Is he that unattractive?"

"No! . . . Say, before you turn into my mother completely, can we change the subject?"

"Alright. We are nearly at your place anyways. Are you sure you don't want me to stay?"

"I'll be alright. I need a moment to myself. Scream, maybe smash something." Luckily, Sam had provided her with new plates.

"Call me when you get the results, alright?" he asked before she got out of the car.

She nodded. "I will. I promise."

And then she was alone. Sam was right across the hall but she couldn't face him right now. Lily was there too, and she didn't want to scare her.

Why? Why had she EVER trusted John? She went to the closet to look at her dress. But even that could not help her. What if she had an STD . . . what if it had made her infertile? What if, god forbid, she tested positive for HIV? What if she had blown her chances . . . thrown her life away on that loser? She'd never find someone, never wear that dress.

She tried to push the negative feelings away, tried to tell herself, that in all likelihood, nothing would be the matter. But it was to no avail – she was scared, mad, and had no one to ventilate these feelings to. Except John . . . but she knew it wouldn't do any good to contact him. He would just blow it off or blame her, like he had done with everything else she had said during their relationship. The selfish bastard. Breaking down crying, she crawled onto her bed. Why?

The phone rang, and she let it ring. She couldn't pick it up, not like this. It rang a second time. Then a knock on the door. Sam – she remembered she had promised to come over for dinner. But she couldn't now.

The key turned in the lock though. She heard his voice in the hallway. "Izzy, are you alright? I saw you coming home and you looked upset. Where are you?"

". . .b-b-bedroom." Her voice faltered, but he had heard. In a few steps, he was with her.

"Izzy, what is wrong?" He said down on the bed beside her and took her in his arms.

He was warm, comforting . . . and she couldn't. She pushed him away. "No, you can't!" she said in horror.

"Are you ill?" He tried to take her temperature.

"No. I mean . . . I don't know . . . I just got tested for STDs. John cheated on me."

"What? When? How do you know?"

She told him everything Mike had told her, and what had happened after that. Sam took her in his arms despite her protest. "You were there for me when it was the other way around, and I found out she had cheated me and I got tested. Remember?" It had been the final straw for Sam's marriage. Izzy had been there to hold his hand.

"But Lily. . ."

"You aren't going to give it to Lily by being around her." Technically, Izzy knew that. They were not called "sexually transmitted" diseases for nothing. And when it had been Sam, nothing could keep her away from him. She had been his shoulder to cry on. But with Lily it was different – she was so young and precious – and even though it made no sense, instinct told her she had to shield Lily from even the slightest off-chance that anything could happen to her. "It's really, really unlikely you have a life-threatening STD anyways. I turned out to be absolutely fine, and so will you," Sam continued. "When do you get the results?"

"Two days. Wait . . . two working days. So Monday."

" Try not to worry, alright?"

She nodded without much conviction, trying to wipe her tears.

"Are you coming for dinner? Please? I already cooked. I turned everything off when I couldn't reach you. I need to get back to Lily. I left her drawing in the living room."

"Yes, yes, of course. Go! Just give a few minutes to pull myself together. I don't want her to see me like this." She was gonna be fine – she had to believe that.

CHAPTER EIGHTEEN

The weekend crawled by. Despite what Sam had said, Izzy lied and said she had a sore throat to keep Lily at a distance. It was horrible to have to lie to the little girl, and not getting hugged by her was even more terrible, especially because Izzy was feeling in real need of comforting. Sam did not hold back though – whenever he saw her sitting in a corner looking miserable, he joined her and tried to cheer her up. "Misery loves company," he'd grin and tried to tell her everything would be fine. She tried to believe it. He had to be right. She had done nothing to deserve this. Well, except date the biggest jerk on the planet – but that should have been payment enough in itself.

Monday came, and Izzy felt like she was on the edge of her seat, threatening to drop off. Any moment, the test results could come. It was making her break out in hives. She would check her messages every five seconds, so her mobile phone was in her hand as she tried to do some work. She had given the clinic her work number too – and as her it rang, her heart nearly stopped.

"Isabelle Stanton," she answered breathlessly.

It was only her colleague, Karin, with a message. "Claire just called to say that she was dropping by later."

Izzy's rubbed her forehead. Claire was coming by? She wasn't ready for her yet. Not in the slightest, and she was suffering from a huge lack of concentration. She tried to focus, but she just could not gather her thoughts. All that came up was pure panic. But if Claire was in fact coming in later, she'd better line up the things that were almost done, so she at least had something to show her. Quickly, Izzy tried to get as much as she could together, writing down a list of details that still needed to take care of. She felt incredibly inadequate, which was something she wasn't used to. Maybe she could call Claire and ask her to come another time? Just as she was about to do so she got the call that Mrs. Thompson had arrived. Too late to back out now. She quickly went downstairs to greet her.

"Hello, Claire! Lovely to see you, but why have you brought forward our meeting? There are still a few things I need to arrange . . ."

"That's not why I came here. Don't worry, this is not a meeting. I wanted to see you. Mike told me . . . you could use a friend." That was sweet.

"Ah, how much did he tell you?" Izzy asked as they walked back to her office and she closed the door. This certainly was not something that she wanted everyone to hear, and so far she had not told anybody at work.

"Everything – including the cheating and the trip to the clinic. Are you alright?" Claire placed a hand on Izzy's shoulder – it was such a reassuring, motherly gesture. Izzy had needed that. She hadn't told her mother, either. She couldn't – not till she was sure either way.

"I'll know that later today. The test results could come in any minute. I have been checking my email all morning."

"You must be a nervous wreck. I'd happily fire that bastard if it was up to me. Anton would too, but he can't get the other partners behind him. So far, he just managed to stall his promotion. I'm so sorry."

"Don't be sorry. And you don't need to fire him. Not on my account." That would only make John hate her more, and he was not a man who you wanted to have against you. Not that he had that much power, but she knew he had a tendency to bully and even haunt people that he thought had wronged him somehow. Little childish antics that could cause a lot of trouble for the person he aimed it at.

Claire disagreed. "He is untrustworthy. The way he dealt with your break-up – keeping it a secret – is proof of that. That's why I want him gone. Cheating, going behind people's back. He's lying to the partners every time he insists you two are still together. Maybe the matter is of little consequence in a business perspective, but if he lies like this about little things, you can only imagine what he'd be like on the really important matters."

Izzy knew exactly what he'd be like on the work floor. "He's an ass. He will always try to hide his mistakes, or better yet, blame them on somebody else. He is the king of that. Worse. . . most of the time, I think he actually believes his own lies and excuses as well. When I just met him, he made it sound like he was always being wronged, and I believed him. It was only later, when he started blaming things on me that I started seeing how petty he was. Still, I thought he was right most of the time, and blamed myself. For somebody who is as sensitive as a rock, he is great at guilt-tripping people. He will start talking and by the end you will think it is totally your fault. Well, I am over that now. My biggest regret is not dumping him sooner. At least I wouldn't have wasted so much time on him." She checked her mail and phone again. No messages. "Sorry about that."

"No, no. Check it as much as you like. I know I would. I can't believe he cheated on you. I mean, you are terrific – how dare he?"

"We were drifting apart. The more I saw him for who he was, the less I liked him. I was trying to make up excuses not to see him, so I did not have to suffer through the tirade of all the things that were wrong with me. I don't even know why I kept seeing him. I think it was just because he made a very handy "plus one," which you often need in this line of work. No more though. I now know I can do it on my own. I don't need a jerk like him to be complete. That is one of my New Year's resolutions, by the way."

"Good on you. I could cut his balls off – I can only imagine how you are feeling." Claire sounded really feisty. Maybe Izzy could borrow some of that, she thought, because today she wasn't feeling very feisty.

"Hmm, that sounds like a plan, I couldn't get past the image of wringing his neck, but I gotta say, to hit him where it really hurts sounds far better." Izzy said, finally laughing.

Claire looked at the door. "Hey, how about getting out of here? I would love to show you the gallery, and the work men are now at a stage where you can actually see the place taking shape. I think it would be great to get a look at the actual space now before we finalize plans."

Izzy looked at her phone.

"I promise you can check you phone every ten seconds if you like. I think it would be good to have your mind on something else though. Looking at that constantly won't make the results come any quicker."

"You are right, and yes, I do need to check out the venue anyways. So let's go," Izzy said, giving in. It was probably for the best since she felt like the walls were closing in on her.

They got into Claire's car and drove to the gallery. It was an old monumental building that was already looking much better on the outside, but inside is where the real change had taken place. So far Izzy had only seen pictures, but what she had seen had looked dank and dilapidated. The building was from the turn of the century. Twentieth century that was, and it had once been a dance hall. In the pictures, you could see it had been beautiful in its heyday, but those times had long gone. The windows had been boarded up, making it dark and spooky, and everywhere bits and piece of the building had been falling down. No wonder it had been on the list for demolition. Claire had insisted it was to be rescued though, and with a wealthy husband in tow, she had gotten her way.

And just look at it now. Elaborate ceilings were now restored, and the hand painted cornices looked beautiful and fresh. Fishbone floors had been sanded back and polished to make it look like decades of dancing had never happened. Walls had either been painted or decorated with wallpaper appropriate for the period. Ornaments had been re-gilded, and as Claire and Izzy came in, workmen were busy rehanging the crystal chandeliers, bringing the light truly back. All in all, the building was starting to look alive again, even if it wasn't quite finished.

Izzy couldn't stop staring, there were so many details to look at whichever way she turned. "Claire, this is beautiful! It's like a palace. Can I live here?"

"Me first! I'm still trying to convince Anton, but he says the rooms are too big." Claire chuckled.

Izzy had a vision of going to a ball here, wearing her spectacular dress, looking for her prince, just like Cinderella. "Do you know, I think we have got the design for the party all wrong – you should have a regency ball here, or a flapper party. Not what we have been planning so far – that could be done anywhere. This place deserves something special – something . . . that fits with the history of the place. A modern fairy tale. This building is crying out for it."

"Yes, but if we throw a costume party, that might scare some of the guests off – especially the older, more reserved ladies. And I spent a bit too much money according to Anton, so I need everybody to come," Claire objected.

"All the more reason to go for it. This way it will stick in people's minds guaranteed. We will keep it from recent history, rather than go all out with "Marie Antoinette" dresses. Imagine . . . Roaring Twenties, jazz band in the corner, waiters going round with cocktails and caviar, and whatever else is appropriate for the period. We have a caterer that is great at that stuff – he already gave me a quote for the party, but I will ask him if he can change that to make it more fitting. Buffet table over there, and lots of old Hollywood glam. Maybe even invite some dancers to liven up the place." Izzy realized three months of preparation had just gone down the drain. But it would be worth it.

Claire was still in doubt. "Love the idea . . . but just how much more will it cost? You'll need to put in a lot of extra work, and there may be extra costs to dress up the place. And Anton is already cross with me . . ."

"Don't worry – I'll throw in the extra hours for free, and I'll make sure everything stays on budget. I have a few people that owe me favors, and it's time I call them in. Now show me more, please."

After all, this was just the entry hall they were standing in. There were lots more rooms to be explored, and Claire and Izzy started to walk around. Izzy snapped pictures of everything she saw, to provide her with even more inspiration later. The stair case was magnificent, and the doors were wonderfully detailed. The original builders had left nothing without decoration. Even the old parts of kitchen had wonderful detailed tiles, making the stainless appliances look dull and boring in comparison. They were necessary though, as this was to be a working kitchen.

"Where are you going to hang the paintings? I'd be terrified to hammer a nail into these walls."

"That's why I'm not doing that. I'm having custom-made exhibition screens built that are in keeping with the place, but reasonably neutral – they're based on the simplified version of a pattern from an art nouveau screen I already own. They can be placed anywhere, be arranged into different set-ups over time and even be wheeled out of the room fairly easily – so, in theory, you could just wheel everything out and turn the gallery back into a ballroom. The carpenter that makes the screens is actually on site today for some other work. Let me introduce you to him."

"Oh no, that's not necessary," Izzy said, checking her phone for the fourth time since they arrived.

"That's him." Claire pointed at a Norse god on the other side of the room. Well, he was a man, but he had all the looks of a modern day Thor. Broad shoulders, green eyes that were dazzling even at that distance, long blond hair tied back in a casual pony tail, all wrapped up in a t-shirt and jeans.

Izzy just gaped.

"Yes, that was pretty much my first reaction too," Claire confirmed. "Do you want to meet him?"

Izzy tried to shake the trance. "No, I am happy admiring him from afar. I don't think I could actually speak to him." She quickly snapped a picture in his general direction, though. "To get a feel of the place."

"Yeah, be sure to send that one to me too . . . believe it or not, he's straight. And single," Claire said meaningfully.

"Him? How does he manage that? There must be a waiting list of women desperate to date him. A different woman every night?"

"Probably. I couldn't blame him . . . or them for that matter. So what do you think? Shall I call him over?"

"Not today. I feel like a rag." It was hard to feel your inner sparkle with a dark cloud hanging over your head. If only she had the results.

Claire didn't press it. "Of course."

"Is he just for show, or actually good at his job?" Izzy asked as they moved on, out of earshot of any of the workers.

"Both, actually. He was the best carpenter I interviewed. The only one with enough vision to turn my idea into reality. And yes, he is very nice on the eyes. I couldn't stop blushing the first time I met him."

"I can see how that would happen."

"Don't tell Anton I said so though. He doesn't need to be jealous. He has nothing to fear anyway – I love him to bits. But yeah, I have been looking. I couldn't help it, that guy oozes sex."

Izzy nodded. "He's not even my type. Too . . . bulky . . . but . . . well . . .

you know. . ." It was the best that she could manage.

"Yup . . . I know," Claire completely agreed.

The girls got out of there in a fit of giggles, hardly able to contain themselves. The builder they passed on the way out gave them a confused look.

"Well that certainly was an effective way to get my mind off things. Thank you so much – I needed that," Izzy said, taking a deep breath. She checked her messages: still nothing.

"Shall we go out for lunch?"

"Yes, please."

There was a lovely restaurant across the street. Claire and Izzy chatted some more and exchanged ideas about what opening night should look like. Izzy felt so inspired, she thought it was too bad she hadn't visited this place sooner. She almost forgot that she was waiting for the test results until the phone rang.

"Isabelle Stanton." A waiter gestured that she could not use her phone here, but Claire went to him and solved the situation. Izzy was oblivious to that, though. All that mattered were the results.

"Miss Stanton, I have your results here. Everything is fine, the tests all came back negative."

"Oh thank you! Thank you so much!" Izzy felt like she could breathe again. The doctor gave her a few details and promised to mail her the results, but she hardly heard it. She was alright, that was all that mattered. Finally she could breathe again. Now to call Sam and tell him the good news. The waiter still looked none too happy, though. She would have to go outside.

"Everything is fine." she told Claire. "I need to make a few more calls though."

"Of course! Mike will want to know.

"Oh, yes. Him too. First, I need to call Sam." There was no one in the world she wanted to talk to more right now.

"Sam?" Claire raised an eyebrow.

"My best friend. Not gay. Not ugly. But I have known him since birth so he is like a brother to me," Izzy explained in one go.

"I didn't ask."

"Sorry. It seems like I need to defend it everywhere I go lately though. That by being single, every relationship I have with a man suddenly is under scrutiny." Or maybe there was another reason. Every time she referred to Sam as a "friend," she felt a pang of . . . something.

"It's alright. Go call him. Shall I call Mike for you and tell him the good news?"

"Oh, yes please." She'd call him later as well, to thank him for coming with her. Now Sam.

He picked up with "And what did they say?"

Izzy smiled. "All clear."

"See, I told you so! I'm very happy for you! We'll celebrate tonight, okay? I'll make your favorite for dinner, and a bottle of fine wine. And lots of hugs from me and Lily."

That made her glow inside – she could already feel his arms around her. She thanked him and couldn't wait for the evening to come.

Claire was approaching her. "Mike is delighted to know you are okay and congratulates you. So now it is time for you to meet my gorgeous carpenter."

"Claire, really . . ."

"Sorry dear, you have to. Daniel just called me to let me know that he has one of the screens with him. He was sorry he missed me and wondered if I could come back. I want you to see them as well, so you'll have to come with me."

"I look horrible!"

"No you don't. You are looking lovely as always, and if he's not instantly charmed by you then that's his loss. So that's no excuse either."

"Alright." Izzy ran her fingers through her hair, trying to tame it a bit. Within minutes they were back at the gallery where the gorgeous carpenter Daniel was waiting for them with a broad smile. He was even more handsome up close, and his enthusiasm was infectious. He spoke with such passion about his work that he became absolutely irresistible. Proudly he showed them the screen which was indeed fantastic. The design was simply beautiful – totally in keeping with the art nouveau style of the place – and it was cleverly designed in a Z-shape so it would remain upright without additional support.

"It's amazing. Can I get a copy of the pattern? It would be great for the invitations, maybe even get it embossed on them . . . if budget allows." She looked at Claire as she said this last part. "Don't worry, the printer that can do that is one of the people that owes me a favor too."

Daniel sent her a dazzling smile. "I'll email you the template, and then you can use it where ever you like."

Did he just wink at her, or had she imagined that? Boy, it was HOT in here. Especially for it being the middle of winter, with the heating off. She could hardly meet his eyes, feeling a bit overwhelmed with his . . . his . . . er . . . masculinity. Izzy swallowed hard, and reached in her purse. "Thank you very much. Here, my card for the address."

His hand touched hers as he took it from her, and it definitely was not by accident. For a second he lingered. He was flirting, and quite obviously too. "Is that your personal phone number?"

She could only nod. This guy could potentially be as addictive as a drug. But if he was, why then was she still thinking of Sam?

CHAPTER NINETEEN

Preparing for Claire's party now became a blast as Izzy got to combine two of her favorite things: party planning and "Roaring Twenties." She kept an eye out for detail. The glasses she hired to serve champagne in just had that extra twist. Flowers adorning the room were those that would have been used at the time. In choosing a band, she had been careful that they not only sounded but also looked the part. The seats were a real good find back at one of the attics of the building. They kept poor Daniel and actually a team of workers busy till opening to get them back up to scratch, but he promised they would last at least another century, so Anton wasn't too mad when he got the bill. They were beautiful, with turned legs and decorative backs.

Claire had asked her along to pick those works of art that were not only lovely to look at but also created the atmosphere they were aiming for. She saw one lovely painting after another. All in all, it was the best party she had ever worked on. Every day was a joy, even if she had to work till late to get it all done.

Now most of it was arranged, though. The last thing she needed was a dress for the opening, to wear on the night itself.

For a moment, she had doubted if she would go. John was also coming and she did NOT want to see him. Claire had told her that she had no other choice than to invite him – everyone else from his work had gotten an invitation as well. Omitting him would have made it look like there was a personal vendetta. Which maybe there was, but he did not need to know that – not yet.

Izzy was over him though, and he was certainly not gonna spoil this for her as well. This was her show . . . Well, technically it was Claire's, as she was paying. But Izzy had put so much time and effort into it, and she felt like it was her baby. John or no John, she was gonna enjoy this. Decision made.

The vintage clothing shop she visited to find the perfect outfit was paradise. So many gorgeous outfits to choose from that it was hard to find the right one. . . But it was a lot of fun trying them all on. She picked out so many until she could barely hold them in her hand anymore and started trying them on.

Then all of a sudden her phone rang, just as she had managed to wrestle herself into a pink number with fringe. John??? Several curses went through her mind, but she picked up anyways. It felt like ice was running through her veins as she heard his voice.

"Isabelle, you *have* to come with me to Claire's gallery opening. You owe it to me." After all this time, he still thought he could make demands like this? Even if she had not known he had cheated on her, she would never agree to it. His voice actually sound panicked though, as if he had just realized they would both be at the same venue. This could actually be fun. Finally, a bit of payback.

"I owe you? For what?" she asked remaining utterly calm.

"Okay, maybe not owe you. But please Izzy? For old times' sake?" He was begging? She did even know he was capable of it.

"Not because you think your career is on the line, dearest?" She felt like a cat toying with a mouse.

"Well . . . yes . . . maybe. . . Please, Izzy, I'll do everything. I'll even pay you. How does $500 sound?" Solve it with money. Yeah that sounded more like the John she knew and . . . definitely did not love.

"What do you think I am? Some cheap floozy? I think you have mistaken me for your bit on the side."

"What do you mean?" He tried to sound innocent, and failed.

"I know." Her words were precise and punctuated.

"Who told you?"

"Does that really matter?"

"Yes. I want to know who said that I slept around on you."

"Wait a minute. . . Was there more than one?" Had he been doing this their entire relationship?

"No, of course not." The high-pitched shriek with which he delivered it revealed another untruth.

"You're lying, and we both know it." Izzy said matter-of-fact.

And then he turned. Maybe she should not have provoked him. "Do you honestly think a man like me can be faithful to you? I have needs, and when they aren't met, I go somewhere else. You frigid bitch, you always gave me the cold shoulder."

Somehow his words did not seem to hit their target just then. Despite the fact that they should hurt, and did to some level, her mind managed to remain clear. Clearer than she had ever been before. There was only one way to end this conversation. "Did you hear what he just called me, Claire?" The silence on the other side of the phone was deafening, and before he could regain his equilibrium, Izzy hung up on him.

But then like always, doubt set in. Was she frigid? Sex with him certainly had seemed like a chore, but that was mostly because John did not possess a romantic bone in his body. Being in bed with him was like performing a business transaction, and an unpleasant one at that – like a tax audit.

Everything was done in a set order – it had been almost mechanical. Had he been different with that office slut? Was it her fault? After all, he had never really had been able to satisfy her. Sometimes she had felt that she had almost reached that point where she would reach some kind of satisfaction, but then he would always pull back. He could have acted differently if he had liked, but he clearly had chosen not to. But then again, maybe she was just too slow.

She suddenly realized she needed to call Claire to warn her. This was only effective if she played along, and she knew Claire would only be too happy to do so. In fact it kind of scared her when she thought of what Claire might do when she heard about this. But on the other hand, if Claire didn't know, Izzy's perfect little revenge would fall apart. So she dialed the number.

"Claire, John just called me."

"What?" You could almost hear Claire's jaw drop.

"Wait for it, it gets worse. He asked . . . no, he *demanded* that I come to the opening with him."

"WHAT?"

"And then, to top it off, he called me a frigid bitch."

There was a short silence on the other end of the line. "Do you want me to strangle him? Honestly, it would be my pleasure. And I am meeting Anton for lunch in a few minutes anyways."

"Well, that was what I am calling about. I . . . kinda let it seem like you were standing next to me, and heard everything. You could hear him simmer on the other end of the line. So I hung up."

Claire chuckled. "Good move. What can I do to help?"

"Just look like you know and disapprove, okay?"

"I have been giving him disapproving looks for months. They don't seem to work." That was John for you. Blind to what he did not want to see.

"Yeah, but now he knows you heard everything. At least, he thinks you did. He'll be on edge. Anything you say might push him over."

"I'll see what I can do. Don't let him ruin your day, alright? Do you want me to set you up on a date with Daniel for the opening? That would really get his blood boiling, I bet."

Tempting ... but ultimately, Daniel made her nervous with his extraordinary good looks. She did not want the added stress of wondering what he thought of her as well on the evening. "No . . . I am hoping Sam will come with me as moral support."

"You are still coming to the opening night, right? You're not gonna let this bastard spoil it for you. I'm planning to introduce you to everyone as the genius behind this party, so there will be lots of PR in it for you. And I will revoke John's invitation if need be." That was so sweet of her.

"I'll be there. John has no hold over me anymore." He just still knew where to hurt her. But maybe she should take his own approach – just ignore it and let it slide off her like water off a duck's back. She talked some more with Claire, who assured her she was happy to do anything that might rile John up. Then it was back to dress fitting, but it wasn't as fun anymore. Izzy had lost some of the joy that she'd had earlier. Most of it, to be fair.

The lady that owned the shop came toward her. "You look a bit lost."

"I got a phone call from an ex who did his best to upset me."

"Looks like he succeeded. Luckily I know the perfect solution. Shoes! My name is Tina, by the way." Tina pulled her along to another room that was shoe paradise. No regular pair of black pumps to be found. It was a multitude of colors, and each pair was a spectacular masterpiece. Of course there were black shoes too . . . covered in lace, beading and gemstones, looking magnificent.

Izzy felt better already, cooing over each beautiful pair. Each time she put one on, John was a little bit further from her mind, till he was almost completely forgotten.

"I can't buy them all, you know?" Izzy said apologetic.

"You don't have to. Just try them on. This is just fun girl time, no obligations." That was easy to say, but the shoes were so lovely that if you saw them, you wanted to own them all. "And now for the pièce de résistance," Tina said in her best French. A golden box was lifted from a centerpiece and slowly the cover was lifted. "I call them my Cinderella slippers, and I do believe they are your size."

Inside the box was a pair of golden high-heeled pumps. The were made of this fine golden mesh that was just slightly see-through and delicately embroidered to enhance the pattern. The heel itself was completely covered in what looked like hundreds of diamonds. Toward the toes there were fewer and fewer diamonds, but they were alternated with beads and tiny white flowers. The perfect match for her dress . . . even if the frock covered them completely. Izzy suddenly found herself wishing they would fit.

"Seeing I don't have a prince at hand at the moment, shall I do the honors?" Tina smiled and bent down.

They were a perfect fit. Even better, they were comfortable to stand in, which almost seemed impossible when you saw how high the heels were. "How much do they cost?" Izzy asked, slightly terrified about the answer.

"$300. Though it will be a pity to let them go. I only made them last week."

"You made them?"

"Well, not from scratch. I buy plain shoes and liven them up."

That sounded like so much fun. "Fantastic. I definitely want them. If you don't mind selling them . . ."

"If I minded, I'd never sell anything. Take a picture when you wear them to a party, and send it to me. Then I'll be perfectly happy. I love seeing my babies going out in the world."

"I'll do that."

"You were looking at dresses when you came in. Were you looking for anything in particular?"

"Yes, something for a 'Roaring Twenties' party. That will preferably make my ex green with envy after that earlier call. It's time for some payback."

"Hmmm. Most flapper dresses look best on a boyish figure, not your perfect hourglass." Izzy blushed – it was a lovely compliment. "I think I have the perfect one, though. Perfect for those shoes, too. So keep them on." Tina disappeared, and came back with a gorgeous golden dress.

Intricate embroidered swirls made it an exquisite work of art. Izzy tried it on immediately. Underneath the beautiful lace, it was really a strapless dress, but ribbon-work brought up to a collar gave it the appearance of capped sleeves, seductively showing the skin underneath. It was pretty short as well, showing off Izzy's legs.

"I've got fishnet stockings if you want to finish off the look, but to be honest, I don't think I would," Tina commented.

Izzy admired herself in the mirror. It did not give her quite the same feeling as her dress, but it came closer than anything else that she had tried on since. And it indeed, looked perfect with the shoes. "This is it. I'll take it!"

"Really? That's fantastic. Well, if this does not make him go bald with regret, I don't know what will."

"Thank you very much for all your help today."

"Are you kidding me? It's my pleasure helping people to get the perfect outfit. That way I get to enjoy it twice. Once picking it out, and the second time seeing the enjoyment on their faces when they try it on and I see that I got it right."

"Well you certainly chose the perfect outfit for me. Can I keep it on?" The dress was so lovely she really did not want to take it off again. And unlike the other dress, this one was easily hidden under a coat.

"Of course. If you don't mind the cold that is. It's quite chilly out there today. And that dress was made for other purpose than warmth," Tina warned her.

"My coat should be warm enough." It was long and heavy wool blend. Besides it would be worth it. This way she could show it directly to Sam as she got home.

"Do you want to keep the shoes on as well?"

"Naw, I'm afraid they'd get ruined with the snow slurries outside. I might keep them under a glass dome till the opening night."

Tina laughed. "Where they rightfully belong. So, are you in theater?"

"No – I have a gallery opening which I helped organize. In the old dance hall on Latimore Street. You should come – the style of the place is totally in keeping with your shop, and there is some of the town's 'high society' coming that I am sure will love your style as much as I do."

"I would love to . . . Unfortunately, I just sold my best dress and shoes," Tina teased Izzy.

"Well, I am sure you'll find something else among the treasures of this shop. Here's an invitation. I'm sure Claire won't mind."

"Claire Thompson?" Tina asked. Izzy nodded. "She's a regular customer at the shop. In fact, she is coming in later this week for a fitting. Well, in that case, I'll definitely come."

Settling her bill and waving goodbye to Tina, she left the shop. She would certainly be visiting this place more often. In the car on her way home, she tried to decide what was the best way to ask Sam to come with her. He probably would – but how much should she tell him about John's shenanigans? She did not want to keep things from Sam, but on the other hand, she also did not want Sam to beat John up. John had certainly earned it – but he wasn't worth the trouble that came with that.

Well, the dress certainly would be a good distraction, even if she was freezing her butt off like Tina had predicted.

The flat was warm and cozy, though. Sam opened the door, and she immediately took of her coat and did a twirl, showing off the dress.

"What do you think?" Izzy wanted to know.

Sam remained quiet, just staring at her.

"Come on," she begged, excited to know his opinion.

"As your father, I am telling you – you are not leaving the house like that, missy."

She grinned. "Oh, Lily is gonna be in trouble when she gets to that age."

"Thirty-five, you mean? Because I am not letting her out of the house before that."

"Little girls grow up a lot sooner than that, *daddy*. And you can't stop it."

"Yes, I know. It will be a while though, luckily."

"So about the dress? Too slutty?" she asked, concerned.

"No, that's not it. But if you go in public, there isn't gonna be a man in the room that won't want to peel that off you."

That was a satisfying thought. "Exactly what I was aiming for."

"What's the occasion?"

"Claire's gallery opening. John's gonna be there."

"Izzy!" Sam looked alarmed.

"No I don't want him back. God no, I'm happy to be rid of him. I just want him to know what he's missing. You know he had the nerve to call me and demand that I come to this opening with him? He still thinks nobody at work knows, and that by showing up with me on his arm, he can just keep up appearances and get his promotion. Well, he's wrong there. You know he got mad when I said no. He called me a frigid b. . ." Little pitchers had big ears, and even though Lily was in the next room, Izzy wasn't risking it. "Well, he called me frigid. Can you believe it?"

"The nerve of that guy." She saw Sam getting hot under the collar.

"Yeah. So I wanna teach him a lesson he won't forget, and hit him where it hurts most. His ego."

"That dress should do that. Okay, on one condition. I come with you as your date. In case he needs some physical hitting as well, which I will be happy to oblige."

"I thought you'd never ask. I'd gladly have you there. You looked so handsome in your tux last time." She hugged Sam, and somehow the moment seemed to linger. He did not push her away, and she did not let go. They just stood there, in each other's arms, neither one ready to let the other one go.

"You are absolutely beautiful, do you know that? He's a fool." Sam softly kissed her neck, and slowly she melted.

"Aunty Izzy!" A girl jumped in their arms. The moment with Sam was gone . . . although Lily hugs were just as special. The few days that she had kept herself from hugging Lily had made that painfully clear.

Sam detached himself. "Shall I go make dinner?"

"Yes . . . I'll go change. I want to keep this dress clean till the gallery opening. I just wanted to show it to you two."

"You look very pretty, aunty! But not so pretty as the other dress."

Izzy smiled. "I don't think any dress can be as pretty as that."

CHAPTER TWENTY

Izzy felt nervous. Very nervous. Tonight was opening night, and everything needed to be ready on time. The last of the builders had left the building in the morning, and from there on, the setting up had started. Rental companies, florists, caterers, staff, everybody was there, and it was Izzy's job to make sure everything ran like clockwork. It was hard work, and by the end of the day she felt frazzled – but that did not mean she was gonna pass on this evening's festivities.

Sam, like always, came to the rescue. Coming an hour before opening while Izzy was still running round like a headless chicken, he brought her dinner and her clothes for the evening, so she did not have to go home to change. Already dressed in his suit, he was looking absolutely gorgeous.

He handed her an overnight bag. "I grabbed everything I thought you would need."

"Do you have my shoes? They were standing right under the dress." Izzy asked worried.

"Yes, I did. For a moment, I wondered if they belonged to your other dress, though."

"They're for both. And not that terribly expensive if you consider that the lady that sells them makes them herself," Izzy apologized immediately.

"I did not ask. Really Izzy, your expenses are yours. And you're gonna look beautiful tonight, of that I am sure. Now eat some dinner before you pass out, jitterbug."

"It's been one hell of a day. But it's gonna be worth it." she said between bites. The musicians had arrived, so she had to go show them where to set up. They complimented the dance hall perfectly. It was like stepping back in time – the only difference being that the dance floor was now full of art, displayed on Daniel's wonderful screens. They had left a space open in the middle though, where, hopefully, people would take to the floor later on – the place had originally been a dance hall, after all.

A few more bites, and then it was time to get dressed. In about twenty minutes Claire would be arriving, and soon after that, the first guests.

Including John probably, seeing he made it a point to be at events like this long before anyone else. In fact, he might be there any minute, knowing his timing. Izzy wanted to be fully dressed by then, not look her current state of panic. She would blow his mind, and make him regret the way he had treated her over the years. Then she'd laugh in his face and make him feel as little and insignificant as he had always made her feel. Well, if everything worked out as she hoped. Revenge always seemed to backfire, though. She would be satisfied if the evening went off without a hitch and John wasn't too much of an issue. She had Sam there to stand by her after all.

As Izzy got ready in the bathroom, Sam stood guard outside. Unfortunately, he had forgotten to bring any hair products, so Izzy did what she could with her brush and a couple of hairpins. Her hair looked alright, but she doubted it would hold the rest of the night. Sam had however thought to bring her favorite perfume, the one John hated. Well, that would be one way to make John keep his distance. She applied it liberally – enough to repel John, but of course, not so much that she would leave the rest of the room in a coughing fit.

"You look absolutely beautiful," Sam said as she reemerged. "And if John can't see that, he's a horse's ass."

"I thought he already was that? Although . . . you shouldn't really insult horses that way."

Sam chuckled. "True. So what do we do now? Is there anything else you need doing?"

"Nope. Now we just wait till the guests arrive. And hope Claire arrives first."

She did indeed, and Izzy showed her round. So far, everything was going perfectly, which was a bit nervewracking. No party ever went completely to plan, but hopefully any hiccups would be only minor. And not involve John. Izzy sighed. She really had to stop worrying about John now, or he'd spoil the whole evening for her before he'd even arrived.

"And this is Sam," she finished off as she and Claire arrived back in the lobby. Sam was already chatting away with Anton, and they looked a lot more animated than she had ever seen him be with John.

"I should have brought my camera. I could have taken some amazing pictures here tonight. But I'll see what I can do with my camera phone," Sam promised.

"Oh I should have thought of that. But then again, I did not want you working tonight." She gave him a hug.

"Daniel is, unfortunately, not coming, Izzy." Claire's tone of voice was strange, and the look in her eyes even stranger.

"That's a pity – he put so much effort into helping to put all this together." Why was Claire putting such an emphasis on telling her? Should she be disappointed? She liked the guy and he was nice to look at, but she certainly did not have any feelings for him. And she had Sam standing right beside her. It made it sound like Sam was only second best and that Izzy was waiting on something better to come along.

"Yes a pity indeed that he can't enjoy the fruits of his labor– don't you think Izzy?"

'Please drop it, Claire' was all Izzy could think. Luckily, there were other people arriving to distract them. Mike, for instance, who hugged Izzy immediately.

"Izzy, you look delectable. If I was into ladies, you'd be my favorite dish of the night." The comment made Sam raise an eyebrow.

"Thank you. But if you wanna lay low, you'd better watch what you say, dear."

"Well actually, I have been thinking of coming out. I am sick of hiding part of myself for eight hours a day. Not tonight though – don't want to upstage Claire's party."

"Do it next time, when we go on one of our gastronomic outings," Claire suggested. "It'll give them another reason to choke on their soup."

Anton looked somewhat disapproving, but couldn't help letting out a chortle as well.

"Some people will freak out, you know." Izzy said. It was sad but true.

Mike laughed wickedly. "Like John? I am counting on it."

"Is this the guy that drove you to the clinic?" Sam made it sound like an accusation, even though it wasn't. It was just one of those rough edges Sam had now and then when he wasn't quite comfortable, and with more and more people coming in he was starting to feel a bit on edge. Maybe she should have let him brought his camera so he could hide. His nerves were rubbing off on Mike, who was prattling around.

"Yes he was," she confirmed. "Sam, this is Mike. Mike, this is Sam."

Sam grabbed Mike's hand, and Mike nearly jumped. In fact, maybe he did. "Thank you so much for taking such good care of her. I wish I could have been there for her myself."

Mike let something out that sounded like a giggle. "Is he always this ardent?"

The giggle was infectious. "Most of the time, yes."

Mike put arm over Sam's shoulder. "I like it."

"Uh . . . let me get you both a drink." Sam suggested, not really sure what to think about the situation and momentarily left.

"Girlfriend, get some sense. You don't let guys like that walk. Especially when they are that into you."

"He's not into me," Izzy denied.

"He's here tonight playing your knight in shining armor, isn't he?"

She couldn't disagree. Sam was back already, champagne in hand. Luckily, Tina came by. It surprised Izzy that she had still not seen John. Maybe he had taken the high road and had decided not to attend? The high road sounded nothing like John though.

"Hello, Cinderella shoes," Tina greeted her.

"Hi Tina! Wonderful that you could make it! What do you think?"

"It's great! The place makes me want to do a fashion show here. It would look totally in keeping with what I sell . . ." Then she noticed the man beside Izzy. "This is not the jerk that nearly brought you to tears in my shop, is it?"

"No! This is Sam. He's here to help protect me against said jerk."

"Ah, good man. Say, you promised me a picture of you in my shoes. Is it alright if I take one of you now?"

"Oh of course. Let Sam do it, he's the master of that kind of stuff." Sam was looking a bit lost in the corner, so this was the perfect way to get him involved.

Sam took Tina's phone. "Her shoes?" he asked, confused.

"Yes, these." Izzy pointed at her toes. "Tina made them."

"Ah yes, you told me they were handmade. Alright, over there perhaps, kick your leg back and look like you are about to do a Lindy hop. Yes . . . gorgeous . . ." Sam was back in his element, and he visibly relaxed. Izzy smiled as he snapped a couple of pictures.

"Ooh, are you for hire? I thought of doing a catalog a while back, and if you are this good with my phone, you must be fantastic behind a camera!" Tina said excitedly.

"He is, and he is indeed," Izzy said, answering both questions in one go. She sneaked a peak at the pictures – as usual, he had made her look great.

"I got a wonderful subject," he blushed.

They chatted a while longer until Claire stole Izzy away to introduce her to people, as promised. Still no sign of John, and they were almost an hour into the party. Maybe he had decided to forgo the party altogether, which would have suited her just fine. Just when she thought he definitely wasn't going to show, as being fashionably late was not his style, Mike ran toward them. "John's here! And you'll never guess who he has with him," he said like a gossipy aunt.

"Who?" Claire and Izzy asked simultaneously.

That moment, John entered the room with a woman in a red dress in tow. "Dress" was not quite the word for it, though. It covered the necessities, but not much else. Men everywhere turned their heads to look – only to meet the disapproving stare of their wives five seconds later when they had quit gawking.

"That's . . . that's . . ." Claire stammered in disbelief.

"Tracy the Tramp," Izzy finished.

Mike snorted. "You can't say that! Even if it's true."

"Well, that is what John always called her, not me. I can't believe it. He would have a fit every time she passed by. Especially the last time he saw her – he nearly choked. Well, actually, that would make sense now."

Sam who already had been standing close by, now loomed protectively over her. She felt safe from anything John might throw at her, but she wondered if Sam was alright.

"Sam, however much he upsets you, think of Lily, alright? I want her to be a mantra in your head so he doesn't get to you," she whispered.

"There is nothing that bastard can say to upset me. If he upsets you however, I am throwing him head first out of the nearest window."

"No you are not – too much time went into restoring the place, and I would be very offended if you did." She giggled and pulled him closer. "What would I do without you."

"Let's hope neither of us ever have to find out." He embraced her and kissed the top of her head.

"Finally made your move, loser?" John. Who else? Sam's embrace tightened. "I knew it only would be a matter of months till you'd try to get in her pants. Took you long enough."

"Ignore him," Izzy whispered.

"I was planning to. Did my lady care to dance?"

But certainly. Sam was a great dancer, and on the floor she could forget all about John, even though every time she looked round, she found him staring at her. Best to focus completely on Sam. They laughed and danced till the band needed a break and Sam needed the toilet.

As soon as Sam left, John cornered her. "You honestly think you can keep up this farce with Sam pretending to be your boyfriend? You don't think people will see right through that?"

Izzy wasn't afraid. His words could no longer hurt her and she saw him for what he was. A cornered predator. "I'm not pretending anything. Sam is here as my friend to celebrate the opening. What, exactly, is Tracy doing here though?"

"She is my date because you did not want to come." The sentence was full of accusation.

"Well, good luck with that," Izzy replied unimpressed.

"She is replacing you."

Like she cared. "So? We are over. I could care less about who you spend your time with, although I do feel sorry for her, knowing all the things you called her behind her back. "

"Just admit you want me. Why else would you come here all tarted up like that?"

"Because, now that I'm rid of you, I don't have to follow your stupid dress code anymore. You might have tried to control me, but no more. I'm free of you, which means that I can wear whatever I like. And I have never been happier."

"Dressed like a common slut to attract the likes of Sam?"

"Whatever you want to think. I really don't care. Apparently Tracy didn't quite understand your dress code. Better get back to her, or she might see the light as well and get someone better. Honestly John, I don't know what I ever saw in you. You must be the biggest jerk I have ever met, although really, even that is giving you too much credit."

"Damn it, woman! You are ruining my career making a fool of me. I still haven't gotten my promotion, and it's all your fault." Just as she thought, he tried to blame it on her.

"You're doing that all by yourself, by lying to everybody. So we broke up – what's the big deal? If you had been honest from the start, I am sure no one would have cared. But then again, honesty isn't your best subject, is it?"

"You little slut . . ."

"No, you're the one that's a slut!"

He grabbed her wrist and she screamed out in pain. "Let go of me!" Everybody looked their way, and he tried to push her back, twisting her arm at a funny angle and making her howl in pain. He pulled back his hand to strike her.

Sam emerged out of nowhere, grabbed John from behind, and threw him to the ground. "Keep your hands off her," he roared.

Izzy was scared – not for herself but that Sam would get hurt. Sam seemed to be in control of the situation though.

"Are you okay Izzy?" he asked, a bit out of breath.

"Yes," she said, rubbing her painful wrist.

"Get off me, you bastard!" John yelled, trying to break free. However, Sam had him in a vice grip though, thanks to years of judo as a kid. Security came and took over. As Sam got up, John tried to take another swing. Luckily, he wasn't quick enough. This time, the security guard, who was built like a linebacker, tackled him, and John fell to the floor like a sack of potatoes. Izzy fled into Sam's arms and hid there.

Both Mr. Thompson Jr. and Mr. Thompson Sr. stood there, shaking their heads. Anton looked pissed, and his father wasn't too happy either.

"How dare you ruin my wife's gallery opening like this?" Anton growled as John was dragged off by security.

John tried to protest. "But she . . ."

"Dumped your ass months ago? Yes, we all know that."

Then Mr. Thompson Sr. got involved. "Consider yourself fired, John.

We do not condone public displays of violence. Half our clients are here tonight."

"She started it!" he yelled like a common thug.

Claire got involved as well. Knowing what he had done to her friend, she had been dying to scratch his eyes out all evening. "She did nothing of the kind and you know it! I saw you corner her the moment Sam turned his back for a second. Get out of here, you bastard!" Then she looked at security. "Escort this man out of here."

John wasn't going quietly though and tried to break free from the bulky security agents' grasp. "I will get you for this, Isabelle!" he screamed.

Sam shielded her, stepping in between them. For the first time, she was frightened. She had never seen John be physically violent before. She had known from the beginning that he might try to pull something tonight, but she had never thought it would go beyond verbal abuse.

Izzy was surprised to find Tracy beside her all of a sudden. "Are you alright? I had no idea he was such a jerk!"

"I'm … I'm fine," Izzy stammered. Pity from the woman John had used to cheat on her. She should know by now that when it came to John, she should expect the unexpected.

More revelations started coming from Tracy's mouth. "He told me the two of you had an open relationship."

"He didn't tell me though." Or she'd have dumped his sorry ass.

"I'm so sorry! I didn't know!"

"When did you get involved with him, anyway?" Izzy wanted to know this – needed to know how long John had been cheating on her.

Tracy's answer was of no use though. "A few months ago, at the Christmas party. You weren't there, and I was kind of flattered he was even interested in me. You are so beautiful and I am just . . . me"

"Well, then he did not lie completely. We had already been broken up for months at that point." So it could not have been Tracy in the office that night with John. It would have had to been some other woman. Izzy wondered how many there had been. What a lying, cheating bastard. "So it was a very open relationship, indeed. You have nothing to be sorry for." Except maybe for dating the jerk in the first place. But then, so was she.

"Really? What an asshole!"

"You are preaching to the choir, honey," Izzy agreed. "But I'm curious. Even if it had been an open relationship – which it most definitely was not – didn't you mind that you were not the only one?"

"Well, those are the only kind of men I seem to get . . . men who are married, or who already have a girlfriend. They are usually very nice to me, though. Buy me lots of things. Although John isn't all that nice, to be honest. Very pushy and aggressive. I only said yes to tonight because he practically made me . . . I'm gonna go home now. I'm really sorry – if I had known the truth, I would never have gotten involved with him." Tracy looked like a sad little girl, and Izzy couldn't help feeling sorry for her.

Claire stormed at Tracy. "Don't you think you should leave, now that piece of scum you have been sleeping around with behind my friend's back has left?"

"Claire, it wasn't her," Izzy said, trying to calm Claire down.

"How do you know?"

"They only got involved this Christmas."

"Really?" Claire might be surprised, but after tonight, there was nothing John could do to surprise Izzy.

Tracy nodded. "Yes."

"I'm sorry I accused you."

"It's alright. I probably deserved it. He did tell me he was still involved with Izzy, but he said they were open that way."

"Yes, very open. The less I see of him the better in fact." Oh, what a night this was turning out to be.

"I think I'll go home now. I don't really feel comfortable here with all these posh people. Sorry for everything." Tracy looked so fragile that Izzy took pity on her,

"You have nothing to be sorry of. He has," Izzy ensured her.

"And we'll make sure he'll be VERY sorry," Claire remarked.

Tracy left, and Izzy felt ready to leave as well. She was tired of all the drama. "I don't think Tracy is a bad girl, just not that strong a personality. She seems very insecure to me," she told Claire.

"Insecure?? Dressed like that?"

"Especially dressed like that. She feels unworthy so she thinks she needs to do that to get attention. Be nice to her. I'm gonna get my coat as well, I think."

"Are you sure you want to leave? Don't let John spoil it for you."

"I have been up since six am this morning and then this . . . I just burned off the last of my adrenaline. I'm afraid I'll fall asleep in a corner if I stay."

Sam, being the gentleman, got their coats for her. She leaned into his embrace as they walked out. She really was so lucky to have him. Her knight in shining armor.

CHAPTER TWENTY-ONE

The drive home was a quiet one. Both Izzy and Sam were just too tired to talk. Tonight had taken its toll, and for now, they were content to just be in each other's presence on the drive home. Part of Izzy had wanted to stay at the party, but after all that had happened, she just wasn't sure she would be up to it, and in the end, she was happy to enter her own building. They dragged themselves up the stairs – and Izzy was very grateful not to find an angry John in front of her apartment door. Somehow she had expected him to be there to give her an earful – or worse. It was another reason she had wanted to get home quickly and get inside in case John was thinking about doing something stupid. She opened her door, glad to be home, and Sam automatically came in with her.

"Don't you want to pick up Lily?" she asked, sitting down on the couch.

"Mrs. Halford has her for the night. I thought it better to leave her there than to drag her out of bed halfway through the night – and drag Mrs. Halford out of bed too."

Izzy looked at the clock. It was barely past eleven, even if it felt like 4 am. Mrs. Halford was probably still awake. And knowing what a night owl Lily was, there was a good chance she was still up too. "It's still early."

"Naw, she'll be fine. I thought we could talk for a while. Relax." He plopped down next to her.

She looked at him and smiled. "That was . . . some night. Thank you for coming. And for saving me."

"Wouldn't have missed it for the world." He meant it too.

"You were like Superman the way you shot past me and threw him to the floor."

Sam undid his bow tie. "I'd like to think of myself as Batman. He has more style, and does it all without superpowers."

"Finally got your revenge on the Joker, Bruce Wayne?"

"It did feel good to have him pinned to the floor unable to move. I had to hold back though not to bash his brains out."

"What brains? It's John – there's only hot air up there."

"And do you feel like you got back at him by showing him what a beautiful woman you truly are?"

"Sorta . . . He called me a slut, of course. Accused me of trying to win him back, and when that did not work, that I wanted to seduce you."

Sam laughed. "You weren't seducing me? Because I am totally mesmerized by the way you look tonight."

She played along, and stroked his cheek. "Of course I was." Something in her wrist twisted the wrong way. "Ouch!"

"What is it?"

"Nothing – my wrist just hurts after John manhandled it. It's just a bit bruised. I'll put some arnica salve on it to help it heal."

"Let me see," he said inspecting it.

"I'm fine!" she tried to insure him. It hurt a little where he touched it, but she was sure it would be fine in the morning. Except for a bruise, maybe.

"I'll be the judge of that." He carefully felt her for wrist bone, and then bent her arm. As he did, he carefully studied her face for signs of pain.

"Sometimes you can't help those daddy hormones kicking in, can you?" She ruffled his curls trying to distract him.

"Not when the woman I love is hurt. Medicine cabinet?"

"Hmm?" Izzy was confused. He said love in a way she had never heard him say it before. There was something different in his intonation.

"The salve – is that in your medicine cabinet?" he specified

"Oh yes, top shelf."

He went to get it, and in the meantime she inspected her wrist herself as well. It didn't feel all that great, but there was nothing that needed urgent medical attention.

He put some of the cream on the tops of his fingers "May I have your hand, milady?"

"Of course you may."

Ever so gently, he massaged it in. When he was done he asked, "Glass of wine? Like you said, the night is still terribly young. I guess it's us who got old."

"Speak for yourself. And yes, I'd love some wine."

He poured her a glass and one for himself.

"I am not sure how happy I should be about the fact John got fired. Knowing him, he'll blame me for that. God knows what stunt he might pull."

"I'm right across the hall if anything happens. And it would be my pleasure to kick his ass."

"I know." She let her head rest on his shoulder.

"I hope you did enjoy some of the night."

"I did. It was a dream until John showed up, And even then. I loved dancing with you. We should go dancing more often."

"I'm not sure. I am not that good." That wasn't true – he was the best dancer Izzy knew. Every time she was in his arms, the rest of the world seemed to disappear. "Besides, we'd need to find a sitter for Lily, and I don't want to leave her too often."

"I guess you are right."

Sam took a big gulp of his glass of wine, downing it in one go. "Would my lady care to dance now perhaps?

"Here? Now?" Izzy asked, surprised.

"Well, your apartment is big enough. And I promise I will be careful with your wrist." He held out his hand and helped her up.

"How about music?"

"We don't need that, do we?" Carefully he draped her injured arm over his shoulder, and swayed her back and forth to an imaginary song. She was drifting again.

And then it just happened. They moved closer and closer, arms entangled, and then he pulled her toward him for a kiss that was anything but brotherly. They melted together as one as they lost themselves. The pins from her hair came loose, clattering through the floor as her hair cascaded down her shoulders.

His kiss surprised her, but her own need for him surprised her even more. She closed her eyes and let him lead her with his lips. Her body curled itself around his. They danced on to the tones of nonexistent music. There was a beat though – that of their hearts drumming in unison, led by the rhythm of their kisses. He leaned back to kiss her throat as his hand ran down her side to her leg. Spinning her round he kissed her neck, his hands on the front of her body, caressing her breasts.

She should put a stop to this right now. This was Sam, and what they were doing would change their relationship forever. Potentially, it could ruin everything. She did not want to lose Sam. But if she stopped him now, wasn't it already too late? What happened could not be undone. And she realized she did not want it to stop. She loved him, more than just a friend or a brother. She hoped he felt the same. And, if his kisses were anything to go by, he did. Well, if not, she could try and blame it on the alcohol and the stress of the night. If need be, if it saved their friendship, she would just say they were both drunk and overexcited, and that it had happened by accident. It wasn't true, though. She was sober enough to know what was going on, and what decision she was making. Right now, she wanted this to happen, more than she had ever wanted anything else. She loved Sam, with all her heart, just like everybody had been telling her. It was time to give in.

They swayed through the room into the hallway. She knew the general direction he was pushing her – the bedroom – and she wondered if it was on purpose. Well, pushing was the wrong word . . . it was more like a slow waltz, with twists, turns, and fervent kisses.

Just before they reached the bedroom door, he picked her up and carried her over the threshold. She couldn't help but smile as a slow fire started spreading from her belly. He put her back on her feet in front of her bed. It was up to her now if this would continue.

"Undress me," she asked, lifting up her hair and turning around so he could undo her zipper.

"Are you sure, Izzy?" Doubt was in his voice. This was her last chance to stop this.

"Go ahead," she reassured him. She could feel his hands shake as they went down her back. There was no way she was gonna stop him now, though. She shrugged the dress off her shoulders and let it drop to the floor. As she stepped out of her dress, she also left her shoes behind. Turning around, she saw him smile like he had never smiled before. She looked carefully, but there was no hint of disappointment to be found in his face. Now it was just her bra and panties left. Before she was gonna take them off, she wanted him to lose some of his clothes as well though.

Starting with his jacket, she pushed it over his shoulders, where it soon met the floor. There was only one way this could go. Sam seemed surprised, but rather than give him time to think about it, she kissed him again.

Her fingers worked the buttons of his shirt in the meantime. One by one, they revealed his chest. She had never known he was so well built – then again, the last time she had seen him without his shirt, he had been a teenager. That slender figure was now gone, replaced by a muscular chest and broad arms. No wonder he'd had no trouble pinning John to the floor. Following the collar bone she kissed her way from his shoulder to his chest.

There were more clothes in the way between her and what she wanted though. Grabbing his belt buckle, she undid it, and then pushed down his pants. She could see that this boldness scared him a bit, as he backed away a bit and tried to cover his manhood with his hands. To be honest, she had no idea where this was coming from – she never had been this forward in the bedroom before. It seemed right though, and, judging by the bulge in his boxers, he had nothing to be ashamed of.

"Izzy, are you sure? After this, there is no way back." So he was thinking the same thing.

"There already isn't." She jumped up in his arms, wrapping her legs around him as they kissed. Through the layers of fabric, she could feel him, and he definitely was not small. And he was definitely ready for her. She ground into him and he stumbled, making them fall on the bed. He took most of his weight on his arms, but he still looked worried. "I'm fine," she assured him and started to remove the final layers of clothing between them by unclasping her bra. Her breast sprang free, and he just stared. Didn't he like them? All men liked breasts, didn't they?

"You are so beautiful," he whispered.

She sighed of relief. As he kissed them, he turned her body on fire. Slowly he kissed every inch of her body. Gentle, ever so gentle he was, unlike any lover she had had. She could see the fire in his eyes, but he held back with what seemed divine respect for her. "Please don't stop," she begged him. The heat in her body was turning into a roaring fire that was threatening to burn out of control.

She found the waistband of his boxers and pushed them down as his erection sprang free. He was even bigger than she thought, which was slightly frightening. She needed to get used to the idea for a moment. Sam rolled on his back, so she could explore him. "Not quite how I remember you," she giggled nervously.

"What do you remember?"

"Well the last time I saw you naked you were a lot smaller, and running away from your mom, who was trying to hose you down." Stupid, stupid – what a way to ruin the mood.

Sam wasn't fazed though. "Well then . . . take your time . . . get to know it," he said, leading her hand around his shaft.

He was beautiful, and she wasn't just talking about the gorgeous cock she was now softly stroking. He moaned softly, bucking under her hand. She kissed his groin, and breathed in his musk.

"I want you so bad, Izzy."

She moved back up to kiss him, straddling him. He helped her out of her panties and ran his over her back. She ground into him, making them both shiver. Flipping her back over, Sam trailed a line of kisses to her sex. She had to clench the sheets as his tongue touched her most intimate spots. No other lover had ever done this for her. As he moved back up, she could do nothing but smile.

"Oh Sam."

"I love you, Izzy." Slowly he entered her. She could feel his manhood enter her shaft, filling her up inch by inch.

"I love you too, Sam.

This seemed to make him start thrusting in earnest. Every move brought her that much closer to the elusive orgasm. Was it really possible, then? He went faster and faster, until she could feel him tense. She was so close as he screamed his orgasm. Nothing. Maybe she really was a frigid bitch.

"Sorry, that was a bit quick. It's been a long time." He softly kissed her and she was ready to move away, wiggling beneath him to let him slip out. "Hey, what are you doing?"

"You came."

"Yeah – sorry about that. Give me a few seconds to catch my breath and we'll do it right. I haven't waited my whole life for you, just to disappoint you." He kissed her again to smother any protest. Slowly he started moving again, and Izzy realized he was still hard. His strokes were long and deep, and created a feeling she did not know existed. He was fully focused on her now, on the pleasure on her face as ecstasy built. She could feel it was really happening this time, she was reaching a peak, and then . . . she exploded into a million pieces, slowly drifting back to earth. She had never felt like this before. All she knew was that she was with Sam, the most wonderful man in the world.

As she regained her senses, he started thrusting again.

"What are you doing?"

"What does it look like?" He had not gotten any softer. She was now so aroused that a second, and even a third orgasm came quickly. He grabbed her legs and rolled so that she now straddled him once again, but with him buried deep inside of her. It was for her to set the pace, and the different angle also brought different sensations. She went faster, looking for one more peak that would surely take the last of her energy. As he grabbed her nipple and pinched it, she came even harder than she had done before. The power of her orgasm was so great that she took him with her, as she finally collapsed on his chest.

"Wow," was all that she could utter.

"Yeah, wow."

He was now finally going soft, and she tried to move off him.

"Stay there," he said, pinning her hips to his.

"I don't think I can take anymore, stud."

"Me neither – but I can think of no better way to sleep than with you splayed across my chest."

"Isn't that a bit suffocating?"

"Maybe . . . but worth it."

So she lay down and eventually fell asleep in that position. As they woke up during the night, she rolled off him to the side, and he spooned her. He could not help himself, and made love to her in that position as he kissed her neck before going back to sleep.

CHAPTER TWENTY-TWO

Izzy woke up to an empty bed. There was a dent in the pillow, but no Sam. Was last night a just a dream? No, it could not be, it had been too real for that. Her body still felt the afterglow of her orgasmic bliss, and the sheets smelled of him. But then where was he, and why was he not beside her? The clock said 8:00 am, which was pretty early – especially after the night they had. Her wrist was now bruised and painful to the touch. Maybe she needed a doctor after all, just to be sure nothing was wrong.

Later, though. First she needed to find Sam. She got up and put on her robe. The fact that she was naked was another sign that last night had happened – she usually wore a nightgown to bed. Her dress and shoes were in the exact position she remembered leaving them, and her undies were dangling from the bedpost. Sam's clothes were gone though, like they hadn't been there in the first place. Quickly she put on some underwear. God, she was stiff. Of course, it had been months since she last had sex . . . if you could call it that. Last night, for the first time, she had experienced what it really could be like. No more was she an orgasmic virgin, and for that she needed to thank him. Preferably in bed. Her body longed for more, and just thinking about him made her nipples react.

Maybe he was in the kitchen making breakfast. She heard none of the usual rumbling of pots and pans, though. The house was absolutely quiet. She knew Sam so well that she was sure he wasn't the kind of guy to love 'em and leave 'em. Quite the opposite. So where was he? Even if something was wrong, he would have surely woken her up.

Unless something was wrong with her. Sam wasn't good at confrontations. Was she frigid after all? Could that be the reason that he had left without so much as a word.

All the doubts John had put into her head over the years now returned threefold. Maybe she just wasn't good enough. Maybe he had expected more of her. Last night had been magical for her, but that pretty much said what she knew about sex. Nothing. What if he thought she was just a mistake and decided to leave so he did not have to face her in the morning.

Maybe he was just trying to think of a way to tell her, to let her down easy.

No, she could not face losing him! Maybe as a lover, but not as a friend anyway, especially since that meant losing Lily as well. And that was what was sure to happen – maybe not today, but in the long run. Last night was not something you could forget about like it had never happened. Which meant they would drift apart. And she would never see him again, never see Lily again . . .

This was no time for tears. She needed to go and see him. Try and save what was possible. So she got dressed. The lovely golden dress got picked off the floor and placed on a hanger. The shoes went in the closet. She looked at the other dress. "Much luck you have brought me so far." She was about to lose everything she cared for. Maybe it really was bad luck to wear a wedding dress when you weren't getting married. So instead she put on a simple gray dress that she'd normally wore to work and a jacket. She combed her hair and put on the first pair of boots she found.

Then she stepped out in the hallway. She paced in front of his door, afraid to knock, afraid to go in. She loved him so much more than a brother, she wanted him as a lover – a life's mate. But how was she ever gonna tell him that?

The door opened by itself. Maybe he had heard her pacing. "Izzy we need to talk. Last was not quite as it should be." In that sentence all her fears were validated. Whatever happened last night it had not meant for him what it had for her. She could break down and cry right now.

Instead she started talking, trying to make things right. If he did not want her, than fine, but she couldn't lose him all together. Maybe if she acted that she was fine with it, all would be okay. "It's alright – last night was kinda weird. It should not have happened. I hope we can put it behind us and pretend it did not happen. I value your friendship more than anything." The words left her mouth but felt hollow. She felt utterly hollow, like she had just lost everything important. And she had. Whatever happened after this, it would never be the same.

"Daddy", Lily called from somewhere in the house.

"Izzy that was not what I meant." There was a lost look in his eyes. He was ready to cut her loose altogether, she was sure of it.

"Daddy!" The cry sounded more panicky now.

"Sorry, I gotta go to her. Come in please. We really need to talk." He turned around, but left the door open.

Izzy couldn't. She felt like she was nailed to the floor. Right now she could not face the rejection, could not hear him say the words out loud. She wasn't sure how she'd react. So instead, she turned around and walked out the door. Somehow she had already grabbed her purse and coat, so there was nothing stopping her, not even the icy winds. She didn't even know where she was going. She took a cab to the mall and wandered aimlessly. She looked at clothes without looking. Tried them on without checking her image in the mirror. Bought a shirt of which she had dozens in the closet, just to keep her occupied.

Her phone buzzed telling her a text had arrived. Automatically she checked it.

"Hi Izzy. Sorry I could not be there last night. Would you like to meet me for lunch today. -x- Daniel"

Daniel. Not Sam. Well, maybe that was a good thing. On the other hand, Daniel was nice, but she wasn't interested in him. She was about to delete the text when she realized her stomach was burning from running on empty. She hadn't had breakfast, and it was nearly lunch time. She had no desire to eat, except the fact that her body told her she needed some nutrition. If she rendezvoused with him for lunch, she would have to eat. Plus, he might be able to distract her from her current thought pattern. Didn't they say it was best to get back on the horse as soon as possible once you had fallen off? Although she had no intention of sleeping with Daniel, it might be a good idea to just go out with him. If only to think about something else for a while. Daniel's good looks sure were a distraction for any girl.

She just hoped she hadn't lost Sam for good – she did not know how to live without him. She knew she needed to go back and talk it over, but she couldn't. Right now she could not handle the rejection, not after he had just given her the best night of her life.

She called Daniel, and they agreed on a place to meet. Getting back in a cab, she got over there. It was a nice French restaurant which had a lovely luncheon spread but was also quite expensive. Oh well, she could afford it. And she was gonna insist on paying – of that much she was sure.

So what if he thought of her as a diehard feminist. For too long she had been depending on men. And now that the last man was gonna leave her as well, she might as well learn to stand on her own two feet.

She found a table by the window, Daniel arrived looking . . . like a poster boy model. Blue lumberjack shirt that totally complimented his eyes. Underneath, a tight white shirt that showed off his muscular body. There was a small row of buttons down the collar, the top one left open, and any woman in their right mind would want to undo the rest.

So it was probably a good thing that she wasn't all there today. In fact, she hardly noticed it. She noticed the hole in his "distressed" jeans where his knee poked though, but rather than appreciating the erotic value of seeing a bit of unexpected skin, she was surprised they had let him in looking like this. After all, it was a classy restaurant. But then again, with looks like that, you could get in anywhere, even with jeans like that.

"Hi," Izzy said with as much enthusiasm as she could muster. He wasn't the cause of her dark mood, after all.

"Hello, Izzy. You look very ravishing."

Like this? Sure. Well, it was nice of him to say so. Of course, he had never seen her in another state besides a mess. "Thank you." She didn't even blush, which normally she would have done.

He placed a red rose on her plate, like a perfect gentleman. Then they ordered lunch. She still wasn't hungry, even if her body had other ideas.

"I'm very glad you wanted to meet me. I was so sorry that I couldn't be there last night, but my roommate had fallen ill, and I needed to take care of him."

"That is very nice of you. Not everybody would do that for a roommate."

"Well, I say roommate, but really he is more like a brother. We set up the business together. I owe so much to him. He is the brains behind the operation. I'm just there to look pretty." He laughed at his own joke.

Izzy was stuck on the word "brother." Sam had always been like a brother . . . and now he was so much more. How could they ever go back to that?

"Are you alright?" Daniel asked.

"Hmm? Oh yes, fine. Yesterday night was rather eventful. My ex showed up and made a scene." Unconsciously, she rubbed her wrist.

"That is quite a bruise. Have you let a doctor look at it?"

"Not yet. I think I will later though."

"Do that. I broke my wrist once, riding my motorcycle. Took me out of business for months. It was awful. Not just the loss of income, but not being able to do what I like. Wood is my passion, just the smell of it. And then there is the texture . . ."

She could just imagine him on a motorcycle. It suited him. Sam had driven a motorcycle when he was younger. Driven his mother nuts with worry. With Lily arriving, he had given it up though.

"Am I boring you?" Daniel asked all of a sudden

"What? No! Like I said, last night took a lot out of me with my ex and all. I am having a bit trouble concentrating, but that has nothing to do with you."

"There is something else though, isn't there. When we met before, I felt like we connected, but now . . . nothing."

"Sorry. My head just isn't in it today." Nor was her heart, if it ever was.

"That's okay. I hope we can still be friends. I would be nice to have a female friend for once that doesn't immediately wants to jump me. Not that I am complaining, but sometimes it would be nice to just have a conversation."

"Sorry that I am not much of a conversational partner either, today."

"Well, I am a good listener too. Tell me what happened. Somehow I feel like there was more to it than just that."

How did he know? "I was there with my best friend. And somehow last night it became more than that."

"And you don't want it to be?" he asked. He wasn't flirting anymore, just being a friend.

She swallowed back the lump that was forming in her throat. "I do. But he doesn't."

"Do you know this for sure?"

"Well that is pretty much what he said this morning."

"Pretty much?"

"We got interrupted. His daughter called out to him."

"How old is this daughter?" He was very thorough in his questions.

"Four."

"So we can pretty much say that he wasn't free to talk."

"Yeah, but . . . He wasn't there when I woke up. He had left me. What does that say?"

"That we guys on the whole aren't the smartest beings on earth. Sometimes we make the wrong decision or say the wrong thing. And usually when we start doing something stupid, we do a whole string of them together, making it worse and worse, until we have completely dug our own grave. So don't judge him too harshly. Go find out what is really the matter. If he is smart, there is no way he'll let you go."

His words were encouraging. "If you are wrong though, how do I get our friendship back?"

"Well not by sitting here and talking to me, that is for sure. You're a woman. You lot always know how to fix things. So go and fix it."

He was right. And yet she was still scared. She finished her meal thinking about it. She insisted on paying for both of them – she owed him that much. "Thanks, Daniel . . . if I weren't already in love with somebody else . . ."

"Yeah yeah, story of my life. All the good girls are taken. Don't worry, I'll live," he joked and made a gesture that said "Get out of here."

So there she was, out on the street again. With a bit more hope, but still not enough courage to go home. It was two o'clock now. He'd be having his father-daughter time with Lily. There was no way they could have a decent conversation like that. Not like the one they needed to have.

Maybe she could hide out at Robert's till it was a bit later. She would also like to hear his opinion. He was the one that had said she was in love with Sam after all, before she knew it herself. Maybe he would also know what to do now. Of course, he probably did not have all the answers, but he did usually manage to give her a good perspective on things. Besides, the bar was the closest thing to going home there was right now.

She entered the bar. It was pretty busy. "Robert can we talk . . ." Orders came in. Normally, she would help, but not today. "Maybe a bit later?"

"Yeah. Go upstairs. I'll see you in a bit." It was a strange reaction. She had never been upstairs so far, even though she knew this was where Robert lived.

"I'm fine here." She settled on a stool.

"No, you're not. Go upstairs. And don't be stubborn."

That was bossy and uncalled for. But maybe she did look like a mess. She certainly felt like it. So she went up the stairs.

"Robert?"

That was Sam's voice – what was he doing here? Was it too late to turn back around and get out of here? Just as she wanted to turn away the door opened.

"Izzy, you're here. I was hoping you would be, eventually. We need to talk." His face was pale, and his eyes were red – like he had been crying. She had not seen him this way since his divorce. And this time it was all her fault . . .

Apologies started flowing out of her. "I know we do. I just couldn't face it yet. I feel like we are on the verge of losing our friendship. I mean, it's okay if you don't want me, I'm much too old for you anyways . . ."

"But I want you. I've wanted you all of my life."

That didn't make sense. "Where were you then this morning?"

"I got a text from Mrs. Halford at 6 am that Lily got sick overnight, so I went to pick her up."

"Why didn't you tell me? And why are you here with me instead of her now?" Lily trumped her any day. If only he had told her . . .

"I did things wrong, okay? From the moment I left your bedroom without waking you, which was a mistake. But it's impossible to choose between the two most important women in my life. Lily was doing better this afternoon, so I left her in the care of Mrs. Halford to find you. Sorry, alright? I'm not perfect. But I love you more than anything, I promise." She could see he was biting his cheek, trying not to cry.

So this was all a bout of stubborn Sam-ness? He was pretty perfect on the whole, but sometimes, if he tried to do everything by himself without asking for help, he messed up big time. Daniel had been absolutely right. She hugged him. "Get your coat, we are leaving. We'll talk when we know Lily is asleep." She put on her own coat and headed for the door. "Oh, I love you, by the way."

"Really?" He grabbed her by her wrist to stop her leaving. I wasn't even hard, but it made her cry out in pain. "Sorry! I don't think I can do anything right today," he said defeated.

"Of course, I love you. You may not be perfect, not today anyways, but normally you're pretty close."

"I love you Isabelle Rose Stanton." He kissed her, pushing her into the wall until there was no room between them." Never doubt that."

As they let go a picture came off the wall. With catlike reflexes Sam managed to stop it falling. It was a picture of a young lady.

"Hmm . . . she looks familiar."

"She looks a bit like you."

"Naw that's not it . . . Oh well, it will come to me." Carefully she hung it back on the wall. "Now let's get home to Lily," she said as she grabbed his hand and they got out of there.

CHAPTER TWENTY-THREE

They were in the car on their way home. Izzy drove as Sam seemed too jittery. She did have a lot of questions, though. So she started with, "What happened to Lily?"

Sam grimaced. "She threw up overnight. Stomach bug probably. She is taking it like a real trooper though. I had a hard time keeping her in bed earlier. Fine one moment, throwing up the next."

"Then you can't leave her with Mrs. Halford. She's not so young anymore – she can't run after her."

"Well, I needed to find you. When I had turned round you'd left. And later on you weren't picking up your phone. I was worried that you'd . . ." He couldn't finish the sentence.

"I wasn't? Oh sorry, I must have turned it off at the restaurant and forgot to turn it back on after I left." She hoped he would leave it at that. She didn't want to tell him that she had been with Daniel. It somehow seemed like cheating, even though nothing had happened.

Luckily other things were on his mind. "Please don't listen to the messages I left. They are a bit . . . frantic." Sam looked embarrassed.

"I won't." She probably would . . . She didn't care about "embarrassing" – all it meant was that he cared for her. But that did not answer why she had woken up in an empty bed. "Why did you leave without a word this morning?"

"It was so early, only 6 am, and we had been through quite a night. You were looking like an angel in your sleep, so I couldn't bring myself to it. Besides, I honestly I thought I could catch you before you woke. I didn't know Lily was that ill. My plan was to take Lily back to your apartment and make breakfast, and then wake you with a kiss. Only it didn't work out that way. I barely got upstairs, and we were back in the bathroom. One moment she'd be fine, and the next . . . well, you get the picture. It cleared up around noon. When I left earlier, hoping to catch you at Robert's, Lily was asleep and I asked Mrs. Halford to call me if anything happened. I haven't heard from her. So she's okay now, I think."

"Let's just get home quickly, shall we?" Keeping her eyes on the road, she grabbed his hand and squeezed it.

"Before we get there, I need you to know one thing. Last night was the best night of my life. You are absolutely amazing, Izzy, and I love you. I don't want you to doubt that for a moment."

That was exactly what she had wanted to hear this morning. It was good to hear it now though. Her heart leaped, and his words made it hard to concentrate on the road. Now that was no good – there was a little girl waiting for them, and they needed to get home in one piece. "I love you too, but can we save it till later? You are turning me to jelly and that's not helping me drive very well." The traffic light in front of her turned red. She took the opportunity to strengthen her words with a kiss . . . until honking from behind them indicated that she needed to pay attention again. Sam simply smiled. Luckily, home wasn't far.

Lily was still asleep when they got there. She hadn't had any more episodes. Mrs. Halford looked worried at Izzy. "Is everything alright between you two?"

She wondered how much Sam had told her, though the old lady could probably guess it was serious if Sam had left his daughter in her care in order to find Izzy. "Yes, we're fine." They would be. After another talk. Lily was their main focus now though.

The little girl was waking up, probably awoken by the noises in the house. "Hi, Aunt Izzy." She sounded so groggy, and her eyes looked watery.

Izzy bent down next to her bed. "How are you feeling, sweetie? Any nausea?"

Lily shook her head. She looked pale though, and Izzy worried. Putting her hand on Lily's forehead, Izzy concluded that Lily didn't have a temperature – which was good – but she did need to get hydrated again. "My throat hurts," the little girl croaked.

"Well then, let's make you some tea. Now, this tea might not taste so good, but it'll make you feel better – so I want you to drink it all, okay?"

Ginger would help the nausea and some honey would help issues with her throat. She went to the kitchen to make some. Sam looked miserable. His daughter not being well obviously was gnawing at him. "Hey, it's alright. Little girls get ill, but she'll be fine," Izzy assured him

"I should have been there last night. Not that I regret what happened between us, but as a father I should have been there for her," he whispered softly.

"I know how you feel." She felt it herself, even though it wasn't rational. Nothing could have prevented this. "These things happen, Sam. You are there for her. Always."

"Except for today," he said full of self-loathing.

"You went to get her as soon as you heard. And you are here now, Super Dad. Just look at her. Yeah she is ill, but she'll be fine." Water was boiled, and she poured it in a mug. Now the tea needed to steep for a while.

"Still, it doesn't feel right."

"Do you feel that what we did last night was wrong after all?" It was an important question for Izzy.

"No! Don't even think that. It was one of the best things I have ever done in my life, even if the timing was all wrong. And that is what I meant this morning when I said last night was not as it should be. NOT that anything is wrong with us being together, understood?"

"Yes." She still did not understand exactly, but it would have to wait until Lily was back asleep. "Tea is ready – want to bring it to her?"

He took the cup from her, and they went back to Lily's bedroom. Carefully they helped her up. She looked a bit peaky, but slowly color was coming back to her face. She was already smiling again.

"How was your ball last night, aunty?"

Izzy felt color rush to her cheeks. What could she tell about last night? She didn't want to tell her about John, and she couldn't tell her what happened after. "It was terrific – your daddy is a lovely dancer."

"He was your Prince Charming?" Such an innocent question. Sam was grinning away like a Cheshire Cat in the background.

Maybe she was getting whatever Lily had. Izzy certainly could not get any hotter. "Yes, he was. Do you want to watch some TV?" Izzy asked, quickly changing the subject to something more neutral. She knew Sam disapproved of the TV as a babysitter, but sick girls needed distraction. And so did Izzy. She popped in the DVD of Mary Poppins and watched the movie with Lily. She made sure Lily drank some more, and it seemed like her stomach had finally settled. Then they tried something to eat – applesauce on toast – which went down well. Lily finally fell asleep, as Izzy was telling her a story. She softly stroked the girl's hair and then tiptoed out of the room.

"Let's talk." Sam whispered.

Izzy nodded. They went into the kitchen where Sam quickly rustled something up. After all, they needed to eat as well.

"I love you. I have always loved you. So what happened last night was NOT a mistake do you hear me? Even if it did not go according to plan." He was cutting vegetables and throwing them into a stir-fry,

"What do you mean by plan?" It was sounding more cryptic by the minute.

"I always thought I would woo you, you'd fall madly in love with me, and then we would get together. But there was no wooing," he said disappointed. "Maybe that was a silly teenage dream."

She grinned. "But I did fall madly in love with you."

"You did? Why?" He served out the food and divided it on two plates. Time for dinner.

That was a good question. She hadn't thought about it, she just did. Slowly she chewed and thought about it. With him she was comfortable, she was herself. There was no show to put on. "Because you are . . . Sam. Sweet, caring, reliable."

"Girls don't fall for that. They want dangerous bad boys. That's why no woman has wanted me thus far." He could be so negative from time to time. Especially if it involved himself.

"Not true – lots of women would want you, you're just not available."

"No, I got you now." He smiled. She liked it when he smiled.

"That too, but to others you can come across as aloof. I know you are not. I know you're a sweet, handsome, caring guy. Somebody with whom I do not have to pretend to be anyone but me. Others don't always get to see that side of you. Which is fine, it means I get you all to myself." She gave him a peck on the cheek between bites.

"So what changed eventually? What made you fall in love? Because I have been trying for years."

"You kissed me." She blushed. "For real, not just a friendly peck." The Taylor party had been the start.

"That was it? That was all I needed to do??" he cried out in surprise.

"Yes. You became a man all of a sudden."

"All of a sudden. What was I before that?"

"I don't want to say. You won't want me anymore." The age difference was really not something she wanted to point out.

"Please, Izzy. Nothing can do that."

"Okay . . . Well, I'm a lot older than you. . ." she started carefully. It needed to be said some day, or it would keep nagging her forever. So why not now?

"Barely six years. Six years minus two days in fact. But who's counting?" That was true . . . He had been born just before her birthday. She had always seen him as a gift. That day she had first held him as a baby had been her birthday, in fact.

"That's a lot when you are kids. I remember you being born!" She wanted him to think about it, to realize it.

"I can't say the same, but Izzy . . . We're not kids anymore."

"No . . . I just got that."

"Just now?" Dinner was done and he cleared off the table. She followed him and they sat down on the couch. She was very happy Lily was asleep – this was a tough conversation. He poured Izzy a glass of wine, which she gladly accepted. It gave her time to regroup.

"Well, for a few months now. I just didn't know how to tell you. It seemed weird."

Sam nearly choked. "But I have been in love with you since I was twelve!"

"Twelve?" That was impossible, wasn't it? Surely she would have noticed. Alright he had acted weird toward her as a teenager. He had looked at her so strange sometimes. But all teenagers acted weird, so she had thought nothing of it.

"You were the first girl I fell in love with. And the one I am still in love with. That never changed."

"But . . . you married somebody else. Surely that means I was just a teenage crush."

"You seemed like an unattainable goal at the time. You still do, to be honest. She reminded me of you in the beginning. Biggest mistake I ever made. It turned out that was all show, but by then I had already married her."

"So why did you never ask me out? I mean, surely in all those years there were opportunities." Why hadn't she realized it herself? It would have both saved them so much grief.

"When? As a twelve year old? You saw me as Sophie's annoying brother for at least the next six years. Then I went to college, and we hardly saw each other, except over Christmas. And I was still Sophie's little brother. I could feel it in the way you treated me. Cute, but definitely a kid. Which was logical – I don't blame you for it. You were twenty-six, out there building your career. I was still stuck in college projects and books. Then I got married, got Lily. You moved here – single, yes, but by the time I got divorced, you were involved with John. I finally became a man in your eyes, but I got pushed into the friend zone. Where I was happy – you are the best friend I ever had. But I want more. Especially if you want me too."

"You really don't mind I'm older?" Maybe he did not mind now, but later as they got older . . .

"Why would I? I love you because you are beautiful, and kind, and funny, and smart. You're perfect."

She rolled her eyes. "A perfect mess maybe."

"No, that's not true." He grabbed her hand.

"Please, I don't do well on a pedestal. I'm so far from perfect."

"No, but you are perfect for me, for us. For Lily."

"You are looking for a mom for Lily," she stated. That would make sense. He would do anything for that girl, and so would she.

"No, she already has one. You. I don't need to sleep with you to make that happen. I want you for you."

"I'm her aunt. Not her mother."

"You're all the mom she knows, whether we are together or not. And I never want to change that, whatever happens between us. But I would really like it if something did happen between us."

"So what are you saying?"

"I already bought the cow, now I want the milk too?" He grinned mischievously with that silly comparison, and nibbled her neck.

She pushed him away. The imagery he brought on was horrendous. "That's . . . you're . . . you . . . argh . . . bad boy!" she slapped him playfully.

"Oh she thinks I'm a bad boy, now I know she really loves me." He grabbed her closer and hugged her.

On the one hand his "insult" was comforting. That was the Sam she knew . . . and loved. If he still dared to make remarks to her the day after they had been . . . intimate, than perhaps nothing was going to change between them. "By the way, you haven't bought the cow till you put a ring around my finger," she shot back.

"Oh I'll happily correct that." He slid off the couch onto one knee. "Would you marry me Isabelle Rose Stanton?"

"What? No! You don't compare me to a cow and ask me to marry you five seconds later. Besides you are not being serious. You told me you never wanted to get married again."

He looked hurt. "It would be different with you. I thought you wanted to get married before you were thirty-five. You got the dress."

"Yeah well, get back to me when you're serious. With barely more than a month to go till my birthday, I have pretty much given up on that. And that's okay. I did not buy the dress because I wanted to get married."

He gave her a confused look. "Then why did you buy it?"

"Because it's beautiful. It makes me feel beautiful."

"You are beautiful. With or without the dress." He got closer to whisper in her ear. "You look especially beautiful completely naked."

"I didn't feel that at the time the time I bought it."

"John." The bitterness in his voice was palatable.

"He's gone now." And good riddance.

"I want to make you feel beautiful every day."

"You do. You always did. I sometimes think that the fact that you were always nice to me and there to fall back when John was behaving like a horse's ass was the reason I was able to stay with him."

"So I should have treated you mean, and you would have dumped the loser?"

"Hey, it wasn't a reproach. And yes I might have dumped him, but I wouldn't be here with you. Or I would have married him by now thinking that all men were like that and I would never find anyone better anyways.

And that would have been really horrible." Sam was so much better than she had dared to dream. "You are everything I ever wanted in a man."

"Who is building pedestals now?"

"Well, it's true. Only thing that I can find wrong with you is that you are six years younger."

"And got a daughter with the wrong woman."

"Well I love Lily, so I don't see a problem there. I don't even want to think about her not being born. It was her time. Just not ours yet."

"You just want me for my daughter?" He was joking, she could hear it in his voice.

"Yes, that was it. That and the fact that you are AMAZING in bed," she fully agreed.

He grinned. "You want more of that?"

"Definitely," she agreed.

"Well then . . ." He pinned her down on the couch and started kissing her neck.

"Stop it – what if Lily wakes up? She can't find us like this," she suddenly realized.

"Then she knows I love you, so what?"

"Let's just take it slow until we figure everything out, okay?"

"I love you – there is not much to figure out there. Unless you don't love me."

"I have loved you from the moment you were born. But those feelings and what I feel for you now are completely different. So things are bound to change now."

"For the best," he assured her.

"We hope," she added. "We can't afford messing up."

"Isabelle Stanton, I would have never guessed you to be a pessimist."

"I'm not, just a realist. And if something does go wrong I don't want Lily to have to suffer. Do you want her to have to choose between us? I love you, and yes I hope and I do believe that we will make it. But just in case, I'd rather be safe than sorry."

"You do realize that I already know all there is to know about you?"

"Yes, and more probably. You sure you want anything to do with me, knowing all that?"

"Of course I do! And it goes both ways. You know more about me than any person on this planet Do you still want me? A single dad with little prospects?"

"Little prospects? You are putting yourself down – you are an amazingly talented man."

"In the bedroom?" He smiled wickedly and nuzzled her neck.

"Yes, there too. I love you."

"Please stop worrying then."

"I will. If we take it step by step. I don't want to risk hurting Lily."

"Alright. So what now? You are going home? I don't know how much longer I can restrain myself." The bulge in his pants confirmed that.

"Well, Lily is asleep. Maybe if we are quiet, and go to your bedroom . . ."

A wicked smile played upon Sam's face. He picked her up and carried her to the bedroom. Peeling off layers of clothes, they enjoyed each other until they fell asleep. Quietly of course, so as not to wake Lily.

CHAPTER TWENTY-FOUR

It was a week later. Izzy had never been happier. No man had ever made her feel like Sam did, inside and outside of the bedroom. He treated her like a princess – but not without his Sam humor, and she was ever so grateful for that. During the day, he was the Sam she knew and loved, and at night . . . he was the man she loved with a passion. There had been some close calls, as Lily had walked into the bedroom and caught Izzy in Sam's bed at one point, but they had explained it away by saying that Izzy had fallen asleep there. Lily had seemed satisfied by that and luckily had not seen that Izzy was completely naked under the covers. Or that her father was too. It had caused them to be extra careful, and get dressed immediately after sex. Izzy was there every night now, though. Where else would she be, except lying in his arms right until morning, after Lily had gone to bed?

They were together on the couch, just having read Lily her bedtime story. "Izzy, you're not settling for me, are you?"

She caressed his cheek. "No of course I am not. Why do you ask?"

"Well you describe me as loving, caring, reliable. That makes me sound like a puppy, not the man of your dreams."

She couldn't help laughing. "Oh dear, I guess it does. Would you rather have me gush over you? Because there is more than enough to gush over. Your beautiful soft curls for instance, your amazing looking bum, or your amazing talent to make me come like no man ever did. Because that's all true, but I am rather bad at saying such things out loud. It is my good-girl upbringing."

"You really think all that of me?" He sounded perked up already.

She nodded and started kissing his jaw. Telling him all this had stirred up lust.

"So you are definitely not settling?"

"No, handsome. I'll tell you a secret, and then I want you to forget all about it or you'll get far too conceited. To be honest, I was comparing every man to you. I wanted a guy just like you, but there was none. I was just too stupid to realize I could have you too. So I'm not settling. I'm going for the main prize."

"Which is?"

"My very own toy boy." That had a lovely ring to it.

He laughed. "Watch it, or I will have to start calling you a cougar."

"Well that is a vast improvement on a cow," she mocked him.

"How many times do I need to say sorry for that?"

"It's not how many times you say sorry, it is how you say it."

"Ahh . . . As your personal sex slave perhaps? I can't resist you anyways."

She liked that description. "Exactly."

"I created a monster." And he liked it – she could tell by the way his hands were caressing her sides.

"You know what they say: Be careful what you wish for, it might just come true." She snuggled closer. "By the way, I have been thinking about what you were saying about having a day to wear my dress and so on. And with my birthday coming up, I'm just gonna do it."

Sam looked confused. "What do you mean?"

"Wear it. Why wait? My birthday is the perfect opportunity outside of a wedding. You told me to live in the now. Well, I might get married, I might not." Which mainly depended on him at the moment. She did not feel that suffocating need for it anymore though. Just being with him was enough. "But that doesn't mean I can't have a sort of wedding-like celebration. That's all I wanted really. "That Day That Every Girl Dreams About." Where you wear the prettiest dress in the world, and all your friends are there. Women plan these things far before they have even met the guy of their dream, so it's not so much about the guy as it is about the dress and other pretty things. So, why not just go for such a celebration, without the groom? I mean, I doubt if men get as much of a kick out of a wedding. And if I am not a bride and I only have a month to plan it, I have no time to turn into a bridezilla, right?"

"I'd happily be part of something that makes you happy. And you'd never be a bridezilla. It's not in you."

"You never know. Anyways a wedding without a groom . . . Well technically that is just a big celebration."

"So you are gonna have a groom-less wedding?"

She nodded, "Yeah, basically."

"Are men still invited?"

"Of course . . . I can't celebrate my birthday without you. I need my Prince Charming to dance with. It will be like a ball."

"A golden ball, with you as a centerpiece in your beautiful golden dress. You deserve that."

"I like the way you think, Mr. Beauforde." She nibbled on his ear.

"Well, I know what my lady loves. What may I do to serve?"

"Oh I don't know. I'll need to arrange it all." A hundred little details, and that in the space of a month. It was good that she was a party planner.

"Just so you know, my offer still stands. I'll happily marry you and make all your dreams come true."

"No rushing into things. I love you, but I don't want to marry you just so you can regret it later."

"How could I ever regret that? I hardly call waiting for a woman for seventeen years rushing into things."

"After your divorce you said you never wanted to marry again." He was so broken back then. And she wasn't sure if he had fully healed.

"Well, I should have made an exception for you. I would gladly be your husband and marry you. Really."

"I think this should just be a birthday. Let's not complicate things." She couldn't explain it, but at this moment in time, it didn't feel right. She felt like she would be forcing him, no matter how many times he tried to assure her it was fine. Besides she might be able to pull off a party in a month, but a wedding?

"Alright, but if you change your mind, I'm available."

She started laughing. "You make it sound like I have a whole host of other offers."

"Well, I hope not. But I couldn't blame them for wanting to marry the most wonderful girl in the world."

It made her blush. "Don't worry, you are the only one I want." She sat herself in his lap and pressed herself as close against him as she could. They kissed before he lifted to the bedroom for more nightly activities. She couldn't imagine being with anybody else.

The next morning, she started planning her birthday in earnest. Sam was with her, trying to help, and so was Lily. What did one need for a ball? Well invites, that was one.

Sam immediately had a good idea. "I can photograph some of the lace on the dress, and then fade it until it is just a watermark background."

"That would be wonderful. Would you do that for me?"

"Anything you ask, you just write them," he offered, picking up his camera already.

"Okay, I need a venue. What do you think of the gallery? I'll call Claire."

"Lovely – it's an amazing place, and you'll look right at home there. It's perfect for a ball. Plus, John should not ruin your memory of that place."

She moved into whisper distance. "What you mean, ruined? John gave me the last push I needed to be driven straight in your arms. I think we should send him a thank you note."

"Tempting, very tempting."

"I am NOT inviting him for my birthday, though."

Sam laughed. "I wouldn't dream of it." Then he headed to her bedroom. To photograph the dress, that was.

Lily came and sat on her lap. "I drew a birthday cake for you."

"Thank you, sweetie. But it's not my birthday yet."

"I know. But maybe you can use it?" The little girl looked so expectantly. She would find a way to incorporate it. She had to now.

Claire was delighted by the idea and even offered to let her use the gallery for the night free of charge, seeing how much work she had put in the opening. "You'll have to invite Daniel, though."

With the phone in her hand, Izzy quickly looked for a more quiet spot where she would not be overheard, and ended up locking herself in in the bathroom. "I'm with Sam now."

"Why are you whispering?" Claire asked.

"We haven't told anyone yet, and he and his daughter are here today. She doesn't know yet."

"Well, I am delighted. But I still think you should invite Daniel. That man does not deserve to be single, and maybe he will meet somebody there. One of your friends maybe, or your lovely colleagues . . . Francesca, Karin . . . Susan might be a bit too old for him, though."

Well, if Izzy could date a younger man, why not Susan? She was a classic beauty. Fran too. Karin, however, she did not wish upon anybody. Izzy owed Daniel one, maybe she should invite him . . . and steer him away from Karin. Sophie would love him, and so would pretty much any other woman she was going to invite. Including the married ones. Could she do that to Daniel? He had said he hated being an object. And how was she going to introduce him to Sam? If he mentioned that lunch the day after the opening, she was not sure how Sam would react. Nothing had happened, but the fact was she had gone out with another man after the most wonderful night of her life. And a very good-looking man, too. She did not want to hurt Sam, or make him doubt her love for him.

On the other hand Daniel would even out the boy-girl ratio of her guest list. Mike hardly counted as a guy, that was for sure, and she did not know that many men in general. If she asked Daniel not to mention anything, he probably would. At this rate everybody except Lily and their parents would know about her and Sam. Oh well. "I'll invite him . . . And thank you so much for doing this."

"Gladly . . . as long as I am invited of course."

"Of course! You and Anton are more than welcome. I was already counting on you coming, in fact."

Venue – done. Invites – in progress. What to wear was an easy one. What else? Food and drink. She would need to ask Robert how to make a

Bohème because she definitely wanted those served. So he was the next person she called.

"Hi Robert, do you know any bartenders I can hire. For one night – preferably cute looking." Else Sophie would be complaining.

"What's it for?" Logical question, maybe she should have mentioned that first.

"My birthday party next month."

"What about me? I'd be happy to do it," he immediately offered.

"Are you sure?"

"What, am I not cute enough?"

Why hadn't she thought of that? Imagining Robert behind a bar other than his own was hard, though. "Of course you are, but I wasn't sure you were okay with standing behind a bar that wasn't yours."

"For you, anything, dearie. I'll take the night off, and I'll be there. Unless you don't want me there?"

"Of course I want you there! But taking a night off just to work at my party, that does not seem a fair trade."

"Izzy, I am happiest behind a bar. Feels safe, familiar. Just standing around with a drink in my hand, poured by someone else feels completely unnatural. So please . . . You need a bartender, and I would love to do it."

"Alright. But I am afraid you'll also have to show my friend Sophie the ropes. She has already been pressuring me about it."

"I'd love to. Any friend of yours is a friend of mine. Now, how are things between you and Sam?"

A blush rose to her cheeks. Of course he already knew everything, with Sam coming to him that day. "Fine . . ."

"Finally! Well, I will happy to see the both of you on your birthday. And any other time you want to drop by in the meantime as well."

"We are taking it slow, though. For Lily's sake. So she doesn't know yet." That was the second time she had to say that, and each time she did, it nagged a little more.

"Alright, I won't tell anyone. So don't worry about the drinks, I'll take care of it all."

"Thank you."

Drinks done. That left food, cake and decorations, but for that she needed to be at work and get her contact list. So all that would have to wait till Monday.

Sam was in the living room with Lily on his lap. He had already taken the pictures, and now he was playing with them on his computer. Lily was there to comment on everything.

"Ah, there you are. Me and my little helper have been hard at work. Tell me which option you like." He showed her three versions: one that showed the dress from the back, one that was a layer of lace on a white background, and one where he had stylized the pattern of the lace to make a lace-like background.

"Number three. A hint of the dress without showing it. They won't know the connection until they see the dress itself. And it has that old-world look about it." She softly stroked his back. "I didn't know you were so good with graphics as well."

"I like that one best too, Aunt Izzy," Lily agreed. "Can I come to your party too?"

"Of course you can." It was Izzy's birthday, and that would not be complete without her favorite girl.

"Can I wear my dress?"

"Yes, that would be lovely. Would you like to be a flower girl perhaps?" It had just popped up in Izzy's head. Because what sort of wedding-like ball would be complete without that?

Lily nodded.

"Do you know what a flower girl does?"

The little girl shook her head. "No."

"It means you get to sprinkle rose petals in front of the bri . . . in front of me on the floor."

A deep thinking frown ran across Lily's face. "Like a fairy?"

Izzy smiled. "Yes, like just a fairy."

"I can do that." Lily looked overjoyed.

Sam let a first draft of the invite roll out of the printer. "The professionals will do a better job, especially if you choose a golden metallic paint for the background. Now just add some text and decide who you want to invite."

"Yeah . . ." Oh dear. She hated that sort of stuff. It was like a popularity contest. She did not want to hurt anybody, but on her birthday, she only wanted to see the people she liked. Besides some people lived so far away it was unlikely they would come anyways. Sophie would be coming though . . . and their parents. Wild horses would not keep them away. She started making a list of people who she would like to come, hoping she would not forget anyone important.

Monday, she told her colleagues of her plans. Susan immediately offered to help. Anything that needed arranging, she would take care of. Knowing, Susan that meant everything would run smoothly.

Francesca, who loved to bake, offered to make the cake. Well, cakes – cupcakes to be exact – sumptuous in taste, gorgeously decorated. It was perfect for what Izzy had in mind. Fran had been dying for such an opportunity to show off her baking skills. And an opportunity to make up for her disastrous date with her cousin, she said.

"But I pay for all the ingredients. I insist. Baking for so many people is a big enough present," Izzy pleaded.

Eventually even Karin offered her help when Izzy mentioned her plans for her amazing dress . . . Izzy did not mention that was a wedding dress. They would see that on the night itself. In her previous job, Karin had been a hairdresser, and she promised to help Izzy with her hair on the big day. It humbled Izzy to know how many people wanted to help. The caterer offered her a discount, the florist promised to bring in her favorite flowers – everybody she ever worked with pitched in to give her party that little bit extra.

Susan came back in. "How about the drinks, an open bar? I don't see that on your list. And if I remember correctly, Claire doesn't have her own staff for that."

"Already arranged. A friend is taking of all that. All I have to deal with is the food"

"Good, I don't like dealing with bartenders. We don't get along."

"I have got a very nice bartender. You will love him." Robert was an absolute dear. And she could not see Susan hating him.

The invites needed to be mailed . . . in golden envelopes. The sooner the better. Lily's drawing would become the seal. You couldn't get any more authentic than that. The guest list was done. There were now about ninety people on her list. She hoped all would come, but she was afraid it was all pretty short notice, especially for somebody that planned all other parties meticulously. Izzy also still needed a text for the invite, so she did some research. She wanted the invite to sound Victorian as well as look it, like it could have been written over a century ago. Using antique invitations as a guide she decided upon the following text:

Dear …., The honor of your presence is requested on the evening of the 27th of March, as we celebrate Isabelle Stanton's 35th birthday at a Golden Ball held at the Thompson Gallery. We look forward to you coming and joining us on this special day. Dress code: Gold. Presents are not required – just your company.

Izzy insisted on that last sentence. She did not need anything for her birthday – just her friends.

CHAPTER TWENTY-FIVE

Izzy yawned. Time to get some beauty sleep. It was the night before the big day. Everybody was here. Her parents and the Beaufordes including Sophie had arrived yesterday, just in time to celebrate Sam's birthday as well – he hadn't want a fuss though. She hated not being able to spend the night with him, but telling their parents what they had been up to this past month, now that would be an entirely different matter. They probably would be happy for them, but . . . they would not leave them alone either, that was for sure. She'd probably be asked to give them another grandchild on the spot.

So there she was on her own couch, not being able to sleep. It was 1:00 am. Her parents were in her bed, and Sophie was on the guest bed. Sam had his own parents sleeping in his bed. She so longed for him. She wanted to be with him on the evening before her birthday. She wanted to be with him every night. Getting his key out of her purse she quietly got up and snuck out the door. He probably was asleep but she wanted to feel his warm body against hers. Even if it was just for a few minutes.

So she broke into his house ever so quietly, like a cat burglar.

Not quiet enough, though. "Lily, is that you?" sounded the groggy voice from the couch.

She knelt down on the floor beside him. "Not quite."

"Izzy, what are you doing here. Come here, it's way too cold without a blanket." Arms went around her, as he enveloped her in his warmth.

"I couldn't sleep." she softly whispered.

"Yeah I am having trouble with that too. But you, you need your rest for tomorrow. Gotta look beautiful on your birthday. Not that you won't, even if you don't get a wink of sleep. But you might fall asleep before the party gets started. And we can't have that, can we?"

"How do you think we ended up on the couch when our family is sleeping in our beds?"

"Extreme lack of planning?" he suggested.

"Hey, I plan everything to a tee." Although this probably the worst she had ever done. She wouldn't have been able to pull it off if it had not been for Susan, who had pulled quite a few strings.

"Said the woman sleeping on her own couch."

"Sophie offered to trade me, but I said it would be okay. I hardly could sneak by her as well to see you, could I?"

"You are missing me that badly?"

"Of course I am. It's horrible watching you and having to hold back. I want your arms wrapping around me at night. How did I ever manage without those?"

"Two more days, and they'll all be home again."

"Maybe we should just tell everybody."

"You're sure?"

Yes, she was now. "I'm sure that I never want any other man besides you. I was afraid things might change between us but that hasn't happened, and I don't think it ever will. I should have remembered that we have practically been living together for the past three years. And what has changed . . . Well that has just added to our relationship." Somehow she hoped he would ask her to marry him again. If he asked now, she would say yes without hesitation.

He didn't though. In fact he remained quiet for a while, before saying: "Well if we are going to tell everybody, wait until the party is over. Else that will be all that is on their mind the whole day. You want to enjoy your birthday first."

A light behind them switch on, and a little girl walked toward them. "Daddy I can't sleep. Oh hi Aunt Izzy." She seemed hardly surprised to see her. Maybe she knew more than the grown-ups thought she did.

"We can't either, sweet pea." Izzy took Lily in her arms.

"Yes, couches are really uncomfortable," Sam groaned.

"You can sleep with me!" Was it fair to take advantage of a little girl's offer? Lily's bed was a small double. It would be a bit of a squeeze to get them all on there, but not impossible. And it would sure beat another night on the couch alone.

"Sure you don't mind, sweetie?"

Lily shook her head, and they followed her to bed. They just about all fit, and with Lily being so little, it wasn't uncomfortable. It wasn't the same as being in bed with just Sam, but it sure was close. Izzy fell asleep in a matter of minutes.

Waking up on her birthday with Lily in her arms, and Sam with his arms around the both of them was just perfect. She could not have asked for a better present. There had been few raised eyebrows, but nobody had even mentioned it, which was a bit of a surprise to Izzy. She was waiting for a sneer from Sophie, but it did not come. Maybe because it was her birthday. After all, the golden rule in their families was "Be nice to the birthday girl!"

Breakfast, at Sam's of course, had come with a with a few presents. More books, and from Lily and Sam a set of beautiful flower pins and a golden hair comb, which she was definitely going to use later tonight when she did her hair. Like always, the presents were well thought out and beautiful.

"Thank you so much," she said, hugging both of them.

Then it was time to plan the rest of the day. The gallery needed to be made ready for the party. Susan would look after deliveries, Robert would be arriving with the drinks, and a crew was coming in to decorate it. Francesca and Karin would be there too at several points in the day, and of course her family wanted to help. Izzy was afraid they would mostly be in the way though. She sent Sophie and both their mothers to Tina's to find dresses almost as wonderful as hers. Gold of course. The men would be looking after Lily until Sam came back from work. She was already wrapping them round her little finger.

Claire was the first to greet her at the gallery. "You really did not need to be here so early – I have the keys, I can let myself in."

"Yes, but then you might have accidentally seen your gift before I was there to give it to you," Claire said, pulling her along.

"Claire, you shouldn't. You're already giving me this space for free."

"But birthdays are nothing without gifts, so come on." There was a curtain draped over a canvas. Izzy slowly pulled it away. It was from the artist she had liked best, found as they had been picking out works for the gallery. A flowery scene in shades of fuchsia.

"Do you like it?" The voice was from Tom, the artist who had painted it.

"Yes it is gorgeous. Oh, I haven't invited you. Do you want to come tonight?"

"Yes, I'd be happy to." Another man on her list. Wonderful.

She went out to find Susan, only to find that she was stuck in traffic, so it was good that Izzy had arrived early. Robert came in with all sort of spirits, and a hug for the birthday girl, of course.

"I have something I want you to try. I know it is early so just take a small sip, but if you like it, I'll serve it next to the Bohèmes tonight." He walked through to the bar. "Wow this place is fantastic. I'd almost trade in my own bar to work in."

"Yes I know. It's very grand. That's why I like it so much."

Placing his bottles on the empty shelves, Robert immediately started mixing. "It's very posh though. I might need to shave before standing out here tonight."

"No, designer stubble is very modern these days. Keep it as you are."

"Alright . . . And one Irish Gold, for the lady. Tell me if you think it worthy to serve at your party."

"I'm sure it is . . ." She took a sip. "Oh my god, this is delicious."

"Now don't drink too much, it's not even past eleven o'clock," he warned her.

Izzy giggled. "It's my birthday, I'm allowed."

Suddenly there was a great commotion from the hall. Glass was tumbling over. "Who put those bottles here?" an angry female voice said.

Robert looked guilty. "Aye, they would be mine. I was getting everything in here to the bar but I wasn't quite done yet, so I left it there."

"Well, don't apologize to me, but to my party planner," Izzy said, recognizing the voice as Susan's.

"I thought you were . . ."

"A colleague offered to take over so I can actually enjoy the day without working. I think she just tripped over your bottles, though. And she does not sound very happy about it."

"I'll go say I am sorry and get them out of the way." With that Robert walked off to find the woman who had stumbled over his wares.

"Suzy? Susan, is it really you?" Robert's voice sounded from the next room. Izzy was surprised. Susan did not seem the bar type – in fact she said she hated them. She did not get time to satisfy her curiosity though. Her phone rang. Mike.

"Good morning, birthday girl! I hope you are having a great day." So far so good. If she just could know what was going on in the next room, it would be even better. "I have a question for you. I have met someone . . . a guy."

"You have a boyfriend?" Izzy asked with a smile.

"Yes, yes I guess you can say that." She could hear Mike perk up. "And I was wondering if I could bring him.

"Of c. . ..Um, wait. Only if you promise to do at least one dance with each lady."

"Are you trying to convert me?"

"Never! But my party has a chronic lack of men and I know you are a very good dancer." Almost as good as Sam.

"Alright, because it's you. And I bet your friends are just as fantastic as you. What if I had said no?"

"Well, nothing. I am very curious about your beau, so I would still want to meet him."

"By the way, how are things between you and Sam?" Of course Mike would want to know.

"Fine." She couldn't tell him as well, it would not be fair to her parents who were still in the dark.

"Just fine?"

Suddenly the noises in the other room got louder. "No, no – you don't get to do this to me, not after all this time." With that Susan stormed passed Izzy toward the back entrance.

Izzy was too stunned to stop her. "Sorry Mike, I got to go," she said putting down the phone.

Robert was still there, looking devastated – as if he had just lost everything. She went over to question him about what just happened. "What's going on? What just happened?"

"That's her. She's the one that got away." There was despair in his voice.

Susan? She is the one you have been pining over?" And suddenly she realized who she had seen in the photo at his apartment – Susan, looking still very young.

He simply nodded. A tear rolled down his cheek and he quickly turned away. "I'll be back later, alright? I promised you I'd do your party and I will. Or I'll find someone to replace me.

"No, you stay right here. I'll go talk to her. She obviously still has feelings for you – otherwise she wouldn't have reacted that way. Don't be a coward now. You have been searching for her for years. And now you found her, you don't just give up – understood?"

"I don't want to mess up her life." She had never seen Robert this lost.

"You're not, there is nothing to mess up – she's single. Has been for as long as I've known her. Just . . . stay here." This was not how these stories were supposed to end. You did not find somebody, just to lose them again. Certainly not on her birthday. This story needed a happy ending.

She found Susan outside on the steps, crying. She had never seen her this . . . fragile. Izzy quickly put her arms around her.

"Twenty years it took me . . . twenty years to get over him. And all he has to say is hello, and it's all back. Everything, the feelings, the pain, all of it."

"He still loves you. He never stopped." If there was one thing Izzy was certain of, it was that.

"How do you know?"

"Because he told me. Before I knew it was you he was talking about. He told me about this woman he loved more than anything."

"He left me. He just said goodbye one day, told me he had to go, no forwarding address, nothing." Susan was shaking and Izzy softly stroked her back.

"He went back to Ireland to take care of his dad," she explained.

"Why didn't he tell me, I would have gone with him."

"I . . . I don't know . . . You'll need to ask him." She did not have the answers. She sure hoped Robert did though.

"I don't think I can," Susan whispered.

"Sure you can – you are Susan, no one messes with you. Besides, even if nothing comes of it, and you just talk, you need closure."

"I wasn't like this back then. I was a bit of . . . a dreamer I guess. And right now . . ." She obviously could not finish the sentence. Izzy felt so sorry for her.

It was hard to imagine. Susan was the most in-control woman Izzy knew. She even aspired to be like her, but most days her head was just too chaotic. "Everybody changes. I bet he did as well."

"He's still as handsome as ever. Different yes, but still . . ."

"Go see him. Talk. For me, if you don't do it for yourself," Izzy pleaded.

"How do I look?"

Izzy opted for the honest answer. "Like a mess – but I doubt he'll care. He wasn't looking much better when I left him. I think he just wants talk to you."

"I was young, only twenty-five back then. Twenty years of wear and tear. I have to make some effort at least."

"Alright, I'll smuggle you into the bathroom. But please tell me you'll talk to him," Izzy begged.

Susan nodded. Izzy went in first to hold Robert back and to see if he was still there, which thankfully he was. He was stocking his bar as promised, and she told him to hold on just a little while longer. Then she went back to Susan to help her.

"I'm sorry, I'm not much use to you, am I?" Susan apologized, washing her face, and gently dabbing it dry, trying to erase the tear stains.

"That's alright, I'll manage. I'm a party planner, aren't I?" Izzy rummaged in her purse to find some makeup to help Susan. If anyone deserved some happiness it was her and Robert.

"The best one I know." Susan agreed, reapplying her washed out mascara.

"After you."

"Not true. You have a natural vision of what the client wants that's better than anybody else has."

"You are better at getting stuff done though." She brushed Susan's hair until it looked back in place again. "There, done. You go to Claire's office, and I'll send Robert to you so you'll have some privacy."

Doing as promised, she left them alone in there. They needed this opportunity to talk, even if Izzy was dying to know what was going on. Luckily, Francesca arrived with the cakes to distract her.

"Here they are, all 110 of them." She carted in five boxes in one go. "I'll be right back with the stand and the bigger cake that you can cut and that that holds the candles."

"Not thirty-five I hope?"

"No, just two number candles – we don't want to burn the place down." Francesca giggled.

"Thanks a lot. By the way, I don't have THAT many guests."

"Best to have some spare I have always noticed. In case extra people come along, or if you have no time to eat lunch. Want one now?" It was just about twelve o'clock. Izzy needed to get a move on – the florist could arrive any minute, and so could the decorating team.

"Oh, heck why not. I do still need to fit in my dress tonight, though." She got handed a cupcake that had been iced to look just like a rose. "Beautiful."

"Oh yes, the mysterious dress. Is it really as gorgeous as the rumors say they are?"

With a mouth full of delicious chocolate cake, Izzy could only nod in agreement. Sophie and their mothers arrived to see if there was anything they could help her with. They seemed very excited.

"That shop is like heaven!" Sophie cheered.

"I know, did you see the shoes as well?" Izzy wanted to know.

"Yes, we had to pry her out of there, or she would have moved in permanently," her mother said. "Where are your helpers?"

"Arriving any minute."

"Where's Susan?" Fran asked, realizing she should be there.

"Talking to somebody. She will be back in a while I am sure." And if not Izzy would deal with things herself.

Sophie let out a wolf-whistle. "Hello gorgeous."

Izzy looked around to see what was the matter. "Daniel, what are you doing here. You aren't supposed to be here till tonight."

"My screens need to be moved to make room for your party. So I thought I'd better keep an eye on things. If you want something done, do it yourself. That's what I learned."

"Sounds to me like you need better friends." Izzy noticed. Everybody was here to help her after all.

He winked. "Working on it."

"Izzy are you dating him?" Sophie whispered in her ear.

"No. And yes you can, he's single. Try to show some restraint though. And for god's sake, let him do his job first. Tonight, however, he's yours."

The screens were really ingenious – he moved them away like it was nothing, paintings still on. More and more people came in to help turn the room into her dream. "Is it okay if I bring a friend tonight?" Daniel asked. "Frank, my business partner and roommate. I think you'll like him."

"But I'm already spoken for," Izzy smiled out of earshot from her family.

"I know – I'm very happy for you that it worked out."

"You were completely right, you know that?"

"That's very good to know, I usually get it wrong when it comes to relationships. Maybe I should start dating men," he laughed.

"I'm sure the female population would be very disappointed. My friend Sophie certainly will be. But bring your friend tonight. I'm sure you'll both have a great time."

Her guest list was growing all of a sudden, with lots of lovely men being added to the equation. Who knows where this night might lead?

Right at that moment, Robert and Susan reappeared, kissing. Francesca's mouth fell open. Izzy, however, could do nothing but smile. Now that was a lovely birthday gift.

CHAPTER TWENTY-SIX

It was time for her birthday party. Her dress was on, and her hair had been expertly done by Karin. She had to agree – she would never been able to do this herself. She looked like a princess – even her mother had said so. So, no trip to the insane asylum just yet. The beautiful comb that Sam's had given her had been placed into her hair, and she was wearing his necklace.

Sam himself had snuck in earlier to kiss her, and she had to say it had been the best part of her birthday. Not that the rest was bad. The day had been lovely. Lots of work – but everybody had pitched in, making it joyous in itself. Lily was playing in her dress, getting petals all over Claire's office, which was now a makeshift powder room. Izzy hoped there would be some petals left to sprinkle in front of her as she went out – but if not, that was fine too.

Thirty-five. This was not how she had expected her life to be at this age. But it was alright. She was at peace with it. She was happy and healthy, surrounded by friends – what more could she want? These last few months had been an education on what really mattered, and today she felt like she was graduating. So some people would probably think it weird she was wearing a wedding dress. So what? She had finally truly found herself. And she was happier than she had ever felt in her life.

Susan knocked. "I think everybody is here. Time for the lady of the evening to take center stage and declare your ball open."

"You are glowing, Susan," Izzy smiled. She was so extremely happy for the both of them.

"Yes, well . . . Yes! Thank you for convincing me to talk to him. I don't know what the future will bring, but it is good to know he didn't just dump me. And who knows?"

Sophie entered as well. "Come on Izzy, you are missing your own party!" Lily showered her in a cloud of petals, getting some in her own hair.

Carefully Izzy picked them out again. "Don't worry, I'm coming." She hated to admit it, but she felt a little nervous. Well, a lot nervous, really, about how people would feel when she stepped out there in a minute. Which was stupid. She wanted this, she had organized all of this. The speech was the finalization, the wedding part of it, vows for herself and to herself, so she would never forget and let herself be taken for granted again. Not that Sam ever would, she was sure of that. Now, everybody out there was a friend of hers, that at one point of her life had been there for her. So what was there to be afraid of?

Everything, apparently, and especially the fact that everybody she knew and respected was out there. They were bound to judge her one way or another. Why did she have to do this? She could just walk out there and party with her friends, but no – she had to take the difficult route. Oh well, the speech was prepared. She closed her eyes and took a few deep breaths to calm herself. They're all your friends, they love you she ran as a mantra through her head.

"But none as much as I do." Obviously she had not just been saying it in her mind.

She felt a kiss in her neck, and opened her eyes. It was just her, Lily, and now Sam in the room. Sophie and Susan had left. "Hey you," she said leaning back into his embrace, "You're looking very handsome in that tux."

"Cocktail for milady? Robert said you might need one." He held a La Bohème in front of her.

"Thank you." She took a sip, which seemed to have the right effect.

"Calm down, beautiful. Everyone is gonna love it."

"And what if they don't – what if they think I am crazy?"

"Then they are not your real friends and I will personally toss them out of here," he promised.

"You thought I was crazy."

"That was different. That was just about the money, never about the dress itself. The dress makes you look absolutely glorious." He kissed her neck. "And you did find the occasion to wear it."

"Yes, yes I did." And people were now waiting to see it. He was right – anybody that made fun of her was no real friend.

"Now, are you ready or is there anything else my birthday girl wants tonight?"

"Yes, you."

"You already got me."

"I meant in that other way, in a bedroom with just a two of us." she whispered in his ear.

"Ah. That one might be tough with both our families staying here."

"I know." Izzy put down the drink. "Alright let's do this before I lose my nerve again. Will you walk out with me?"

"Gladly." He took her hand, and Lily opened the door for them.

The little girl looked ever so happy. Twirling around like a real fairy, she spread the petals around, covering everybody, like a floral baptism. Izzy could not help laughing, and neither could the guests. Everyone looked beautiful and had managed to keep to the "gold" dress code stipulated in the invitation – even the men, who had tiny gold details on their tuxes. Mike had even taken it a step further, and was wearing a golden dinner jacket. Well, any last doubts about his nature seemed to be laid to rest by that, and indeed he had a very cute man on his arm. Izzy felt happy for him.

Everybody was looking at her, but nobody seemed to be judging her, which was a relief. Her mother was crying though, overcome with emotion like a true mother-of-the-bride. Izzy took center stage, looking around her. Almost everyone had come, even though it had been short notice.

A little nervously, she coughed. It was all or nothing.

"Yes, you are seeing it right, I am wearing a wedding dress. And no, I am not getting married tonight." Maybe she should have taken Sam up on his offer of marriage. It would have been a lot less scary, and he would have been here beside her now. But she did not want to make him do anything he did not want to do, just so she could have her wish come true and be married at thirty-five. This speech, this vow was about freedom – how could she take his, just to fulfill her silly childhood fantasies.

People were waiting for her to continue, though. "I bought this dress six months ago, in a state of . . . delirium. But I couldn't help myself – I saw it and had to have it, for it was and is the most beautiful thing I have ever seen. It was probably the silliest thing I have ever done, and as Sophie will testify, that is saying something. It's probably also one of the best decisions I have ever made. Why? Because I found myself. Perhaps that sounds silly to you. But ask yourself the following question. How often do we take ourselves for granted? Too often I bet. So was I. Until I saw this dress, and bought it. Sam will tell you it was ridiculously expensive. It is – it's worth more than my car is. Which is why I had to smuggle it past him the day I bought it. It took me a week to own up."

"Just for the record, I'm fine with it now," Sam interrupted. "I think you look absolutely beautiful in it."

"Hear, hear!" some people in the crowd cheered.

Izzy continued, "Anyways, there I was with a beautiful dress, and no idea what to do with it. I wondered if I had done the right thing. But every time I put it on, I fell more in love with it – and there was no way I could return it. So what to do with it? What do you do if you have a wedding dress and no wedding?"

"You get yourself a groom!" somebody at the back yelled. She wasn't sure, but it might have been Karin.

"Wrong." Izzy let out a nervous laugh. "I got to admit that was exactly what I thought at first, though. I thought having the dress meant I had to find the guy to go with and thus started a desperate search to find Mr. Right. What I found was exactly the opposite. Active seeking seemed to lead to the most self-absorbed pricks you can imagine. Of course, I met some nice guys too, mostly by accident . . ." She looked at Robert. ". . . But they were not for me. And it seems silly. The road to love may lead to a few toads, but to kiss them all just so you can wear a dress is not the way to go, I can tell you."

People laughed. With her, Izzy hoped, not at her.

"But that is what happens. We have got it in our mind that we need a man to make the most special day, the day we dreamed of all our lives, possible. And that is not right. We are setting ourselves up for disaster when we do that, believe me. Because it tells us that we are not enough on our own. That we need a man to make the picture whole." She took a deep breath and paused a second. "Luckily, I have a few good friends to tell me that I am enough."

"More than enough. You are terrific." Sam. Who else?

"Thank you." It nearly brought tears to her eyes – and she wasn't done yet, so she had swallow them back. "And that helped finding myself, along with a wonderful dress, which let me know I was beautiful, and gives me that feeling every time I put it on. Such a dress is worth a party. Even if it's without groom. So here we are."

People applauded, but she had more to say.

"Of course, in the end, the dress is not important. The way it makes me feel *is*. I feel special when I wear it. It's a feeling every woman, everyone should have every day, without having to wait for anybody else. And that is what today is about. To remind myself I am special, and that I always should be true to myself. Now, you might not need a wedding dress to do that, but anything can make you feel that way. If you find that, don't let it go. Go for it, even if it is silly, and have no regrets. That way you can celebrate your beauty, your uniqueness every day. What I want to say is that you need to value yourself. And sometimes you need a push in the right direction for that. Like a wedding dress . . . but really, it can be anything you like – just as long as you don't let anybody take you for granted." Like John had done over the years – but she did not want to think about him on a day as wonderful as this. He wasn't worth wasting another second worrying about, because there was no way he could hurt her anymore. Sam would never take her for granted, or put her down. He never had in all the time she had known him, and that was a lifetime. If only she had known his feelings earlier, she would never have gotten involved with John.

She looked around the room at the faces of her friends. They were all smiling, Sam especially. "But enough of this. Since I am wearing this dress, and it is my birthday, let's cut the cake and party."

Fran had been waiting for this moment to wheel the tower of cupcakes in. On the top tier, there was the normal-sized cake, with two candles burning, shaped like a three and a five. Izzy blew them out and cut a slice from the cake. She had to admit Fran was a terrific baker – it was delicious. Time to hand out the cupcakes. Even if she wanted to keep them all to herself.

After singing the obligatory "Happy Birthday," everybody cheered, and the music started again. People came up to her to congratulate her, most of them bearing gifts, even though the invite had said not to bother.

Tina, who also had been invited, came up to her. "Your speech was so inspirational, it makes me want to create a dress like that . . . Though I am not sure I can top yours. It's not even that 'wedding-like'. If you hadn't told everybody, I think most of them would have just thought you were wearing the ballgown of the year. Maybe I should just stick to shoes."

"Well they are fabulous." Izzy stuck out her foot from under the dress. "And I bet they inspire others as well."

"Oh my, you are wearing them, I hadn't even seen it."

"The dress covers them completely, so that's no surprise. They just make me feel good, just like the dress does. And when I run off at the stroke of midnight, just before my car turns back into a pumpkin, my prince can find the shoe, put it back on my foot and marry me."

"I thought you were done looking for a prince? Wasn't that what you just told us?"

"Well I am done actively searching, because that is when it goes wrong. I won't complain if he happens to find me." She leaned closer to Tina. "And to be honest, I think he already did. Just when I had stopped looking."

"Sam?" she asked, and Izzy simply nodded. She needed to tell her family soon or she was just gonna burst. . . Either that or jump his bones. "By the way, who is Mister Blond God over there," Tina wanted to know.

Izzy did not even have to look. "Daniel. He's single but you'll have a lot of competition." Sophie was already over there, though right now she seemed to be talking to the friend he had brought along.

"Is that the carpenter Claire talked about?"

"Yes."

"Is he any good? The shop is in dire need of some new display closets. "

"I think so, but go have a look at the screens he did. Ask him about it, if you're interested." She was kind of betraying Sophie, but knowing her so well, she knew he wasn't her type anyways. He was too calm – Sophie needed somebody that gave her as good as she got. Someone whom she could spar with.

More people came by to congratulate her, and tell her they admired her speech. Some told her they admired the guts it took to wear that dress. Mike came too, with his new boyfriend.

"Can I have this dance?" he asked.

"Thought you'd get it out of the way?" she giggled.

"Not at all dear, but you look so magical, we both feel the need to dance with you." He introduced Lucas, a handsome young man, with an undeniable sense of style. Lucas said he thought her speech was spectacular, and congratulated her on her courage. They all danced together in a strange nouveau-regency kind of way which made her laugh, conversing as they moved through the room. People looked bemused, but Izzy could care less. This was her having fun. She couldn't possibly make more of a spectacle of herself than she already had, and Sam was right. Anyone making fun of her was no real friend. Lucas was delightful, the perfect match for Mike. Claire joined their circle, also very curious of Mike's new beau. More and more people joined until all of a sudden they seemed to be in a circle dance, which unintentionally complimented the spirit of the evening perfectly. It brought a tear to Izzy's eye.

After dancing she caught up with Robert. He only had eyes for Susan though, and she couldn't blame him. "Thank you so much. I don't know what you said to her, but it helped." He poured her a cocktail.

"I just told her she owed it to herself to talk to you. The rest you did yourself."

"Well I feel like my life just turned over a new leaf. So thank you."

She was happy for them but slightly jealous. Everybody seemed to have found somebody and she just wanted one thing. Sam.

Her mother joined her. "What a great party, dear. I always thought I would be dancing on your wedding by now, but this seems to be the next best thing. It's lovely."

Stick the knife right in, won't you? Izzy loved her mother dearly, but when it came to old-fashioned ideas, her mom's bluntness bordered on cruelty.

"Does this mean you are giving up on men altogether?" her mom continued. "It's alright if you are lesbian, you know."

Izzy choked on her cocktail. "What???"

"Well I saw you dancing with those gay men . . ."

"Mother, dancing with gay men does not make me lesbian. Sorry – I need to go. I love you but I need a glass of water. " One minute longer and she might start screaming. Izzy knew that tone in her mother's voice all too well.. What was wrong with being lesbian anyways? Nothing. She wasn't, though. She was in love with the most amazing man in the world. And she needed him.

She looked for Sam, who seemed to be lost in the crowd. Finally she found him. With his camera of course, blending into the background, snapping pictures of her guests having fun.

"Hey, what did I tell you about taking photographs at my party?"

He took a picture of her. "That it was alright?"

"As long as you took time to enjoy the party as well. And dance with me."

"Does milady want to dance?" He immediately put down his camera, and led her to the floor.

She laid her head on his shoulder. "We got to tell them, or honestly I am gonna go mad, Sam. My mom just asked me if I was lesbian."

"She did?" He started laughing and couldn't stop.

"Hey, this ain't funny," she poked him.

"Well I can go vouch for the fact that you're not gay. I'll even give her a demonstration if she likes," he snickered.

"Still not funny," she moped.

"My mom has been asking me if I was gay for years. Especially after I got divorced. I think they have the idea somewhere in their heads that they failed as parents if we are not with somebody. So if we're gay, they're off the hook. Or at least have something else to blame for it."

"Really?" It was like an epiphany. So that was how deep-rooted the problem was, and why she had rather been with John all those years than alone. Because that was what she had been taught. Well she would NEVER do that to her own children, that was for sure.

"Alright we'll tell them, but in the right order," Sam said.

Izzy agreed completely with that. "Yes, Lily deserves to know first, than our parents and Sophie. You think she'll be happy for us?"

"Lily? Ecstatic. Sophie? I honestly have no idea. It might go either way with my sister. There is one person I got to talk to first though. Let's go somewhere private," he suggested, leading her away from the crowds.

CHAPTER TWENTY-SEVEN

There were many rooms in the gallery, and Sam seemed to be leading Izzy through a jungle of corridors, until she had lost any sense of direction. They ended in a room full of flowers and candles, mirrored from all sides. It was magical, and she couldn't remember having been here before, even though she was pretty sure she had pretty much been everywhere in this building. Or had she? It was like stepping out of reality, into a bubble. Was she even still on the planet? Oh well, as long as she was with Sam, what else could matter?

In the middle of the room was a table completely filled with flowers, and a chair beside it. "Please, be seated my lady," he said, helping her sit down like the true gentleman he was. "What's going on? Where are we? And what are all these flowers and candles doing here?" she asked, confused.

"You have very good friends who all pitched in to help you . . . to help me tonight." That still did not make any sense, but she decided to see what would happen.

He sat her down on the chair and then went down on one knee. He was . . . oh my . . . he was doing it properly this time. And she even hadn't seen it coming.

"I know you did not want to marry me today. And you are right. This was your day, and adding a man to the equation would have ruined it. I'm proud of what you did tonight. But I do want you to know that I love you. I have loved you for as long as I can remember . . ."

"Hmmm yeah, you are ahead of the competition there," she giggled.

He raised an eyebrow. "There is competition I need to worry about?"

"Not at all, handsome." She kissed him. "They got nothing on you."

He continued. "I have tried asking you twice before now, so this time I'd better get it right. Isabelle Rose Stanton, will you marry me and be mine for eternity?"

"Eternity? Now that's pretty long time."

She saw a desperate look on his face. That was not what she wanted, she was just teasing him. "Alright then," she agreed, pulling him into a kiss. "After all, you are the only man I want."

"Is that a yes?" Sam wanted to know for sure.

"Of course. After all, I already loved you since . . . forever."

"Hey, that's my line."

"I'm stealing it, just like I am stealing your name. Beauforde – I was always kind of jealous of that, it sounds so regal."

He laughed. "Well you are welcome to it. Just as you are welcome to this." Out of his pocket came a box that looked a bit old and worn.

She immediately recognized the ring inside. The beautiful band that looked like a branch encrusted with diamonds. "But this is . . ."

"My grandmother's engagement ring, yes."

"We used play with this as kids. It was in your mother's jewelry box. Doesn't Sophie mind?"

"Well she said I could only have it if I ever married you. I think she thought that would never happen, but here we are. So I guess it's yours," Sam explained.

"She won't like that," Izzy worried

"Then she shouldn't have said that. I'm planning to keep her to it now."

"I'll take it, but only if she agrees on letting me have it, alright?" The last thing she wanted was to start a family feud.

"And else the wedding is off?" That was all that matter to Sam at this point.

"No, of course not. You just will need to find me another ring if she wants it. It's not worth fighting over."

He slid it around her finger. "Perfect fit. I think you are supposed to have it. And I'll take care of my sister." Well she hoped so – Sophie was the last person in the world she wanted to fall out with, certainly not over a ring.

"What's going on?" Sophie asked suddenly appearing out of nowhere. It was as if she had heard her name being spoken.

"They're getting married!" Claire cheered. Apparently she had been in the room the whole time, filming the whole engagement. "I'm so happy for both of you. I think I recorded it all, Sam, just like you asked. I'll put it straight on my computer and email it to you now so nothing can happen to it." She pulled Anton away with her as well as she left. Izzy hadn't even noticed them.

"Finally!" was Sophie's response.

Izzy had hoped Sophie would be happy for them, but this was more than she could have hoped for. She felt a huge relief wash over her.

"You aren't mad?" Sam asked, mildly surprised.

"No, of course not. You are making my dream come true! Izzy will finally be my sister. In law perhaps, but I did not need to sell my soul to the devil or trade in my baby brother."

Sam looked slightly disturbed by the revelation that selling him had been an option. Izzy however was completely used to remarks like these from Sophie.

"It'll cost you grandmother's ring though." Sam said, pointing at Izzy's hand. "You said I could have it only if I married Izzy. Guess what?"

"Yes I did, didn't I? And she always loved the ring, even more than I did. So I guess … Wait a minute actually, I do have some demands before you can have it." Trust Sophie to come up with that. "Alright, number one: You better be very nice to my soon-to-be sister. Anything happens to her and I'll have your balls for breakfast, do you hear me?"

"Sophie, I love her with all my heart. I would never hurt her," Sam assured her.

"Good answer. Now Izzy, I know my brother is a big dope, but I do love him, so same goes for you. Hurt him and I'll make you kaput, capisce?"

"Hey you were the one that was always pestering him, not me. He is the best friend I could ever have, and the best lover. He's the only man I'll ever want." She kissed him.

"But what about me . . . I thought I was your best friend?" Sophie asked with an undeniable sense of hurt in her voice.

"He is my best male friend. You are my best female friend. Sophie, how long have we known each other? Do you honestly think anybody can take your place?"

"No . . ." Sophie agreed. "Okay, last demand: I get to be your maid of honor."

"Like we were ever gonna pick somebody else?" Izzy smiled.

Sam was laughing. "Well, I'm not sure if I want this trouble maker at our wedding, you know?"

"Are you telling me who I can and can't be friends with? Because then this wedding is off, buddy," Izzy poked him.

"Like I could ever pry you two apart. You're like twins. Of course you'll be her maid of honor. Who else?" Sam and Izzy both their arm around Sophie and gave her a hug. Izzy was ever so happy that Sophie had taken it so well.

"Well, I guess the ring is yours then. Let me look at it again." She picked up Izzy's hand. "It is truly gorgeous. And it fits perfectly on you. So you have it. Just take care of it."

"Don't worry, I will."

"Where's Lily? You were supposed to take care of her," Sam asked Sophie.

"Don't worry, she is with our parents."

Sam left to get Lily. He had wanted her to be the first know, before they would tell the rest. They both felt that way. So he went to get Lily before she heard the news from someone else.

"So what does he have that I don't?" Sophie asked when he left.

"What? Are you suggesting I should marry you instead?" Izzy laughed.

"No, but . . . You seem so close."

Oh god, Sophie was jealous. What was Izzy going to do about that? "Sophie, you know I love you. There is no comparison between you two. I have known you all of my life."

"You have known him all his life, too."

"Yes, and I love you both. I just love him differently, not more." Well maybe a bit more, but she wasn't going to tell Sophie that. The feelings could not be compared.

"I just don't want to lose you."

"How can you lose me? We are gonna be family. That makes us even closer."

"You're right. So how did you end up with Sam in the end? You have been dancing round each other for years. I had just about given up on you two."

"Well, things changed when I broke up with John . . ."

"Finally!" Sophie interrupted.

"Hey, if you know my love life so well, why don't you arrange it for me?"

"I try to, but you never listen." That made the both laugh.

"Anyways, he kissed me a while back, and from that moment on he stopped being your little brother. It took me a while to wrap my mind around that though. But well, when we ended up bed eventually . . ."

"I don't think I want to know more."

"He's an amazing, amazing lover, made me come like no man ever has." Izzy went on. Sophie always was very candid about her love life – too candid – so this was a little bit of a payback.

"Really Izzy, I'm happy for you, but he's also my brother. I don't want to know such things about him."

Izzy giggled. It was fun to watch Sophie squirm. "Are you becoming a prude?"

"My brother does not have sex," Sophie stated.

"Sure, and Lily was brought here by the stork." Not that Izzy wanted to think too much about how Lily had been made herself.

Mentioning people tonight seemed to make them appear. "Hi . . ." Lily said, sticking her head around the corner.

"Daddy and Aunt Izzy are getting married, Lily!" Sophie said, before anyone could intervene. Izzy had rather told it to Lily herself.

"They are?" the little girl asked.

"Yes!" Sophie was jumping up and down.

Sam and Izzy looked closely for any disappointment. Lily looked confused for a moment, but then it seemed to hit her. "That's great!" she cheered, immediately jumping into Izzy's lap. "Does that mean I can call you mommy from now on, Aunt Izzy?"

This proposal hit her even more than Sam's had done. Tears welled in Izzy's eyes. "If you like."

"Not if it makes you sad," the girl whispered, afraid she had said the wrong thing.

Izzy hugged her tightly. "Oh my sweet Lily, nothing would make me happier than to be your mother. These aren't sad tears, they are happy tears."

"I'm gonna tell grandma and granddad!" With that she ran off again

"So you are just marrying me for my daughter after all." Sam whispered in Izzy's ear playfully.

"Of course, I already told you. That and your talents as a stud. Oh, and your last name, of course."

He grinned "Hmm, we are making babies tonight. After all, I am sure her next demand will be a brother or sister."

Sophie stuck her fingers in her ears.

"What's up with her?" Sam asked surprised

"She can't handle the word S-E-X." Izzy spelled.

"Since when?"

"Since you have it!" Sophie shouted.

"If you think I am gonna be pregnant on my wedding day, you have another thing coming, by the way." Izzy warned him.

"Why not? You already had your party today, dear. Next one will be mine. For I get to marry the girl of my dreams. And nothing will stop me, not even her being eight months pregnant."

"So shall we make it your birthday then? After all, next year you are hitting that big Three-Ooh."

"Yes and I always thought I would be married, live in a house with a white-picket fence, have two kids and a dog by then," he joked.

"Well I'll see what I can do, but the dog is out of the question."

"I thought you liked dogs?"

"Yes, but if you get everything you wished for, you'll get far too conceited."

He let out a fake sigh. "Well, I guess I'll just have to settle for less then."

Just as he was about to ravish her, their parents walked in. "So it is true," Ann said. She sounded upset. This was more like the reaction Izzy had expected from Sophie – not her mom.

"We are getting married, yes." Izzy replied. Wasn't that what her mother had always wanted? Just moments ago, she had seemed terrified that her daughter might be gay.

"You are marrying Sam?"

"Yes." Wasn't that obvious? He was the man she was holding in her arms after all.

"You are not doing this because of anything we might have said over Christmas, are you? Because that was just a joke." Oh, that. She had forgotten about that.

"No, of course not. Like I ever would. I'm doing this because I love Sam. They don't make guys better than this." She kissed him again and again.

"And apparently because he is great in the bedroom department." Sophie added.

"Sophie! You don't say that stuff," Izzy chided her.

"What? You told me."

"What's daddy good at?" Lily wanted to know.

Sam shot Sophie an angry look. "Um, making beds?" she came up with.

Lily seemed satisfied with that answer.

"Well if this is what you both really want, I am very happy for you." Ann said. She did not look very happy though.

Her father tried to calm her. "Mother, they seem very in love."

"Don't you go hurting my boy." Sylvia now finally got a chance to say.

"I wouldn't dream of it. Sophie has already said she would hurt me if I did."

"Of course, we will be expecting more grandbabies now." Sylvie winked, she obviously couldn't help herself.

Sam started laughing "I should have put a bet on how quick you'd mention that."

"I had always expected we would have lots of them by now. Not that I am complaining about this one," Sylvie said picking up her granddaughter. "And I bet you would love a brother or sister, to play with, wouldn't you?"

Lily seemed to have to think about that one, because she did not react.

"Please mother, don't encourage her."

"You don't want more children?"

"Of course we do." Izzy said.

"Yes but we do not need outside pressure for that, alright?" Sam defended her.

The news of their engagement seemed to have spread – people started coming in to see them and congratulate them. Mike, Susan and Robert, Francesca, Karen, Tina, Daniel . . . the small room seemed to hold an infinite number of people, and the many mirrors made it look like even more. Everyone wanted to wish the happy couple the best of luck.

"So, what will you wear for the wedding?" Tina wanted to know.

"Well, seeing even princesses and queens now wear their ball gowns more than once, I guess will follow in their footsteps. Sam already thought it was a ridiculous expense when I bought this one, so I don't think he'll be too happy if I buy another one. Plus, this is the perfect dress – nothing can ever top that."

"You can't wear that dress. He has seen it. That means bad luck." Fran came from a very Catholic, very superstitious family.

"With Sam? Impossible."

"I don't care what you wear. Come naked for all I care, as long as you will be my wife."

"The naked part is for the wedding night, Sam dear," she whispered.

"TOO MUCH INFORMATION!" Sophie screamed, plugging her ears again.

"If I had known it was that easy to tease my sister, I would have asked you to marry me years ago."

"Well, I have other techniques to drive her up the wall as well, and since you are going to be my husband, I will have to share them all."

"Traitor!" Sophie stuck out her tongue. "By the way, think there is a way I can marry you – I mean, do the ceremony. Just like all those years ago, but for real."

"I think it's possible. You'd need to do a course and get a special dispensation I think. But who will be my maid of honor?" Izzy worried.

"Maybe I can do both?"

Sam wasn't sure. "Wait a minute. If you are gonna do this, it needs to be serious."

"I can do serious. I'm not silly all the time. And if I were to do your wedding ceremony I wouldn't make a joke about that. I'm just so happy that you are finally with somebody that is good for you. I wouldn't mess that up. Honestly!"

"We have a year to plan it. Let's not get ahead of ourselves. Let's just enjoy the night." Sam said.

Robert had been handing everyone a glass of champagne, and now raised his glass. "To Izzy and Sam."

"To Izzy and Sam!" everybody agreed. Sam simply pulled her into a tight embrace.

And suddenly the realization hit her. There she was, age thirty-five. All her hopes, her goals, had been met just at the finishing line. She had the wedding, the man of her dreams, and the daughter she had always wanted. Alright, there had been a few hiccups along the way – she wasn't married yet to the man, and the daughter wasn't hers by blood – but those were minor details. This was real life. And it didn't get any better than this.

ABOUT THE AUTHOR

Jolene Marselis loves to write. Yes, I know, who would have expected that from a woman who just committed 87,000 odd words to paper? But it's true. With an overactive imagination and a need to commit that to paper (mostly so she could read it back later), she started scribbling down little stories as soon as she could write. Little stories at first of course, about squirrels in the forest, and later about a vampire that wasn't very good with blood but fell hopelessly in love with the heroine, only to run off with her. Yes, that love for the romantic genre was already there by the tender age of nine – and was only made worse when she got her hands on her mom's old Barbara Cartlands by the age of twelve. Luckily, those novels are very tame if you compare them with today's books from this genre, and don't go any further then a kiss at the end – so not as unsuitable for a young teenager as you might think. Furthering her education with Austen, Brontë, and a profound love of fairy tales, the tone had been set. What else could she be than a hopeless Romantic with a quirky sense of humor?

Printed in Great Britain
by Amazon